What They
Don't Know

Eight of the stories in this collection were previously published in the following journals:

"Miss Kelly Citation Tire," *Pithead Chapel*, February 2014

"Body Parts," *Prick of the Spindle*, Vol. 7.1, March 2013

"The Luckiest Man Alive," *The Summerset Review*, Fall 2010

"A Devil of a Girl," *The Dickens*, 2000

"Boondocks," *The Dickens*, 2001

"Each After Its Kind," *Other Voices*, 1989

"Intruders," *The Florida Review*, 1988
   (reprinted in *Redux*, #129, May 2014)

"What They Don't Know," *Room of One's Own*, 1986

Exerpts from "The Luckiest Man Alive" and "Art Class at Harmony Villa" were performed at the New Short Fiction Series in Hollywood, California, on October 12, 2014.

The verse quoted on p. 146 is from Edward Fitzgerald's translation of *The Rubyiat of Omar Khayyám*, 5th edition, Quatrain XII (1889).

What They Don't Know

SELECTED FICTION

Jo-Anne H. Rosen

What They Don't Know: Selected Fiction
© 2015 by Jo-Anne H. Rosen

ISBN: 978-1-941066-07-2

Library of Congress Control Number: 2015934509

Cover photo from www.istockphoto.com

Wordrunner Press
Petaluma, California

This book is dedicated to
my mother, sisters and brother:
Mildred P. Sandy Rosen
Ava H. Rosen Rich
Louise J. Rosen Franco
Richard T. Franco

and to the memory of my father,
Morris Rosen
(1914-1979)

Contents

What They Don't Know

Maggie crouches near the edge of the garage roof, poking at loose slate with her rubber knife. She wants me to sneak into the coalyard on Halloween. We can get ink blotters from the night watchman.

"I can't," I tell her. "My Mum takes us trick or treating. Me and my sisters."

"Ya still a baby?"

I'm no baby. I climb up garages after dark. I jump from roof to roof.

She pitches a piece of slate into the yard below, and says, "Tell 'em *my* mum's taking us."

"Nah, they'd find out."

"They think you're at my house now, right?"

Before I can answer, a door creaks open below, lighting up the garden.

We drop flat on our stomachs. The beam from a flashlight swings over our heads. I hold my breath.

The light wavers. "NEXT TIME I CALL THE COPS." The door slams.

We lower ourselves to a ledge on the fence and drop down into the alley. I walk as fast as I can without running. Maggie whistles. When we get to our store, she asks if I'm going to ask my father, can I go out with her Halloween. We look at him through the window that says Moldoff's Groceries Drink Salada Tea on it. He's standing behind the meat cooler with the white butcher-apron on and the phone at his ear. I shrug and go in.

The bell above the door jingles. My father turns to face me with bulging-out eyes, the phone at his ear. Look at the floor. At the brand-new sack of sugar as high as my elbows. I know how to scoop sugar out and pour it into paper bags and weigh them, one pound, sir, two or five, ma'am. His telephone voice is buttery: "Here she is now, Mrs. Sullivan. That's alright Mrs. S, good night now." He hangs up without taking his eyes off me. "What took you so long?"

Say the wrong thing and he blows up; say nothing then. "What are you standing there for," he asks, each word a soft nail. "Go on inside. Your mother's worried sick."

I run out of the store down the long, dark hall into our kitchen with his eyes still on my back. Only one plate and one glass on the table. I tiptoe in.

Mum is wiping the cabinet doors with a sponge. When I clear my throat, her shoulders jerk. "Don't sneak up on me like that," she says. She goes over to the stove and lights it. "Your supper's cold. This isn't a restaurant, you know, you can walk in anytime and get served."

I go to the sink and wash my hands. Is she watching? Yes. She grabs me from behind and hugs me to her. "You little bum," she says. "I bet you're starving. I made your favorite."

Baked beans, hot dogs, and chips. She heats up the beans, but the chips are cold. I eat every last bean and carry the plate and cutlery to the sink and wash and dry them all myself before I ask, can I trick or treat with Maggie. If Mum says no, that's the end of it.

"Who's taking her?"

"No one."

She doesn't answer right away. She looks at something I can't see.

"Oh, I don't know," she says. "I think you're old enough, but you better ask Daddy."

That is what I do not want to do.

I watch the shadow slide down the hall every time a car goes by, to make sure it doesn't come into my room. It looks like a horse. They're arguing downstairs in the hall between the store and the kitchen, each at one end, his voice hammering hers down.

Tomorrow, I'll ask him, only I won't say about the coalyard. It's way over on the other side of Lansdowne, close to where Isabelle Rafferty lives. Maggie says that Isabelle and her gang stay up past midnight and torture alley cats. If they torture cats every night, what do they do for Halloween?

I'm not sleepy. I lie on my stomach and spread my arms like wings. What if we fly over the coalyard fence. A crook is robbing the night watchman! Down we go, pow, knock the gun out of his hands, whoosh, up and away. Who are those masked girls, they ask.

Then I turn over on my side and cross my legs like fingers when you want good luck. I rub them up and down against each other. I'm the only one in the world who knows how this feels. Like blowing a slow secret bubble that floats between my legs, growing bright and dizzy as candy floss, till finally it pops. I pop it three times. But the first pop is always the best.

Halloween: Maggie looks so know-it-all. I walk home from school the long way without her. I hop along the tracks where trains don't run anymore; with my arms out like a trapeze artist, balance on the rails. I run by the factory with broken glass in the windows, as fast as I can, because ghosts are in there still working, and I have to crunch on the glass that fell down since the last time.

A paper skeleton hangs in the window of our store behind a pyramid of tinned peas and beans. Daddy is getting the shell-out box ready. He's hopping up and down and all over the store.

"Hiya princess," he says. "Look what I made for you."

A stick with a silver star taped to one end is propped against the cash register.

"For me?"

"I put it there for good luck," he says, his eyes laughing at me. "Come over here and sit still. If the crown fits, you wear it." I climb up on the big sack of sugar, like it's a throne. The white cloth crunches under my bum. He puts a cardboard crown on my head.

"Your royal highness, did I tell you the horse manure story yet?" I already know that long ago he shoveled horse shit off the streets and sold it for fertilizer, but I pretend I forgot. "On Halloween," he begins, "I used to put paper bags full of it against the front doors of the houses on my block, you know, lean one up on a door, like so, then I'd ring the bell and quick duck behind the verandah to see what happened."

"Were you as old as me then?"

"I was as young as you."

"But you didn't have to go with Bubbie Moldoff, trick or treating, did you?"

He steps back and narrows his eyes. I wait. Am I old enough yet?

The telephone rings. "Hello, Moldoff's." The buttery customer-voice. His forehead creases up. Then the bell jingles and in comes Mrs. Murphy, bent over her cane, and dressed in black from her shoes to her beaded hat. A dirty hearing aid is buried in one ear like a seashell and her thick glasses are tied on at the back of her head with a white string. She needs a bar of bittersweet baker's chocolate and a pound of raisins. She's baking for tonight. Remember that. I get the raisins and the baker's chocolate from a bottom shelf. Mrs. Murphy takes the packages in a hand, clawed and yellow as a chicken's foot. She smells of vanilla.

"What are you dressing up as Nora," she asks in her hoarse, wet voice.

"A fairy princess."

"Eh? A hairy princess, did you say? Well, that's very original, isn't it?" And she sputters and sprays her joke into the air, while I politely smile.

She doesn't give me money to ring up, which I know how to do. My father, still on the phone, writes the amount with a black wax pencil on a piece of cardboard that he keeps beside the cash register. Underneath the counter there's a stack of cardboards covered with names and numbers and tied with a rubber band.

"I will take care of that next Friday, Mr. Moldoff."

He hangs up the phone. "Thank you, Mrs. Murphy, Friday will be fine."

Off she hobbles. The bell jingles behind her. My father leans back against the shelves with his arms folded across the white apron and gives me a hard look.

"You think you're a big girl, eh? Okay, you're on your own, you and Maggie Shmeggegi. You show me you got a real kep on your shoulders, understand? Next year you take your sisters with you."

"Okay," I sigh.

He looks at me with eyes narrowed again. "You sure that's okay with you, your royal highness? What do you want to bet I can make you laugh?"

My hand goes to my mouth to cover the smile. He pulls it away. "I know you're always thinking something," he says. "A chip off the old block, you can't help it."

After supper, Mum pins and tucks me into her wedding gown. It is short-skirted and gray on account of the war, even though her parents could afford a long white satin one.

The gray crepe feels soft on my skin. Now I am a Little Woman with a pearl necklace and eau de cologne behind my ears and on my nose from one of the glass bottles on her bureau tray. We both giggle at the square shoulders.

"Now pay attention, this is serious," she whispers. I look around. My sisters are playing jacks at the other end of the hall. "I don't want your Bubbie and Zaydie to know we're letting you go out on your own, so I'm telling them you're going with Maggie's mother, okay? And maybe you'd better tell your sisters that too."

I ask her what she did on Halloween when she was a kid. She went to a party with her sisters and dunked for apples, but she never went out to trick or treat. Her mother wouldn't let them.

Next she paints two splashes of rouge on my cheeks and a red cupidsbow on my lips, the same color and shape she always has on hers. My grandmother doesn't wear lipstick because Zaydie won't kiss anyone who does, not even his own daughter. I kiss her hard on one cheek and leave the mark of my lips there, which makes her smile, when we look in the mirror. She has two mouths. She touches the shadows under her eyes. Then she looks me over one last time. "Okay doll, you're ready," she says. "You're a princess tonight, a real little lady."

"Here comes the bride," my father sings as I walk down the aisle, canned food on one side, bread and toiletpaper on the other. "Stepped on a banana peel and went for a ride."

"No I won't."

"You better not," he says. "Not in that dress."

He fastens the crown on my head with three bobbypins. It's covered with crinkly silverfoil and has a little silver star on each point like the big star on the wand. If the wand were really magic, we could get into the coalyard without anyone knowing.

The shell-out box is filled with penny candy and chocolate bars, but no fruit. Fruit splatters on the sidewalk. He lets me take a handful of pennies from the till and throw them into the box. Outside in front of the store a few kids are hanging around and the street is shadowy.

With the wand in one hand and a trick or treat bag in the other, I go out into the street, taking little steps like a princess. The kids all watch me carefully. They are waiting for my father, the King of the Block, to shell out.

Down at the end of Lappin Avenue a fat orange moon is rising over the Toronto Dominion Bank. Clusters of ghosts, witches, pirates, gypsies, cowboys, supermen and Indian Chiefs head for our grocery store. The ones already gathered begin the chant.

"SHELL OUT! SHELL OUT! OR WE'LL BREAK YOUR WINDOWS INSIDE OUT!"

The sidewalk in front of our store is packed with hollering kids. I squirm through looking for Maggie. There she is, poking her rubber knife into the neighbor's fence where the vines with pink and purple flowers hang over on our side. She has a bright red bandana wrapped around her black hair and dangly earrings. I drop some of the candy my father gave me into her bag and she gives me a lopsided grin. Her teeth are growing in crooked.

The hollering turns to cheers. It's my father on the front step holding the shell-out box. He tosses candy kisses and pennies by the handful into the air, each time in a different direction. Everyone, except Maggie and me, scrambles on the sidewalk, pushing and shoving and shrieking. Fingers get stepped on. The smaller kids run to their mothers.

They pick the sidewalk clean and take off for the drugstore on the next block. My father spots us. "Don't do anything I wouldn't do," he says, and goes back into the store. What does that mean, Maggie wants to know. I think it means I shouldn't mess around in my gown and Maggie says likewise about her skirt which is red with purple flowers on it and a stiff crinoline underneath.

We go down the block to watch Mr. McCarthy, the druggist, shell out from the roof of his building. While we're waiting, Maggie goes up to Joey McCarthy, he's standing in the middle of the crowd, and she says, "Cross my palm with silver, I'll tell your fortune." "G'wan silver, what're ya talking about?" Sounds like he's interested though. He's wearing a paper skeleton, the ready-made kind, doesn't cover his bushy red hair and big ears. Maggie, she really looks like a gypsy.

"I'll give you my wax lips," he says, poking around in his bag. "They're for girls."

Wax lips. Bright and red, you chew 'em like gum afterwards. Cost three cents. Maggie's waiting with her hand out.

"First tell my fortune," Joey says. She stands on tiptoe and whispers in his ear. He pushes her away and puts the lips back in his bag. I can't hear what they're saying. Everyone's shouting SHELL OUT SHELL OUT. That's Joey's father up on the roof, a long shadow leaning over, flapping his arms like a stork. The trick or treat box is on the edge.

Suddenly the entire box falls down smack in the middle of all the kids, but not on anyone's head. The girls scream. Joey and his friends dive on the box and pile up in a heap of arms and legs. Mothers yell and run up and down and into McCarthy's drugstore. Did he throw it? Did he trip? Was he drunk again? Was it a trick instead of a treat?

"C'mon, let's go," Maggie says.

"What did you tell him?"

"That he'll marry a princess," she giggles.

"Yuck." That bully. Chased me down the back alley once, punched me in the stomach. A long time ago he kissed me.

Next, we go to all the houses where we might find baked goods. Mrs. Murphy is giving out fudge brownies, just as I guessed. She gives us extra big ones. "For two pretty girls," she says, patting Maggie's bandana with her clawed yellow hand. "It's little red riding hood, isn't it? You better watch out for the big bad wolf, dear." Maggie looks disgusted.

A lot of people recognize me, the Moldoff girl, right away. Maggie says they give us more because they know me. This one lady I don't know says we have to do a trick before we can have a treat. "Can you dance or sing or stand on your head?" she asks in a silly baby voice. Maggie right away stands on her head. The skirt falls down and covers her face and the crinoline stays up stiff as meringue on her legs. My trick is to sing "How Much Is That Doggie in the Window," but I can't finish on account of the expression on Maggie's face. She's hopping mad because the lady gave her an apple, a plain old macintosh, with no taffy on it.

At the corner of Lappin and Lansdowne, I hear Maggie's voice in my ear: "Dare you." She takes off and stands on the other side. "What are y'waiting for?" she hollers.

Lansdowne has streetcar tracks and offices and stores that close at five every day and don't open on the weekend, not like ours which is open all the time. The other side's dark and far away. Wait till there's no cars coming. Now run like the wind.

The street we go down looks like ours. Houses with wooden verandahs and small patches of grass in front. Some with jack o'lanterns on the verandahs. They could be ghost houses though, the kind you go into and never come out of, or if you do, you're a hundred years old, wrinkled up and ready to die. Not too many kids on this street. Maggie goes right up to a door and pounds on it. "SHELL OUT SHELL OUT OR WE'LL BREAK YOUR WINDOWS INSIDE OUT," we holler. "TRICK OR TREAT!"

A gorilla with a party hat on his head answers the door. We scream and jump back. The gorilla says in a slurry voice, "Don't be afraid, girls, I'm a good-natured beast at heart." Behind him I see more grownups in costumes with drinks in their hands. Music is playing and in the hall a nun and a monk are dancing. Then this clown comes up behind the gorilla and says in a lady's voice, "What do we have here, a gypsy and a queen." And the gorilla says if we kiss him, he'll turn into a prince. "Do we have to, to get a treat?" Maggie asks. "Of course not," says the clown. She sounds angry though her red mouth smiles. She gives us each a *nickel*.

We knock at two more houses after that where no one answers, though lights are on.

"I don't like it here," I say.

Maggie says she knows a short cut down an alley, but I like this even less than the street. The moon is overhead now, shriveled and white. The shadows are pitch black. We hold hands and walk slowly, scuffling our feet in the dirt and humming to let anyone or anything know we aren't afraid. It goes on twice as long as our alley, there are twice as many garages with who knows what inside them, and a cat yowls like someone cut off its tail.

A street at last with lamp posts. Where are we?

The street comes to a dead end at a high wooden fence with barbed wire on top. The back side of the coalyard. We turn around.

"Freeze!" Maggie whispers.

Way down at the end of the block on the other side of the street four dark shapes are coming toward us.

Isabelle Rafferty and her friends. If they see us on this dead end street, we're goners. I point to a hedge on the next lawn. Maggie nods and we tiptoe over and crouch behind it.

Isabelle and her gang come galumphing loudly down the street, making horrible animal sounds. I wish they would turn into pigs. They are almost opposite us when they stop and quiet down. We can see them through the holes in our hedge, but they don't see us.

"What are you two doing here?" Isabelle sneers. "Are you following us?"

I stop breathing. A voice further away whines, "I wanna go home now."

We pull the branches back and look out. The voice belongs to a small boy. He's tugging the hand of a girl about our age. Both pirates, standing under a street lamp two houses down. Isabelle and the others are in the shadow of a tree. They look like four bats.

"I want to go home now," one of Isabelle's sidekicks mimics in an oily voice.

Isabelle bellows, "First you have to pay us a fine."

"Why?" asks the pirate girl, backing off.

"Because," answers Isabelle. Grunting and snorting, the four dash to the street lamp. Before the two can move they're surrounded.

"SHELL OUT SHELL OUT OR WE'LL BREAK YOUR FACES INSIDE OUT," they chant and oink and heehaw.

"Leave us alone," cries the girl.

"Give us your candy we won't beat you up," someone says.

Behind our hedge, we hold our treat bags closely. Maggie whispers in my ear, "They won't get away with this, the lousy crooks."

"What can *we* do?"

"Rescue 'em." Maggie takes her rubber knife out of her belt.

"With *that* thing? They'll murder us."

She hesitates.

"Somebody help!" cries the boy.

We look out. The bats have dumped candy out of the pirates' bags onto the sidewalk.

"It'll be four against four," says Maggie. She straightens up, still holding her bag and steps boldly out of the shadows. I grab her arm and whisper, "Hide the bags."

Quickly we hide them behind the hedge, and Maggie charges across the street with her knife pointed straight out. I follow, waving my wand and wishing I was home in my bed. Maggie whoops "WAWAWAWAWAWAWA" like an Indian. The four bats jump back from the pirates and start to run away, but come back when they figure out who we are.

"Leave 'em alone or we'll murder you," Maggie hollers.

We glare at each other. They have one big one, we have one little one and three of us are scared stiff. Then Maggie takes a giant step forward, right up to Isabelle Rafferty, who could never disguise herself even in a mask, and Maggie says, "You lousy stinking tub of lard, you'll pay for this." Isabelle sneers, "Sticks and stones'll break my bones."

"A rubber knife sure won't," says one of her friends.

"Or a shitty little stick," says another, the one with the oily voice, and she grabs the wand out of my hand.

"Give that back!"

"You can't make me!"

I try to grab it. She shoves me. Her sweaty hand's on the sleeve of the gown. My mother's gown she's putting her filthy hand. She snaps the wand in two and crumples the star. Ruined it! My face goes hot as fire.

Out swings my arm. I feel paper ripping. Smack, it's the sound of my hand! She's bending over and falling. She's down on the sidewalk in the middle of all the candy, crying. I did that?

Everyone stands there looking at me. My hand sticks out, curled into a fist. My knees wobble. The batgirl pulls off her mask and shows us a face as white as chalk.

No time to feel sorry in. Isabelle Rafferty jumps toward me. In the same moment, Maggie lifts her skirt and kicks Isabelle in the butt.

"Why you..." roars Isabelle, whirling around. The two other batgirls put up their fists and come toward me, and those pirates, they stay stock still. We are goners.

THEN: a window rattles open in the house we're standing in front of. "WHAT'S GOIN ON OUT THERE?"

"They're beating us up and stealing our candy," cries the pirate girl.

"I want to go home," says the little boy.

"SO GO HOME."

The white-faced batgirl I punched gets up and runs snuffling down the street, still holding the broken halves of my wand, followed by the other two and last of all by Isabelle Rafferty, shaking her fist at us.

"YOU BRATS THINK YOU OWN THE WORLD DO YA?" BANG. The window slams shut.

"How'll we get out of here?" I whisper. "They'll be waiting for us around the corner." The pirate girl says she knows a secret way home along the coalyard fence. Maggie asks if she knows how to get into the coalyard. "That's easy, I'll show you."

While the pirates pick their candy off the sidewalk, we run back to get our bags. We follow them back to the dead end and through a break in a hedge. Between the hedge and the high wooden fence is a narrow path, the pirate girl says goes through to the next dead end street where her house is.

"What if they come after us again," I look around. "They could come down your street."

"Nah, they got scared off," says the pirate girl.

"Pow!" Her little brother makes a fist and punches the air. "Pow! Bam! Pow! Pow!"

"Here's where you go in," says the pirate girl.

A board is missing in the fence, leaving a narrow space we can step through sideways. Inky dark on the other side.

The pirate girl won't come with us. She has to take her brother home. "Besides, I don't want any more blotters," she says. "That weirdo can keep his blotters."

Maggie asks how we can find the night watchman.

"That's easy. On the other side is a pile of wood. You have to turn this way," she points. "Then walk between the fence and the wood till you come to a big yard. You'll be able to see the light in the shed at the other end of the yard. But watch out for the old bugger."

I pretend I know exactly what she means. Maggie pretends to sharpen her knife. She slaps it back and forth on the broken edge of the fence.

"Goodbye," says the pirate girl. She and her brother walk quickly off down the path and vanish in the shadows. Maggie steps sideways through the fence and vanishes too. "C'mon," she whispers. "What're you waiting for?"

My wand. That greasy batgirl ran off with my wand. Leaned it on the cash register for good luck, Daddy said. It's broken, it's gone for good.

So I cross four fingers on the hand that still tingles from the punch and with them rub the skirt of my mother's wedding gown, and then I step sideways through the fence into pitch blackness.

I hear Maggie but can't see her. "It's a tight squeeze, go sideways," she says.

I touch pieces of wood that stick out every which way, rough and splintery with powder all over. Coal dust. Better watch my step. Something rustles close by inside the wood pile. Something's alive in there. I go as fast as I can sideways with one arm out to feel my way. Look up instead, way up, a bright black ribbon above my head with one small star sparkling in it. Wish I may, wish I might. . . Then my hand touches something warm. It's alive. *What?*

"Hah. Scared you," says Maggie. "Look where you're going!"

I look. She's standing in the moonlight. The wood pile ends right where I am, and the black hills stretch out before us with metal dinosaurs sleeping in their shadows. Or only dozing? Far above us on a cable hang the coal carts, looking like coffins. Red smoke puffs out of three chimneys. It blows up the sky and across the moon, making it red too.

It is quiet in the coal yard. No cars screeching. No kids hollering. No windows slamming or doors creaking. But rats are skittering in the dark. If I see one I'll scream.

Straight ahead in the night watchman's shed shines a dusty-yellow light.

Maggie and I make for it. We pick our way around piles of coal dust, holding up our skirts. How does coal dust feel? Another time we can stick our hands in it. Though we lift our feet carefully, our shoes still scrunch on the gravel. As we come closer we hear music. It's the McGuire Sisters singing, "Be my little sugar, and love me, love me, love me all the time."

The shed has a door and a window. We should peek in the window. But before I can say a word, Maggie goes up to the door and knocks and says "Trick or Treat" in a not so loud voice, so I say it too.

"Trick or Treat!" We say it three times.

The radio stops playing. For a moment it is dead quiet in the coalyard and inside the shed. Then a deep tired-sounding voice calls out, "Come on in. Door's open."

That look on Maggie's face, she wants to turn back too. But she pushes the door open and we step in.

It smells of cigarette smoke and something else, sour and stale. A bright light blinds me for a moment. "Come on in, girls, don't be shy now," says the deep, tired voice. "Aren't we pretty tonight?"

The night watchman is sitting behind a desk facing the door. He has a gray shirt on and gray slicked back hair. His eyes are black and glossy. On his chin and cheeks a gray stubble. And along one side of his nose, and on down to the corner of his mouth, runs a skinny, crooked purple scar, I can't help staring at. Did someone try to cut off his nose?

"Trick or treat," says Maggie in a small voice.

"You've come for some blotters, eh?"

We nod. He pulls open a drawer in the desk, takes out a stack of blotters and puts them on top of the desk in the middle. "How about a trick first?"

We say nothing.

Ping ping, bugs bounce off the lightbulb that dangles from the ceiling. Next to it curls a long strip of fly paper covered with dead bugs, no room for more. A spider crawls down the wall behind the desk. On the wall are pictures of ladies in bathing suits, smiling at us with red mouths. The night watchman's eyes skitter back and forth like two black beetles from me to Maggie to me. He rubs his nose with the back of one hand, making the scar jump around. His other hand is behind the desk. Slowly he stands up.

"Don't be afraid," he says.

The zipper on his gray pants is wide open in front and out hangs his thing, his gray fat thing that he takes in his hand and puts on the desk near the blotters. Gray and black hair curls around the bottom of it.

"Touch it," he says. "Go ahead. Touch it and you get all these blotters."

Touch? I feel Maggie shrink back with me to the door as if she were my legs, but we didn't move.

"I sure wish you would," the night watchman continues, his voice so deep now it scrapes the bottom. "Look, it's easy. It don't hurt. It'll make me feel good, see. Come on over here."

I can't move. I'm like a tree with eyes. It's alive. Hair at the bottom, a nest. Is it warm? cold?

The night watchman says, "I'll give you a quarter if you touch it. A quarter apiece."

"It's full of pee," says Maggie, and I know her face looks disgusted.

"Oh it's not full of pee now," he growls, patting it like it's a small dog that grows fatter and twitches as I stare. "It's full of something else, something special. Wouldn't you like to see what it's full of? Come here and I'll show you."

"I'll show *you!*" says Maggie. And she jumps in front of the desk with her rubber knife stuck straight out. With a loud groan, the night watchman falls back in his chair. Maggie sticks the knife in her belt and grabs all the blotters.

"Run for it," she says.

Out of the shed we run, not shutting the door behind us, and as fast as we can, with our treat bags banging on our knees, race through the long yard, past the coal hills and the giant machines, all the way back to the woodpile, where we have to turn sideways again. I take one last quick look at the night watchman's shed with its dusty-yellow light and the door still open. Faint and far away music is playing again. Then I slip between the fence and the woodpile, this time bumping into things.

We don't stop running till we get to Lansdowne. Then we divide up the blotters. In the light of a streetlamp I see coal smudges on Maggie's face and on her costume. She says I'm smudged too and look funny, but neither of us laughs.

Slowly we walk down our street. Dark and empty now, like all the other streets.

"I'm gonna get it," I say.

"Me too," sighs Maggie. "If my mum's home."

Her too? That means I'm really going to get it. But Maggie's house is dark and she bounces up the steps and smiles a crooked goodbye .

The door slams and a man steps out of the store. My grandfather! Standing straight as a tin soldier and wearing one of his 500 hats, a plaid tam. Did my crown fall off? No, I can feel it's there, with the foil ripped. I bet he's got butterscotch lifesavers. Walk faster. Jump over the cracks or you break your mother's back. What if they know that Maggie's mother isn't home. I stop where I am.

"Nora?" Zaydie takes a few stiff-legged steps toward me. "She's here!" he calls back over his shoulder. My mother rushes out of the store, and behind her, Bubbie. Next my father's head pops out, then back in.

My mother lifts me off the ground. On her breath I smell butterscotch. My legs dangle past her knees. She puts me on my feet and my grandmother grabs me by the shoulders and pulls me up on tiptoes close to her face. She's been crying. Smack, a big wet kiss. Her lilac perfume, she lets me put on. In her chest a wheezy sound.

Then my grandfather bends over and reaches for my bag. "I'll carry that for you."

"No," I say and hug it to me. "No, thank you, Zaydie."

"Tsk tsk tsk tsk," says Bubbie.

My mother takes my hand and we all walk into the store, jingling the bell. Behind the counter, my father is talking softly on the phone. To Maggie's mother? Did she come home? He looks at me with his popping-out eyes. Bubbie sits on the sack of sugar. CRUNCH goes the sack as she sinks down. Her shiny taffeta dress rustles up. She smooths it with a hand that is crooked and blue veined like Mrs. Murphy's, only fatter and has rings on three fingers, and also bakes brownies. Did she bring any?

My mother gets down on her knees so her face is level with mine. Her eyes are red along the bottom.

"Didn't you know how late it was?"

I shake my head no.

"Look at your face! How did you get so dirty? And the dress, it's black too. Look at this princess of mine."

"Since when does a princess wander around by herself after dark?" Bubbie asks.

"She was with a friend, Mother. She wasn't alone."

"You girls never went out alone after dark."

"I know," is all she says back.

"Eight years old is much too young, period," Zaydie snaps. At the door, he fidgets with the knob. "It's past *my* bedtime, by Godfrey."

"I'm almost nine," I say.

BANG, my father hangs up the phone. "I told the police she's home."

The cops he called. What for? He glares down at me.

"I drove all over looking for you. Where did you go?"

"The other side of Lansdowne."

"So far away? What were you doing?"

"Trick or treating."

"Don't get smart with me. The streets were empty."

"We got lost and these kids stole my wand." I stop, on account of it's not ladylike to fight.

"What else?" His voice getting colder.

"There was . . . there was this party. They said we had to do a trick to get a treat. So Maggie stood on her head and I sang a song, and the clown gave me a nickel. I'll show you. Maggie got one too. The gorilla said we were very pretty."

"A gorilla? What were you, a monkey? Where did this schmutz come from. Come over here. Let me have a good look."

I step up to the counter. My father's belt is even with my eyes. A silver M on the buckle. He leans into my face.

"Was this party in a coal cellar?"

I shake my head no.

"So how did you get covered with coal dust?"

One hand taps on the counter; the other's hooked into his belt by the thumb. Hasn't hit me since I was little. Never with a belt. I look back at my mother. Zaydie used to hit her with a razor strap, she said, because she wouldn't eat potatoes. After I was born he melted like butter. Her eyes want to help.

"Look at me, Nora. You were in the coalyard weren't you?" my father asks softly. Yes, nods my head.

"In your mother's wedding gown you roll in the dirt. What are you, a girl or a pig? You couldn't figure out what time it was? You forgot your Mother gets sick headaches when she worries?" Now he's hot and cold at the same time and his voice is rising. "That Maggie's a wild little *shicksa*, but you, you should know better. Why would you want to fool around in the coalyard in the first place, answer me that."

"To trick or treat," I whisper. A big clump of tears in my throat. I won't cry though.

"I'm warning you for the last time." His face is turning bright pink.

"It's true," I say. "We wanted ink blotters. For school. Look!" I pull all the blotters out of my bag and throw them on the counter. Don't want them anymore.

He turns them over carefully. "Who gave you these?"

"The night watchman."

"I see."

What does he see? Blotters? A zipper undone?

"We didn't touch anything," I blurt out. "Only the blotters. Maggie grabbed them and we ran. We tricked him."

My father looks at me and then at the blotters. He presses his lips together and nods his head slowly. "You tricked the night watchman, eh? Instead of a princess my daughter's a little *gonif*." Behind me the sugar sack scrunches. Zaydie clears his throat loudly. I feel my mother's hand on my shoulder.

"Never mind about that," my father continues. "At least it wasn't a total loss." And he winks at me.

Then he gathers up the blotters and drops them back into my bag.

The water turns gray, swirls down the drain, gone forever. Mum sponges me with a washcloth to make sure the dirt is all off. Her face looks sad. Because she lied to Bubbie about Maggie's mother? My fault she was caught. Sadness is all around us like water around two mermaids.

The wedding gown is on the floor near my bed in a gray heap. Mum picks it up and fingers it with a faraway look in her eyes.

"Maybe I can clean it," she sighs. "Or dye it."

"I'm sorry, Mummy."

"Don't you worry, dollface. I never liked it much. I think I'll just give it away."

She kisses me goodnight and switches off the light.

I watch the horse shadow slide down the hall. After it's gone I shut my eyes and pray she'll keep the wedding gown, though I know it won't do me any good. It never helps to pray or wish, no matter how much you want a thing.

Cloudland

My parents were arguing about the money Aunt Rose sent for my ballet lessons.

Aunt Rose lived in the States with her husband, a furrier, and they had no children. Once a year she came up to Toronto on the train. She was tall and plump and had rings on all her fingers. She said we were like pioneers, because we lived behind a grocery store and had a wringer washing machine instead of an automatic. But she would trade all her furs and diamonds for one little girl. And my father had said, "So make me an offer."

They had forgotten I was in the pantry, drying the same green glass plate over and over again so I wouldn't have to go to bed. The sink could not be seen from the table where Daddy was reading the evening paper. I poked my head out for a quick look. He had taken off his glasses and the apron he wore in the store, then his shirt. Sweat stood out on his forehead and matted the hair on his chest. Mum was over at the stove with her back to me, scraping at some grease spots.

She was telling him my little sisters should have ballet lessons as well, but as usual there wasn't any extra money.

"If we give to one, we give to all," she said.

Dreamily I stretched on tip toe with one foot pointed out. I raised my arms, still clutching the plate, and hopped across the pantry floor. I slid through a soapy puddle, lost my balance. My feet shot out from under me and I landed in the puddle on my tailbone. The plate crashed to the floor. I was too surprised to cry.

My mother ran into the pantry.

She crouched beside me picking up the broken pieces, whisking green glass crumbs into the dustpan.

"Can't you dry the dishes just once without breaking them?"

"It hurts," I protested.

"Where does it hurt?" Now she looked worried. My father came over and stood in the doorway.

"My bum hurts."

"Let's take a look and see if it's broken," he said.

I already knew that stupid old joke about the crack. But they were both smiling, so maybe it was worth a sore bum.

"These lessons could do her good," my father told my mother.

"What about Ellie and Sarah Jane?"

He shrugged.

"You can't tell your sisters about the ballet lessons," said Mum, helping me to my feet. "They'll want lessons, too."

Upstairs in the bedroom we shared, my sisters were hanging upside down from opposite sides of their bunk-bed and talking boodjah — a private language they'd invented.

"Boodja boodja?" Ellie inquired.

"Boodja boodja!" Sarah Jane replied. They giggled maniacally.

I ignored them. I got into my nightie and then into my bed — a single in the corner. Before Mum came up to turn off the light I thumbed through our Children's Golden Treasury of Verse looking for color drawings of fairies, because they looked like ballerinas. It was the costume that I wanted more than the dance lessons. The silky fit of the bodice, the starched crisp skirt. And, if only it could be managed, a pair of delicate wings springing out of my shoulder blades.

It was a muggy Indian summer night in Toronto's west end. The windows were open. Waxy smells from the nearby shoe factory drifted into our room along with the smell of cabbage cooking. Restless, we climbed out of our beds to look out the window. Above, the sky was indigo blue with puffy pink-stained clouds piling up behind the house next door. They looked good enough to eat.

"That's all cotton candy," I declared. My sisters stared hungrily skyward. All that candy, looking close enough to touch from the neighbor's roof — fine spun and rain fresh, not flyspecked or stale like the cotton candy at the Exhibition. If only we could fly.

The ballet lessons took place on Saturday mornings in the basement of a church within walking distance of our store, the same place where my Brownie pack met on Wednesday nights. I had joined the Brownies as soon as I turned eight, having looked forward for months to wearing the crisp brown uniform and soft beret. The meetings were boring though, except for signaling in semaphore and dancing around a toadstool. I was now Sixer of the Fairy Circle, a kind of captain appointed by the pack leader.

"Where are you going?" Sarah Jane demanded, watching me dress.

"Brownies," I mumbled. "It's a special Fairy Circle," and rushed out of our room and down the stairs before she could question me further.

Light slanted weakly through the sidewalk-level windows onto the scuffed floor where about two dozen small girls were lined up in rows. A few wore flounced skirts with tights and ballerina slippers, but the rest of us had shorts and blouses on and lisle stockings clipped to garter belts. I was a late comer to this beginning group, older and taller than any of the girls, who were closer to my sisters in age, between five and six. This did not fit well with the self-image I'd been concocting of a wee sprite in satin and gossamer. The teacher, a thin, nervous woman with a foreign accent, thumped out brisk rhythms on an upright piano.

"Girls, make your legs vide enough for a pussycat to jump through!" she commanded. Her name was Masha, I found out later, and she had been a displaced person after the war.

She came over to me and adjusted my legs and arms. "Stand up very straight," she said. "Your shoulders must not look defeated."

On the way home I crawled under the barbed wire fence that bordered the train yard. The fence was as derelict as the box cars and rusted rails, and the factory with broken windows. I strode along the tracks with my shoulders thrown back and head held high, and pretended I was hopping a train to California where I would get a job dancing in a movie. Then I climbed on top of a freight car and lay on my back and stared at the vast sky with its fluffy clouds. What if I really did have wings? What would I find up there? Real fairies — I could almost see them — lighter than air, they lived in cloud castles and nibbled sugar plums endlessly with their tiny diamond teeth that never got cavities.

When I got home Ellie and Sarah Jane were waiting impatiently for me. I had forgotten about the matinee at the Lansdowne Theater, where they could not go without me. I bolted down a peanut butter sandwich and milk.

Every Saturday, Daddy took three dimes and three nickels out of the cash register for us. The movie cost a dime; the rest was for candy that we bought along the way — caramels, bubble gum, marshmallow yo-yos, licorice jump-ropes, fizzy powder, tiny maple sugar tarts, edible wax lips and mustaches. It was always a tough decision. It was a heroic effort not to eat the candy until after the film began. "Let's make believe everything is made of candy," I said as we hurried along with our sweets tucked in a paper sack. "That fence is butterscotch."

"That house is chocolate," Ellie rhapsodized. "Everything is made of chocolate."

Sarah Jane stuck a thumb in her mouth as she trotted down the street. Not only was everything in the world made of candy in this game, it grew back after we ate it.

That afternoon we watched a re-run of the Coronation along with several cartoons, a Superman serial and an Esther Williams movie. We had seen the Coronation newsreel twice before; it was still wonderful, with an abundance of ermine-lined capes and diamond tiaras and the new Queen kneeling to accept her bejeweled crown and scepter. Esther Williams was queenly, too, diving into a turquoise blue pool, regal as a ballerina in a bathing suit. I dispensed candy at regular intervals from the sack.

A few hours later we came blinking out of the theater. We wandered off toward home in a daze. A cool breeze had sprung up, the first harbinger of autumn. Clouds seemed to tumble across the sky like acrobats.

"Cotton candy!" I cried out.

Ellie and Sarah Jane nodded eagerly.

"Fairies live in those clouds," I improvised. "They're dancing. That's why the clouds are moving so fast."

The story spilled out then without my thinking about it. Right above our heads fairies were celebrating the coronation of their new queen which had taken place that very morning. They were performing a ballet; every one of them, even the Queen, dancing effortlessly on their toes because they were suspended in air. Afterward they would dine on chocolate and maple sugar Laura Secords. I had been invited to the coronation ceremony that morning because I was Sixer of the Fairy Circle of the 49th Brownie Pack. But I had to leave before the dancing and the banquet started so I could take my sisters to the movies. Luckily, the Queen liked me and had invited me to visit her in the clouds once a week for a short time on Saturday mornings. Humans weren't supposed to be there. It was a tough magic spell to cast, just keeping one kid my size afloat. Fairies are very tiny, no bigger than Sarah Jane's baby finger; they could shrink me to their size but couldn't give me wings unless I decided to live with them forever.

I glanced at my sisters. They were staring up at the sky in wonder. They believe me, I realized astonished. They think it's real. An unfamiliar excitement grew in me.

"Promise you'll keep it secret," I said solemnly. "If you tell anyone, I could die."

They both promised, looking somewhat startled.

"The spell could break," I explained. "I could fall out of the clouds."

I went on to describe the fairy coronation I had witnessed, followed by an account of fairy diet and hygiene. Fairies never had to take a bath since, living up in the air, they didn't get dirty. All that twirling around kept the cotton candy clouds clean as well. Because they ate nothing but candy all their lives (which spanned hundreds of years), they peed pure lemon fizz anywhere and anytime they felt like it. They pooped tiny chocolate nut turds all over the clouds.

We giggled explosively, a chain reaction.

Sarah Jane laughed so hard she sat down on the curb and wet her pants. Then she burst into tears.

"It's lemon fizz," Ellie tried cheering her up.

"It is not," she sniffled.

"Anyway, most of the time they pee into little pots." I hastily revised the story.

"Like ours in Belle Ewarte?" Ellie asked.

Belle Ewarte was a small village on Lake Simcoe, an hour's drive north of Toronto, where our grandmother had a summer cottage. The cottage had electricity but no indoor plumbing. Water was supplied from a pump in the yard and the toilet was a double-seater outhouse. My sisters and I had chamber pots made of enameled tin with our names painted on the sides. Even though we were all old enough by then to manage the high wooden seats in the outhouse, we still used our pots at night.

I told them that I floated up to Cloudland seated on a pee pot made of spun gold that was lighter than air.

"I find some place nobody can see me. Somewhere in the train yard." They listened eagerly. The train yard was forbidden and they had never been inside it. "Then I think the magic words and the pot comes floating down to get me. They're not words you can say out loud. It's thinking without real words."

"Like boodja talk," Ellie nodded thoughtfully at Sarah Jane.

"Kind of. And as soon as I sit on the pot it floats back up to the clouds."

They were really hooked now. Why else would I go out on Saturday morning alone?

I began to dread the ballet lesson. Masha nagged me intermittently, droning instructions. I felt loutish and confined in the church basement, and I knew I would thump across the boards like a baby hippo. I couldn't concentrate on pliés and relevés; I'd much rather think about Cotton Candy Cloudland. I had to think about it. A new serial was required by my sisters every Saturday en route to the matinee at the Lansdowne.

I thought about it all week long in school. It was more interesting than Dick and Jane stories or multiplication tables. On Wednesday nights I was filled with scorn for the mundane activities of the 49th Pack. A real fairy would not have to earn a badge for sewing. A real fairy would simply wish for an embroidered handkerchief — or a tutu. Despite my ineptitude on the dance floor I still longed for a tutu.

We had a new game to play. My sisters were bored with Sheba of the Jungle and Dale Evans, Queen of the Cowboys, even with Witch in the Cellar. They wanted to pretend they were visiting the court of the Fairy Queen.

I complied gladly at first. The dark hallway between kitchen and grocery store served as a secret place to think the magic words that summoned down our golden pots. We pretended to sit on them and float up the stairs and along the upstairs hallway to our parents' bedroom, which we made believe was Cotton Candy Cloudland. This room was large and sunny with bay windows and a window seat that we climbed on to observe the world below. We dared not linger long. Pleasure was edged with danger. At the stroke of 12, down we came or forfeit all.

I explained that if we were to stay up in the clouds we would never see our parents or grandparents or anyone we knew again. It was something like immigrating. You can't ever go back to the Old Country.

Eventually we grew bored with that game, too, and instead played in the backyard. We dug worms up out of the iron-hard ground and housed them in a shoebox, the Orphanage for Worms. The worms were assigned beds and names. We hovered over the box to make sure our charges stayed put, didn't track dirt in and didn't talk back. By the end of the day, deprived of earth and food, they had all died. The next day Ellie busily nailed living worms to a board, to my disgust. She wanted to feed the robin red breasts. Sarah Jane and I had a big fight and she broke an arm off my favorite doll.

The days grew shorter. It was too cold and nasty to play outdoors.

One night as we were going upstairs after supper, I asked my sisters, "Want to go to Cloudland?"

"Really? Now?" they both shouted. Their faces lit up. "Can we really go?"

"I mean make believe," I said quickly. "You can't really go."

"Not ever?" Ellie asked. They both looked ready to cry. "Can't you ask the Queen?" Ellie pleaded.

"I could try," I said finally in a small voice. That seemed to mollify them. I no longer had the heart to play the game, but they insisted and didn't notice how woodenly I went through the familiar routine.

After we got into bed and lights were out I lay awake for a long time. I felt trapped in the hugeness and complexity of my lie. I put my hands together in what I hoped was the correct position for prayer. I had learned about God in school. But my family did not pray nor did we attend religious services, so I was not clear on procedure. I *thought* my prayer as hard as I could, several times over and in explicit detail. Dear God, make it all be true and I will believe in You forever, was the gist of my request.

Make it be true, I prayed at school during the Lord's Prayer, which wasn't a Jewish prayer anyway, so I thought the God of my Fathers should not take offense. Whenever I thought about it, which was often, I fired off a quick silent prayer. I prayed myself to sleep every night. I supplied all the minutiae necessary for God to undertake this creation.

Daily my sisters grew more expectant and I, more miserable. I couldn't look them in the face anymore when I made up my excuses. I told them the Queen had quite a temper, she was hard to approach, I had to wait for the right moment or she'd lock me up for a thousand years or fling me out of the clouds — without the pot.

Days went by, then weeks. The prayers weren't working. Maybe only old guys with beards and shawls prayed, maybe I was not supposed to pray. Maybe I was doing it wrong or my prayer wasn't important enough. Maybe God was a lie, too.

The more I thought about it, the madder I got at Aunt Rose and the ballet lessons, which seemed to be the source of all my problems. I asked my mother finally if I could stop studying ballet.

"I wish you'd told me sooner," she sighed. It turned out that Aunt Rose's money got used up and my parents were paying for the lessons now, so they'd be happy to have me quit. But this wouldn't solve my problem at all, I realized. I burst into tears to my mother's amazement.

She took me in her arms to comfort me. When I could talk again I explained somewhat disjointedly what I had been telling my sisters I was doing on Saturday mornings.

"You've got some imagination," she said. Her mouth twitched like she was trying not to smile.

"What can I tell them now?"

"Oh you'll think of something. What about the truth?"

The truth? But the truth was that I lied to them. The truth was that I didn't want to give up that other, perfect world of my own making.

My sisters and I were in the kitchen eating rice and milk and butter. It was raining hard outside. Thunder rumbled in the distance. Ellie wanted to float up to Cloudland after supper. I shook my head, no.

"I mean make believe," Ellie said eagerly.

"When it thunders!" Sarah Jane chimed in.

I didn't answer. I couldn't invent anymore, it seemed, or even talk. Sarah Jane tugged at my sleeve.

"It's all make believe," I managed to whisper, looking into my empty bowl.

They stared at me, not quite understanding.

"It never was real. I never ever went there. I was taking ballet lessons and Mum said not to tell you, so I made it all up."

Ellie looked shocked; Sarah Jane angry.

"You, you," she sputtered. She threw her spoon on the floor.

We all went up the stairs without speaking, undressed and got into bed, though bedtime was an hour away.

They didn't talk to me that night. I lay wide awake listening to thunder coming closer. I felt light-headed, relieved of a crushing burden, and this was so pleasant a sensation that I swore a mighty oath never to lie to anyone again. I watched over my sisters who were sleeping soundly despite the storm. Lightning illuminated their faces. I would save them if the house caught fire. Then they would forgive me.

A few years later we three went up in the air with our mother in a four-prop plane that was taking us to live in the States. Our father would join us once he had sold the grocery store. Mum was stylish in a new shirtwaist dress, her eyes shiny with excitement. We all chewed gum and flew straight toward a bank of tumbled white cumulus clouds.

Although I had studied the water cycle in school, I was not prepared for the disappointment I felt when, having penetrated a fleecy cloud, I found myself staring out at dreary fog.

I saw the same disappointment on my sisters' faces.

"A cloud is the same as fog," I lectured. "It's the condensation of water that rises..."

"Blah blah blah!" Sarah Jane snapped.

Even Ellie looked disgusted with me. She put her hands on her ears. "Ow, shut up," she said.

We sisters were in a foul mood until the plane rose up and soared above a cloud bank, stained pink and orange by the setting sun. We flew on through a starry night to our new home in a land where, we had been told, coconuts and oranges would drop out of trees into our outstretched hands.

Queen of Egypt

The Polowskis arrived late on Christmas Eve, long after the children had given up watching for a white Cadillac convertible with a black top and gone to bed. The drapes were pushed back in the living room so that anyone passing by could look in. The street lamp near their apartment cast a bluish-green glare over the road.

"That must be them," Brenda said. A white and black sedan lumbered slowly through the intersection and disappeared, lost among the dozens of identical two-story apartment blocks.

In a few minutes the car reappeared, and Dave snapped their porch light on and off several times. "Hey y'all!" he hollered. "You all get your sorry bums off the road, you hear?"

"You all yourself, you crazy bugger," they heard Roman snigger in the car.

Their visitors carried suitcases inside the apartment. The men shook hands. The women pecked each other's cheeks.

Dolly, pale and plump, bright blond hair swept up in a French twist, wore tight toreador pants and a low-cut halter. "Brenda, you're looking great," she cooed. "What a marvelous tan."

"How you all doing, colonel suh," Roman drawled. "How's the missus, eh?" He was taller than Dave and long in the jaw.

Brenda offered soda or tea.

"Got anything stronger, sugar? We've been on the road since dawn."

Dolly looked around the room. "We don't want to crowd you," she murmured.

"Don't think like that," Dave said. "It's like being on a cruise ship, a little tight but everyone fits."

It was only a week since Dave told her he'd invited the Polowskis to stay with them, and Brenda was still bewildered. Roman and Dolly Polowski had been their neighbors and Dave's poker buddies back in Toronto. But she didn't consider them friends. "Where will they sleep?" she'd ventured.

Dave had arranged to rent a sofabed at a discount from the furniture store where he worked, and Roman would help him move it once they got here. He had it all planned. Why didn't he ask her first, she wondered. He had also decided to uproot her and the children without consulting her. She didn't so much mind being transplanted to another city and country as not being asked. "We're moving to the States," he'd announced, and that was the end of one life and the beginning of a new, which, he assured her, would be an adventure for all of them.

It was their first winter in Miami. The three girls slept in one bedroom, she and Dave in the other. The rent was cheap and the pool across the street — for tenants of the Coral Springs Manor — made up for their cramped quarters.

While their daughters were in school, she swam and sunbathed. Weekends the family spent the entire day poolside. Brenda's skin glowed like burnished bronze. Men still turned to appraise her in a bathing suit but Dave never seemed to notice. He roughhoused with the girls, tossed them into the water, taught them how to dive. Once he swam underwater and pinched Brenda's behind.

"Oh you!" she sputtered, and for the rest of that day felt loved.

It was too late to fetch the sofabed. The guests were given the back bedroom, Dave slept on the couch and Brenda slipped into a twin bed with Nora, their oldest. Nora was a restless, sharp elbowed sleeper in early adolescence. Her sisters, one dark, one fair, small replicas of Brenda and Dave, shared the other bed. She lay awake for a long time, watching a sliver of blue light where the drapes didn't quite close and listening to the children breathe. She heard Dolly's husky laughter through the walls and Roman's baritone rumble. She knew Dave lay awake, too. He was over 40 and selling furniture on commission 1500 miles from what had been their home, but it was better than working seven days a week in their grocery store while supermarkets opened all over the city and former customers avoided them in the street.

She recalled how he'd cheer up whenever Dolly Polowski sauntered into the store for a pack of cigarettes. Brenda never knew what to say to her. Not that it mattered, since Dolly didn't linger when Dave wasn't there.

"We made a bet," Dolly said the next morning. "I said you guys do Christmas on account of the kids. Roman said you don't on account of you're Jewish. So, if you don't, then consider these house warming gifts."

"Pay her off, Roman," Dave waggled one finger. "It's like an extra day of Hanukah. That way the kids never feel left out."

Still in their baby doll pajamas, the children filed into the livingroom. Nora was a head taller than Ellie and Sarah Jane.

"How you've grown!" Dolly exclaimed.

"She's a young lady now," Brenda said, and Nora flushed.

"I'd give anything for a daughter," Dolly sighed.

The girls stared shyly at their visitors.

Dolly piled gaily wrapped boxes on the dining table. A pound of Laura Secords chocolates was opened and passed around. Dave got a bottle of Crown Royal; the girls, travel kits with Elvis Presley logos, and Brenda, a silver bangle bracelet. Dolly watched intently as she slid it onto her wrist. "You look just like that lady," she said.

She pointed at a woman's head in profile on the bangle. There were two kneeling bas relief figures on either side of the head, one of them playing a stringed instrument. The woman wore a strange sort of tall hat. The bangle wasn't really silver; it was tin or aluminum.

"She's the Queen of Egypt," Dolly said. "Her name is on the tag."

Brenda read the tag. Queen Nefrititi, it said. She wasn't sure this was a good thing. Maybe she'd been spending too much time in the sun. Fair skinned Dolly and flaxen haired Dave were laughing at something Brenda had missed, and Roman said practically in her ear, "Y'all lookin' right pretty, Nefrititi."

Dolly said, "That southern accent is driving me nuts, will you can it!"

Dave took the bottle of whiskey out of its purple bag and gave the bag to Ellie for her marble collection. "Tell you what. We're throwing a New Year's party," he said. "Our first party in Miami."

Brenda made dozens of tuna and egg tea sandwiches for the party. She got her daughters to tidy their bedroom before they went to South Beach with the Polowskis and Dave. She didn't mind not going. It was a relief to be alone and her head hurt. Roman and Dolly were still strangers to her, though not to Dave. He was all keyed up. Playing cards late at night, shouting happy insults. Flirting with Dolly, yes he was, he always had probably. And then Roman would tease her and the girls.

Dolly seemed to want to be her friend. She washed dishes and helped prepare dinners. One afternoon when they were alone in the apartment, she confessed to Brenda that she'd been seeing another man back home.

"I know I can trust you not to tell."

Brenda nodded, puzzled.

"Maybe you noticed, Roman has a roving eye," Dolly went on. "But he'd kill me if he found out. See what I mean? It's alright for him, but not for me. I bet you think it's wrong, no matter what."

Brenda tried to see it from Dolly's perspective.

"Maybe it depends on the situation. If the man you're seeing is married, for instance, that wouldn't be right."

"What if he's not happily married?"

"But what about his wife? If she loves him? Somebody's going to be hurt."

"It sure does get complicated," Dolly said. "That's why, mum's the word."

After cleaning the apartment, Brenda showered and changed into her good taffeta dress with a starched crinoline beneath. She brushed her black hair till it shone, clipped on silver earrings and slipped the new bangle on her wrist. She regarded herself in a full-length mirror. Her waist was slender, breasts small. She used a pocket mirror to examine her profile. The nose was too long, the chin too short for beauty, she decided.

Roman and Dolly had picked up streamers and hats. Whistling, Roman tacked a banner over the entrance to the kitchen that said HAPPY NEW YEAR 1958.

Ethel and Irv Levine and the Blattners arrived in one car. They were all transplants from suburban Toronto and had never met Dolly and Roman before. The women wore flower print dresses and little heels. They tried not to stare at Dolly's tight skirt and low-cut peasant blouse.

Brenda shooed Ellie and Sarah Jane off to bed. Nora wanted to stay up till midnight. "I'm not a kid anymore," she insisted.

That was fine with Brenda, and Dave was already too jovial to protest.

Dolly had brought some new 45s along and she gave them to Nora to play. The girl listened wide-eyed to Ray Charles singing "I've got a woman, way over town, she's good to me." She played it five times in a row.

"Sugar, you need to dance to that music," Roman took her in his arms and whirled her around the room. Brenda watched Roman's big hand on her daughter's slim waist and felt queasy. He postured dramatically, swaying his hips, and Nora didn't know where to put her feet. Her cheeks were bright pink. After that dance, she sat in a corner sipping coke for awhile and then slipped into the bedroom.

The Crown Royal got polished off first. Brenda drank too much too fast and the party rolled forward like a jerky old-time movie. Dolly was working the room, flattering the women and flirting with the men. She and Dave volleyed jokes back and forth nonstop. They had nicknames for each other Brenda had never heard before, Blondie and Bubba.

"Blondie and Bubba," Irv howled. "They could be on TV, right hon? The Blondie and Bubba Comedy Hour." He was a big, good natured man, easily amused.

Ethel ignored him. She was fussing over Brenda's new bracelet. "It's so unusual," she cooed. Not "it's lovely" or "it becomes you." *Unusual.* Brenda twisted it on her wrist, to hide the profile of the queen.

At midnight everyone kissed everyone else. She saw Dave kissing Dolly slowly. Dolly kissed all the men at great length, without discrimination, but this was too much for Brenda. She was crossing the room to claim a kiss from her husband, when Roman grabbed her. His tongue went into her mouth and she almost gagged. She broke away and ran into the bathroom. Shaking a little, she pulled the bangle off her arm.

When she came out again, Dolly was dancing with Irv. He held her close, swung her away, pulled her close. Dolly didn't take her eyes off him. His wife watched, too, face sharp as a cleaver. Suddenly, Ethel elbowed her way through the dancers and spat out, "Hands off him, shicksa!"

Dolly threw her hands up and laughed. "Look ma, no hands."

"Now, Ethel, honey," Irv began.

"Don't you honey me."

"What did she call her?" Roman asked.

"A shicksa," Ethel repeated. "In plain English, a floozy. A cheap tramp."

"Son of a bitch," Dolly breathed.

The two women squared off. They were a whirlwind of crinolines and fists, and finally had to be pulled apart.

And that was the end of the New Year's Eve party. Ethel huffed off with Irv and the Blattners trailing behind.

Dave tried to smooth things over. "Don't mind Ethel," he said. "She's always been the jealous type, isn't that right Brenda?"

Brenda shrugged and said nothing.

Dolly would not be placated, and Roman scowled. "I knew we shouldn't've come. What'd I tell you, Dolly?"

In the morning when the children got out of bed to greet the New Year, Dolly and Roman were gone. Off to stay in a motel, Brenda told them.

"But they promised they'd take us to the zoo," Ellie cried.

"In the Cadillac with the top down," Sarah Jane added.

Dave came out of the bathroom holding the bangle. "Brenda, how did this get in the garbage?" He sounded annoyed.

"I threw it away."

"Now, why would you do that?"

"I don't like it."

"It's pretty," Nora protested.

"You can have it," Brenda said.

Dave rolled his eyes and handed the bangle to his daughter.

The girl looked startled and pleased. She turned it around carefully and touched the profile of the Egyptian queen. "She really does look like you, Mum."

"Let me take another look," Dave said and Nora passed it back to him. He held it between thumb and forefinger. "This does look like you, hon. It was thoughtful of Dolly."

But Brenda turned away from him. "It's a piece of junk," she said.

Miss Kelly Citation Tire

The opening day crowd at the track pressed through the gates and swelled toward the betting windows, parting before me like a stream around a rock. For a long moment, I couldn't move or speak. I was the only person in a swimsuit at Hialeah Racetrack.

My father got me this job. What was he thinking?

I was wearing a one-piece swimsuit and high-heeled pumps. A wide green ribbon, pinned diagonally from shoulder strap to hip, announced I was Miss Kelly Citation Tire 1965. I'd been hired to hand out promotional pamphlets for new tires.

At first I tottered like a colt in the shiny white pumps I'd bought to wear to interviews. There had been no interview for this job. My father and the tire store manager, Al Brown, were lodge brothers in the Knights of Pythias. Daddy was really pleased with himself. He'd sold Al a life insurance plan and snagged me a job. "It'll be a piece of cake," he said. "You walk around, you smile, you make forty bucks."

Al drove me to the track in his Lincoln Continental. He was a little younger than my father, his hair a mat of tight gray curls, square-jawed face deeply tanned. I'd met him a few years before at a Pythian family picnic. His wife was tall and thin with breasts like giant grapefruits, and they had a chubby little girl who'd played horseshoes with my father.

Al kept looking at me as if trying to figure something out. I wore a shapeless floral print muumuu over the swimsuit. It was what I put over my costume every night for the drive to and from my shift at the Tiki.

"Maybe this is a crazy idea," he mumbled.

"Hi!" I trilled, showing all my teeth. "Here's a special offer for y'all."

That worked alright until a guy in checkered Bermudas and a black t-shirt stretched over his paunch leered, "Anything else on offer, babe?" Then I switched to: "Hi, here's a real deal on tires for y'all."

It didn't matter what I said. Men took the flyers automatically.

Some women went out of their way to avoid me; most seemed startled or amused. A wrinkled redhead in tight toreadors grabbed several, her ruby nails like claws. "I don't have a car," she murmured, "I'll take these for my boyfriend."

I glided through the crowd, head held high, smiling graciously. Princess Grace Kelly Citation Tire. It wasn't a bad gig, after all.

When the supply of flyers was gone, I walked over to the snack bar to get more from Al. The crowd was thinning now. People either looked me over or tried not to look. Without the stack of paper in hand, I felt self-conscious again. The pumps hurt my feet.

Al looked up from the racing form. "How'd it go, sweetheart?"

"They snapped 'em all up."

"I knew it. Sit down, sit down. Take a break."

I dropped into a chair, grateful to be off my feet. The plastic stuck to the back of my thighs. Now Al was looking me over, just like everyone else.

"Dave was right. You're a babe."

"My father told you I'm a babe?"

He reconsidered. "Aw, not exactly. He said you look good in a swimsuit."

I shivered. "Boy, it's cold in here." I pulled the muu-muu out of the bag I'd left with Al and draped it over my shoulders. Then I took out my compact and checked my make-up in the mirror.

"Are you really 21, Nora?"

"Would my father lie to you?"

"Maybe."

"Well, I wouldn't," I said a little crossly, eying my reflection. No matter what I did with mascara and lipstick, I still had a round baby face.

I was the youngest cocktail waitress at the Tiki. The skirt of my sarong draped around my hips just below the navel and fell to mid-thigh, with a slit to show more thigh as I moved; the top piece was a cheap bra covered in the same fabric. Although my mother wasn't convinced the job was respectable, she had helped me sew the costume.

My station was at the bar facing the front entrance. Small fluorescent lights behind the bar made my earrings glitter.

"Aloha," I'd say, greeting everyone who came in with a cheery smile.

"Aloha," they'd chorus in passing.

The bar was rarely busy, even weekends when a hula troupe performed in the main dining room. I felt like an animated figurehead at the prow of a ship, alluring and only occasionally useful, until late at night when the serious drinkers staggered in from shows in the big hotels. They were usually conventioneers on a binge. Sometimes I picked up extra tips by posing with customers out on the floor, their arms draped around my shoulders or waist. The cigarette girl who doubled as photographer whispered instructions in my ear. "He won't bite you, kid. Sit on his knee."

Once, my parents came to the Tiki for dinner with their friends Betty and Leo Roth, and had their picture taken with me. "Sweet Leilani and the Gang," my father wrote on the border of the Polaroid print, which he pasted into the family album.

Al went off to buy us coffee. While he was gone, I looked at his racing form. I liked the names of the horses: Sir Bontempi, Desert Moon, Celestial Jade, Finnegan's Whiskers, Lucky Redhead. Miss Kelly Citation could be a horse's name.

My father used to read the racing news every day. I was a little girl then and we lived behind our grocery store. The store was often quiet. Supermarkets were opening nearby and we had ever fewer customers. Daddy would open the newspaper to the sports section, pen in hand.

I remember looking up at him behind the counter, smiling down at me. I'd just discovered words can be spelled.

"Spell sugar," I demanded. "Spell eggs. Tea."

"Enough!" he said finally.

He came around the meat cooler and picked me up and deposited me on a large burlap sack of sugar. Then he folded the newspaper and put it on my knees and pointed to the columns where horses' names were listed.

"Try to spell the names of the horsies," he said.

I didn't know, until my mother told me, that for several years my father ran a bookie business out of the grocery store. Customers placed their bets while picking up a pack of cigarettes or a ham sandwich.

During those years my mother worried he'd be caught and put in jail. Or that her family would get wind of it. The idea of her parents finding out struck terror in her heart.

"He had to bribe the cop on our beat with a ham every Christmas," she said. "I was miserable when we had the store."

I was still living at home because I couldn't afford both college tuition and rent. Sometimes I'd go out after my shift at the Tiki and listen to music or eat breakfast on the 79th Street Causeway in the middle of the night. Even on my nights off I'd get home quite late, slipping into my room before anyone was awake. One night I didn't make it in till after dawn.

I had been in bed with my boyfriend Thunder. He was not the kind of boyfriend I'd introduce to my parents, so they didn't know he existed. I didn't even know his real name. His glossy black hair was longer than mine, his eyes as green and impenetrable as the swamp. The sinewy arms holding me were tattooed with snakes that wrapped around and swallowed their tails. Thunder's gig, trapping water moccasins in the Everglades to sell to pet stores, excited and frightened me. He was a man of few words, and sometimes I imagined my own words ricocheting around inside his head like ping pong balls. Yet he was a gentler and more experienced lover than any previous boyfriend. His skin felt like something I could sink into.

A pet gecko lived in the house where Thunder rented a room. It made loud gek gek gek sounds on and off through the night; maybe it was lonesome. The gecko woke me up that morning. Gek gek gek.

I gunned my car down hushed thoroughfares. A pale blob of sun had just cleared the horizon. Dew glistened on the cut grass and hibiscus bushes outside our house. The windows were all dark. I unlocked and opened the front door quietly.

My father was sitting in the Florida room next to the fake rubber tree plant, arms folded over his chest. He was dressed for work in lime checked slacks and a white shirt, his thinning hair damp from the morning shower, face freshly shaved.

"Good morning, Daddio," I said.

He managed a thin smile. Calling him "Daddio" was his idea, not mine. He wanted to be a cool, with-it dad.

"Where were you all night?"

"At a jazz club."

"All night?" he persisted. He stared at me and his face got bright pink.

"Clubs don't stay open all night," he snapped.

"This one does," I improvised. "They locked the doors, the band wailed, and we boogied the night away."

He took a deep breath and spoke slowly with that penetrating gaze that was worse than being slapped.

"I don't really want to know what you were up to, but as long as you're under my roof, I'm asking you to come home at a decent hour."

"That's ridiculous." I fumed. "I'm 21 years old. And believe me, I'm moving out of here as soon as I possibly can."

"You're behaving like a tramp," he spat out.

I stormed down the hall to my room and shut the door and fell on the bed.

Within reach of my bed was a bookcase my father had custom built for me because the room was too small for standard sized shelving. When I was younger, he'd hide my weekly allowance between or inside the books and I'd have to hunt for it.

I looked at the book spines and put my face in a pillow and cried, soundlessly. After a while, I grew drowsy. I must have fallen asleep.

Three men in suits came into the room and sat on barstools next to my bed, drinking and talking, blah blah blah. It was shadowy at first, then daylight streamed through the window. I struggled to wake up, but could still see them clearly. They were standing now and clinking the ice in their glasses. Irritated, I wondered why my mother had let them into the house. "Leave me alone," I pleaded.

My mother opened the door cautiously.

"Who are you talking to" she asked.

I sat up in bed and looked around, astonished. It had been so real.

"Don't mind what your father says, Nora. He's just worried about you."

"What about you? Were you worried?"

There were dark circles under her eyes. She shrugged. "I trust you," she said.

The next day, my father acted as though nothing had happened. Presto, once again he was the cool Daddio who didn't want to lose his little girl. And didn't want to know he already had. Maybe he got me the job at the track to make up for our quarrel.

He didn't go to Hialeah the day I was Miss Kelly Citation Tire. I think he didn't want to see his daughter parading unprotected and half naked through that mob. He rarely went to the track, anyway. He'd rather bet on cards than horses. In fact, he was something of a card shark and we'd all go out to dinner whenever he won big.

Even though he didn't go, he tipped off his friends, who stopped to talk with me, people I'd known since I was a gawky, tongue-tied adolescent. Betty Roth laughed when she read the ribbon. "Aren't you glad they didn't make you wear a tire, dear?"

Al bought me a glazed doughnut with the coffee and watched while I wolfed it down.

"So how many boyfriends do you have, Nora?"

"One's plenty for me."

"You like him a lot, huh?"

"Yeah, sure."

"What's he like?"

"Tall, dark and handsome."

"Oh, really?"

"Well, he's an older man. He's twenty-eight."

Al looked a little startled.

A bell rang. He checked his watch.

"Next shift," he said. I took off the muumuu, gathered the flyers and stood up.

"Once more after this, Nora, they should all be gone. Say, you want to watch a race?"

"Sure," I said. "I've never seen one."

"Let's make it race number seven. Around four o'clock."

Al placed bets for both of us. I didn't want to, but he insisted on lending me a five spot.

"If you lose, I don't want it back. If you win, you owe me five. A deal?"

"A deal."

"Okay, now you choose from these three here that I've circled."

"I wouldn't know," I began.

"Doesn't matter. Just pick one. Beginner's luck, right?"

So I chose the name I liked best, Birdland Blue.

Al grunted and took off for the betting windows.

I had slipped the muumuu on and I'd have kicked off the heels and gone barefoot, but the floor was sticky with gum and spilled soda and beer. There were heaps of paper everywhere — torn tickets and some of our pastel fliers.

Our seats were halfway up the grandstand. It was a sweltering, muggy afternoon. I tugged at the muumuu till it slipped down my shoulders.

"I'll be ready for a swim when this is over," I said. "Which horse is ours?"

Al leaned over to point and his arm brushed across my breasts. I edged away from him, hoping that had been unintended. He was in pretty good shape for an old guy, but he was married. And he was my father's friend, wasn't he?

The horses were off and running. "Go Birdland, go!" I shouted. I had no idea which horse was Birdland Blue, but it didn't matter. It was like going to a football game, where I had only the fuzziest notion of how the game was played, but could howl there with impunity. I really did feel like roaring. I'd just smiled about a thousand phony smiles and I was tired of being nice to drunks every night.

"Rahhhhr Birdland," I growled. Everyone was standing and yelling now.

"It's Birdland Blue under the wire," the announcer cried. "Birdland Blue by a head, at five to one."

"Yowser!" Al shouted. "You did it, sweetheart!"

I jumped up and down, I was so excited. I gave Al a quick hug.

He grabbed me and hugged back. Then he pressed himself closer. Damn, the man was hard. He tried to kiss me with his tongue. I squirmed and pushed him away.

"Sorry," he said. "A guy's gotta try, right?"

"I wouldn't know."

"Oh, I think you do."

"You have a daughter, don't you?" I asked.

"What about it? You're not my daughter."

"And a wife?"

He shrugged and looked at his watch. "You just made an extra 20 bucks, kiddo. I made a pretty good haul myself. So thanks for the good luck. No hard feelings, okay? Can't win 'em all."

Al drove me to my car, which was parked at the tire store. He gave me a check for forty dollars, a twenty dollar bill and his business card. "Call me if you change your mind, doll," he said.

Asshole, I thought and drove off.

I tore the card in half and tossed it out the window. But that didn't erase the bad feeling. I thought Al might know something about me now. His embrace had, briefly, aroused me. Recalling it made me a little sick.

Then I thought about the extra twenty in my wallet. My parents were only going to hear the good news. I would take them out to dinner with my winnings. Daddio would be proud. That's my girl, he'd say.

Intruders

Every morning at six, weather permitting, Herr and Frau Leopold climbed the wooded hill next to the inn where they vacationed and descended to a clearing, ringed on the north with tall firs and opening on the south to the lake. They deposited deck chairs and baskets, stripped to their bathing suits, donned plastic caps and ran without a word into the water. Franz Josef cut effortlessly across the surface. In the water he did not feel his seventy years. Karla preferred to float on her back and look up at the circling gulls. If she tilted her head she could see the snowcaps on the Alps.

Then they returned to the clearing, and as the day progressed, moved their deckchairs around it in a semi-circle, following the sun.

Early in the morning Franz Josef read the newspaper from beginning to end. As the sun rose, his eyelids grew heavy. He adjusted his chair to a semi-reclining position and took out a volume of Schiller to read between naps.

Karla busied herself knitting scarves for her husband and son. At least that was her intention. Anything might distract her — a bird, a squirrel, a cloud. While Franz Josef dozed, she would swim again or stroll along the shore and look at the sunbathers. She would have liked to speak to some of these people, but of course it was not possible to sit down half-naked and insinuate herself into a conversation. From a distance, then, she wondered who they were and where they came from.

By late morning, the Leopolds might be joined by a few guests from their inn. No one so invited was gauche enough to play a radio or tape-recorder. No one wished to sit in the shade. Thus they all moved in quiet stages together around the clearing. When it had filled completely with shadow, Franz Josef and Karla returned to the inn for dinner.

From the window of their room, Karla had a view of the plum orchard and the highway sloping downhill past the wooden stations of the cross. But not of the mountains. It was just as well, she thought. Too much mountain-gazing made her restless. She would have liked to visit the Swiss Alps, but her husband dreaded traveling abroad. They had not so much as been to Austria in thirteen years, though the border was forty kilometers from their inn. Whenever she suggested they try some place more exotic, Franz Josef would remind her that outside of Germany, and sometimes inside, Germans of their generation were barely tolerated. At least on the Unterhimmelsee they were known and respected. It would be stressful to vacation elsewhere, and therefore pointless.

The Leopolds took all of their meals at the *Stammtisch,* the big oak table near the entrance that was the prerogative of the village elders. Occasionally other guests would seat themselves there before the Leopolds arrived. The inkeeper Frau Müller would gently request that they sit elsewhere, if you please, and when the Leopolds claimed their rightful place, report the incident to them, a flick of her eyes indicating the unthinking intruders.

Every morning at quarter of six, the innkeeper set out coffee and rolls and a picnic basket for the Leopolds on the *Stammtisch* and then went off to dust and sweep and cook and change the flypaper. Where else could they find such old-fashioned *gemutlichheit*? If only Frau Müller could organize the weather as successfully as she did her inn. Thunderstorms plagued the first week of their vacation. The days were swollen with rain and arthritis and marked by the slap of cards in the *Gaststübl* and the whine of mosquitos. When the sun finally came out, the beach was mobbed.

Even their "own" special spot was not proof against spillover from the grassy meadow where people sunbathed elbow to elbow. One cloudless morning, a large and noisy Turkish family marched into the clearing. The Leopolds stiffened in their chairs, whispered uneasily. "They have as much right as we," reasoned Karla. But Franz Josef disagreed. Year after year he had been required to deal with the public. In his retirement had he not earned the right to peace and quiet? Reluctantly he got to his feet. He stepped firmly across the clearing. He explained politely and patiently to a short mustachioed man who seemed to be in charge that this space was reserved for friends who were coming soon. The man shrugged.

No one joined them that day. The Turks spread their gear all over the clearing. The women in long dresses and bright shawls sat on blankets in the shade and prepared coffee and grilled meat. A radio played loud, highpitched music while several small children fought with plastic water guns. The boys had hair cropped close to the skull and they looked like ugly little soldiers, but the girls were exquisite, Karla thought, with their black curls and long-lashed eyes.

Franz Josef moved their deck chairs as usual around the clearing with the sun, until at one o'clock, he was practically on top of a blanket full of giggling adolescent girls. An older woman barked out a guttural command and the girls moved out of his path.

Karla fled to the lake and swam vigorously. When she looked shoreward, she saw only a dense clump of fir protecting their camp and the green rolling hills that, dotted with farms and cows and cross-stitched with fences, covered her angst like a quilt.

Following the "Turkish affair," Franz Josef spread their blankets and chairs strategically around the clearing early every morning, securing it against invasion. He insisted that — until reinforcements from the inn arrived — either he or Karla stand guard. That meant they did not swim together at dawn.

"Now you're going a bit too far," she protested mildly. "I don't want to worry every minute."

"If we take a few simple precautions, we won't have to worry."

She decided to humor him.

Franz Josef was at bottom a mild-tempered, retiring man whose back went up in unfamiliar situations. Only when they were in their own home was he truly at ease. He would have been content to stay at home with "his best friend" as he called her, and never leave. It really is a shame, she thought, not for the first time, that he has no close friends. He was a little jealous of hers. He had been jealous of their son, especially when Ulrich was small and demanding.

Franz Josef remained fiercely loyal to the memory of two young men who had been "friends beyond compare." One had died on the eastern front; the other, in France. Their framed photographs hung in his "museum," a little room under the main staircase that had been off limits to their boy unless he were accompanied by an adult. There too were housed collections of antique carpenter's tools, dueling pistols, nautical instruments, rare leather bound books, some Limoges platters, and Franz Josef's prize possession, a three-masted ship in a bottle which had been assembled by his great-grandfather in the last century and which one day, he fretted, would fall into the careless hands of their only child, that thirty-year-old university student and motorcycle bum.

Ulrich Leopold had never vacationed on the Unterhimmelsee. He traveled instead to places like Thailand and California. These vacations lasted six months. Afterward he came home without money or a job. Franz Josef did not bother to hide his disappointment. But Karla still maintained that the best time for a young man to see something of the world is before he settles down.

"And when will that be? Your young man is over thirty."

"Soon. He's calming down already."

Her hopes were based on the fact that Uli had been with one woman for eighteen months and that Franz Josef himself had been 33 and more dead than alive when Karla met him. "Those were different times," he countered, "And I was not handed the world on a platter. I tell you what, he doesn't need the love of a good woman. He's had that already for 30 years, perhaps too much of it." How many times had they argued thus. It was as close as they ever came to anger, the little cold war in the closet, Karla called it. Her position strengthened considerably when the American girlfriend convinced Uli to move out of the *Besitzwohnung* where they had squatted all winter with a band of fellow anarchists, and not a moment too soon, for the following week the police raided the building, tore down the red "occupied" banner and hauled the occupants off to jail.

"How long can he get by on luck and charm," Franz Josef queried icily. "As for what's-her-name, grinning at me like a monkey, I suppose she thinks she's charming too."

"Donna is a go-getter," Karla shot back. "She'll see to it Uli makes his diploma."

"What about the way she dresses. Just barely." He was referring to the *Amerikanerin's* flimsy low-cut blouses and tight leather pants.

Karla replied, "It's the style, isn't it? You are too old-fashioned. Besides, the leather keeps her warm on the motorcycle, she told me."

That motorcycle. She could not refrain from teasing him. Nothing irked Franz Josef more than Uli's motorcycle unless it were the mopeds which the last few summers had been whining up the trail past their clearing on the Unterhimmelsee. He hated the noise and the smell. Karla secretly liked the smell. It reminded her of gas stations early in the morning of a long trip.

Karla woke up abruptly. Her sleep had been undisturbed. Night had not leaked into the dawn. The day might be extraordinary; it could not possibly be bad. It was foolish, she knew, but sometimes just pulling a fresh sundress over her bathingsuit made her heart beat a little faster.

At six o'clock they left the inn and crossed the deserted highway. A fine skein of dew lay over grass and trees. The sky was delicate and cloudless.

They climbed the hill slowly. They were carrying deck chairs, picnic basket, towels, books, newspaper, knitting needles and yarn. Karla felt oddly unencumbered, as if she were many years younger. She glanced at her husband. He was deep in thought, his sparse hair lifting in the breeze.

At the top of the rise they paused to catch their breath and to appreciate the view of lake and mountains. Cowbells clanged lightly. Otherwise no sound disturbed the early morning quiet. They moved more swiftly downhill on a damp trail between the firs. Karla shivered. Franz Josef transferred the deck chair to his other hand and with the free one, vigorously rubbed her bare arms.

When they came to the hedge which separated the trail from their clearing, he stopped suddenly. He could see over the bushes, but she on tip toe could not.

"What's the matter, dear," she whispered.

"A bicycle," he replied simply.

"A bicycle at this hour? It's not possible."

Each mirrored the other's incredulity and disappointment.

"Someone must be sleeping there," Franz Josef whispered.

Quietly they walked around the end of the hedge and peered into the clearing. There at the spot where they normally deposited their chairs at this hour stood a bicycle. On the ground nearby, like a giant dark slug in their path, lay a sleeping bag.

Franz Josef raised his voice to just above a whisper.

"He'll be on his way before too long. Meanwhile we'll have our swim." He lowered his voice. "And we'll take all of our gear down to the shore."

The gear now seemed a burden. The silence they shared had grown heavier too. At the beach they deposited their belongings, removed their outer clothing, put on their caps and plunged joylessly into the water.

Karla thrashed about for several minutes, warming herself up. Then she floated on her back and looked at the snowcaps on the mountains. But this only disheartened her further. She lowered her feet to bottom and found Franz Josef also standing waistdeep in water and staring toward shore.

"Did you see anyone leave?" he asked.

"No. I wasn't looking."

He turned glumly toward her. "This corner of the world has become altogether too crowded. We should really look for something better next year. Don't you agree?"

She shrugged. They fell silent again. Their lake was as serene as ever. Why always assume the worst? Might they not be pleasantly surprised? "It's only a youngster on a bicycle tour," she said finally.

"I've slept in the woods like that," Franz Josef murmured. He was thinking back over fifty years to his boyhood. "We were *Wandervögel* then, free as birds."

"So have I," she smiled. "You can't have forgotten."

"I remember everything. We couldn't find a room."

"We couldn't afford one. We spent too much for lunch."

"We'd been walking all day," he continued dreamily. "The sun was setting. And there was a perfect stand of fir off the road without any underbrush, a bed of leaves, a roof of branches and the stars shining through.

"I couldn't sleep. I imagined someone would report us to the military police. Or what if a land mine or an old grenade had gone off. You heard stories like that all the time."

"Oh you slept. I watched you. You looked like a wood nymph with fir needles in your hair."

"A wood nymph? What am I now, a mer-matron?"

She laughed, showing large slightly buck teeth. He looked down at her fondly. She might be placid as the lake on a summer morning. Then a sudden joie de vivre would erupt in her. Or a storm of tears. He never knew what to expect.

"Franzl?"

"Hmm?"

"Why are we making a fuss over one young man who is communing with Mother Nature?"

"I won't make a fuss. My dear Frau Leopold, if you wish, we can invite him to commune with us over breakfast."

"Let's see what sort of young man he is first," she replied, smiling up at him somewhat coquettishly.

He took her arm and led her out of the water.

They climbed the trail, chatting loudly and rattling their baskets and chairs.

The bicycle was gone. But the sleeping bag remained, spread on top of the hedge, along with bright red saddle-bags and a pair of hiking boots planted at their seven o'clock position.

Franz Josef spread the contents of their dufflebag all over the clearing. Then he paced back and forth between the saddlebags and the entrance to the clearing where an-other dirt trail sloped downhill through the trees to the highway. He inspected the sleeping bag without touch-ing it. Goosedown and quiltstitched, a quality item. The saddlebags bulged insolently.

"What galls me is the complete lack of responsibility," he said. His voice did not sound angry; he spoke slowly and methodically. "Think how long you would have to work to buy a sleeping bag like this. Would you leave it on a hedge?"

"Certainly not." Karla's knitting needles clicked.

"It is exactly what your son would do."

"Oh please, let's not start on that."

"Very well."

He would not discuss Ulrich, then. Nor the irrespon-
sibility of an entire generation to whom everything in life
had come so effortlessly. He paced the clearing, looking
frequently at his watch. What was he going to say to this
fellow? This young man in leather jacket and cutoff jeans,
how was he going to defend his behavior?

It is true, Franz Josef reasons, that we do not own this
land. But certainly, we have seniority. Year after year, you
see, not just one night's worth. And then, what about a
little respect for my gray hair?

Gray hair, the bicyclist says. That doesn't even give
you the right to be alive. Get out of here, fascist swine.
I'm taking over.

Franz Josef inquires calmly: What makes you think you
are any better than I am?

But when had he said that before and to whom? He
recalls the sound of his own voice. High pitched, a kind of
strangled scream. Uli must have been in his teens. *What
makes you think you are any better than I am?*

Uli is rummaging around in the little museum under
the staircase. It looks like a diploma he's dug up but it's
not. He's holding it between his finger and his thumb as
if it were contagious. Certified Denazified, it says.

What did you do, he asks.

Stamping birth certificates and such, oh that was the
final straw. Racist, fascist, bureaucratic cockroach, guilty
of every word in that mountain of paper I stamped and
sealed and filed away in the cellar of the city hall. Better
to have rotted in a camp, he says. Better to be dead.

What about the time we pamphleteered for the Reds
and the Brownshirts beat us up. He doesn't believe we
ever did it for the Reds, but it's a fact. Alright, the SD
too. I admit we really did it for the money, though never

indiscriminately. Willie, now, he only worked for the Reds. His father was a party man. They broke Willie's jaw. They broke my glasses, knocked out a tooth. Broke Jörgen's arm and two of his ribs. I was the lucky one.

That story has a beard, he says. What about the rest of it? The rest is simple. I kept my mouth shut. I survived. Simple. I was in the cellar of the Rathaus when our house was hit. Your grandparents and my first wife and little girl, your half-sister, they're all dead. Willie blown to bits at Stalingrad, Jörgen no one knows. Perhaps you're right. I should have died as well and never met your mother. She brought me back to life, you know. You were the child of our love.

Franz Josef looked over at his wife. She was a small round woman with deep creases around her eyes and short gray hair, and he was a tall bony man. Funny how well they fit together.

Karla looked up.

"Come and drink your coffee," she said and patted the empty chair beside her. He did not move. "I can hear you thinking. You may as well let me in on it."

"You won't like it," he managed.

"Not if it's about Uli again. It isn't fair. He isn't here."

"But he is." Franz Josef tapped his chest and then pointed at the saddlebags. "He's here and he's here. In essence."

"Ach!" Karla handed him a mug of coffee. "It doesn't do a bit of good to get worked up. When the fellow comes back, you'll talk to him. Meanwhile, won't you sit down?"

"As you wish," he said stiffly.

By 8:00 they had finished the rolls and cheese and a cup of coffee each. Karla was knitting. She lost count, dropped stitches. So the rows are uneven, she thought, cross with her clumsiness. Franz Josef had pulled out the *Frankfurter Allgemeiner*. He read an item aloud to her, and his voice cracked a little.

She dropped needles and yarn to her lap, exasperated, and folded her hands and waited. They were waiting, she realized, exactly as they had once waited for Uli. She felt as uneasy as she had then, and she was asking herself the same questions. If he never comes home? When do we stop waiting?

"Franzl, what time is it?"

"Half past eight."

Finally they heard the clicking of bicycle wheels down the trail. Franz Josef folded the paper neatly and put it back in the basket. He walked slowly to the entrance of the clearing, where he waited with arms folded across his chest. Karla remained seated.

Up the trail clattered a bicycle, an old one judging by the sound of metal being rhythmically scraped. Through the trees they saw it, clanking up laboriously, a figure rising and falling, then disappearing behind the hedge, a light thud — the rider dismounting — and Franz Josef stood yet straighter. His heart beat faster. How he hated the whole business.

Then around the corner came a slender, young woman, pushing a solid, antiquated lady's bicycle. Momentarily Franz Josef was speechless. Behind him, Karla sucked in her breath.

"My God," she said. "*You* spent the night here? Alone?"

The woman put the kickstand down and looked around the clearing warily. She spoke slowly with a heavy American accent.

"Yes. A lovely spot, isn't it? Do you come here often?"

"We have been coming here every morning for thirteen summers, Fraulein." Franz Josef, too, spoke slowly and precisely. The woman was standing about a meter away on the other side of the bicycle, panting a little from the uphill climb. He became aware of his crossed arms and let them drop.

"How lovely," she said.

"We stay here all day. Following the sun in a circle, you see." He swung one arm in a slow semi-circle. "You can tell the time of day by where we are sitting, you see."

"I see."

"How could you have slept here alone?" Karla'a voice rung out imperiously. No woman she knew would wander the countryside without protection — not even Uli's American girlfriend.

The young woman shrugged. "I couldn't find a room," she said. "That inn down the road was full." She came forward cautiously to where her saddlebags lay, Franz Josef following behind. She was not, after all, so very young, Karla observed. Her hair was streaked with gray and there were webs of lines under her eyes — heavy-lidded eyes that, accented by high cheekbones and a beaked nose, gave her a sorrowful air. Perhaps she was part American Indian? Her hair was tied in two shoulder-length pony-tails and she wore cut-off jeans and a t-shirt, which accounted for the first impression of youth. "I think it must be dangerous for a woman alone," Karla continued softly. "Weren't you frightened?"

"A little, yes. I was frightened when you walked by." The hooded eyes widened suddenly in comic alarm. "I pulled the bag over my head."

"So sorry," they chorused.

Franz Josef considered. His daughter, had she survived the war, would have been this woman's age. He would be remiss in his duty should he not speak.

"If I may offer advice, *Fräulein*. It was ill-considered to abandon your belongings here. I suggest greater caution in the future."

"Oh I know I took a chance." Now she spoke in a rush, cutting off ends of words. "I woke up hungry and tired and these packs are so heavy, you see. Then I saw you two in the lake, and I thought, there's nothing to worry about. I could tell that you were trustworthy. So I went back to that inn without the saddle bags. She was surprised to see me again, the *Gastwirtin*. I was never served so enormous a breakfast."

"To be sure," Karla murmured. She felt uneasy, having a room in that inn. "Please do join us for a cup of coffee," she offered.

"Thank you, no. I have had two already."

They watched as she knelt to roll up her sleeping bag.

"Isn't it lonely for you, traveling alone?" Karla asked.

"Not at all." She looked up from her task with a quiet radiance on her face that threw Karla into further confusion. Was the woman perhaps mentally unstable?

"So long as you are happy, then," Karla said.

The woman tied up the sleeping bag with a flourish and sprang to her feet. She seemed much taller suddenly and she shifted from foot to foot as if there were hot sand instead of grass beneath her. "I dreamed for many years about doing this," she said earnestly. "Now here I am."

"Ach, so."

Karla straightened up. She felt old and fat and Franz Josef looked rickety. As long as she did not move from the deck chair, she would retain her dignity.

The *Amerikanerin* fastened the saddlebags and the sleeping bag to the bicycle, while Franz Josef held it steady.

"Be careful," he said. "We don't want to read about you in the newspaper."

"I *am* careful."

And where was she going? First, for a swim. Then to the highway and north to visit the cathedral in Ottobeuren. Franz Josef advised her of an excellent bicycle trail that had been built along a former railroad bed. No automobile traffic, quite serene. Exactly what she wanted, she thanked him enthusiastically, and with good wishes on both sides, off she clattered down the trail to the lake. The sound died away.

"Americans are all cowboys at heart," Franz Josef observed.

Does she have a husband, Karla wondered, or children? What is she doing in Germany? I don't know her name.

They didn't quite settle down. They were waiting still. The *Amerikanerin* had to come back up from the beach in order to reach the highway. When she did, they stood up to wave goodby. "I can see it's almost noon," she called through the trees. Then she was gone for good.

That evening the Leopolds dressed more festively than usual. Franz Josef wore the most flamboyant in his collection of clip-on bowties — his "little wings," he called them. Other than that one gay spot at his neck, he dressed soberly, as befitted a retired official of the Bundespost. Karla tied a batik scarf around her neck — made in India, it was a gift from Uli she had not yet dared to wear.

Arm in arm, they descended the stairs to the *Gaststübl*. As they crossed the hall, the door leading to the garden swung open and in sailed the widow Müller carrying a large bowl of plums. Seeing them she smiled mischievously before disappearing into the kitchen.

What was that about, Karla wondered. Does she know we found that *Amerikanerin* in our spot?

Franz Josef opened the door and ushered her in with a courtly bow. She looked eagerly around the room, which was empty, except.... Her heart sank. There at the *Stammtisch*, his back to them, sat a stranger. She felt her husband's arm, still linked in hers, stiffen. Frau Müller must not have seen the man come in. He turned in his chair, then got to his feet, facing them. He was tall and fair and clean-shaven.

Karla stopped where she was, bewildered. Uli? Afterward, Franz Josef confessed that he too had failed to recognize their son. "It is because he shaved his beard off," was his explanation of the phenomenon.

"Mother. Father. How are you?" He came up to them and took their hands. Then Karla recovered and hugged him to her. She could still feel the delicate bones of the child and his cheeks were smooth again. "How you startled me," she cried.

They sat at one end of the *Stammtisch*, Karla between the two men. She observed that Uli's eyes were red-rimmed and the skin blotchy beneath. He slouched over the table. Franz Josef sat bolt upright. Even the bowtie seemed to stand at attention. Suddenly she laughed aloud. Father and son looked at her, the same high, puzzled forehead times two. She controlled herself with difficulty.

"It's the little-wings, Franzl. Remember how you'd tell us they were propellers. Do you remember, Uli? And if we spun them around, off we would go, *eins zwei drei, AUF!* Straight up in the air." She beamed at her two men. "Franzl, you look ready for take-off."

Franz Josef shifted uneasily on the bench. He also remembered that the boy had mocked him, for the story, for the old-fashioned bowties.

But Uli said, "Sure I remember. I used to love that story. Straight up in the air. Like magic."

Franz Josef was touched and embarrassed. Just then a girl came in with a pitcher of beer and three steins and took their orders. Uli drank thirstily, the elder Leopolds slowly. They watched their son and waited for him to explain why he had come. He had never in thirteen years visited them on the Unterhimmelsee. They scarcely saw him at home. He must want something, Franz Josef thought; and Karla, he is in trouble. Indeed, he seemed troubled, distracted. He was on his way to a *Skat* tournament in Friedrichshafen, he said. They wished him luck.

"It isn't luck," he said impatiently. "It is skill."

They nodded politely, their faces impassive. Karla, sensing her husband's repressed outrage (that their son was, in his words, "a confirmed gambler, a card shark"), quickly changed the subject.

"It has been a day for surprises!" She described their encounter with the American lady-bicyclist, and Franz Josef commented that they need not go anywhere; the world would parade by them for a visit. Last week, they'd had an encampment of Turks. Next week, who knew what — Eskimos, perhaps. Uli nodded politely through all of this. "Very interesting," he said in a dull, far-away voice. "I'm glad you still enjoy your vacations here."

"Indeed we still do," his father replied coldly.

A long pause. Then Karla inquired a little anxiously after Uli's *Amerikanerin*.

"Could Donna not come with you?"

"She has an important assignment this week. Improving the English of some bigshots from Krups." He stared into his glass. "Anyway, she won't ride the motorcycle now."

"Why not," rapped out Franz Josef.

"She is pregnant."

Silence. Uli drained the glass.

"So now you know," he said.

"You aren't delighted with the prospect of fatherhood?" Franz Josef asked sarcastically.

"Were you?" Uli snapped.

Father and son glared across the *Stammtisch* at each other. Their anger was so palpable that Karla almost succumbed to it herself. It was a dense, familiar thing, somehow, a beast let out, a ridiculous, unnecessary two-headed beast, and it was intolerable. "You are a fine pair of fools," she said sharply.

They turned to Karla astonished by her outburst.

"Oh you are both looking at me with the same face, exactly the same. I can not bear it," she spluttered. "Now listen to me!" She lifted the pitcher and filled all three steins, then raised her own.

"Here's to a healthy baby. Well, what are you waiting for? Here's to the mother and the father. And the grandparents. *Prosit, um Gott es willen*, pick up your glasses, you idiotic men. *Zum wohl!*"

They lifted and clicked their glasses and drank. Father and son regarded one another warily. Karla was now a little tipsy.

"Will you — well of course you will, now, I suppose," Franz Josef fumbled.

"Get married, he means," Karla finished for him.

"Not unless we live in America." Uli spoke into his glass. "Then I could get the American green card. If we live here, Donna stays single. She is eligible for *Versorgengeld*."

Franz Josef pressed his lips together. They knew his opinion. Who paid the taxes to support these good-for-nothings!

America? Karla thought with a pang. Well, then, we will visit. She eyed her husband doubtfully. Or I will. At the prospect, her heart beat quickened. Of course, I could.

Dinner was served. The food absorbed their attention, soothed them. When the coffee was poured, Uli looked out the window. He could reach Friedrichshafen while it was still light, he said. They walked outside to where his motorcycle was parked.

Once mounted on the machine, he looked taller and more self-assured. He did not slouch. The engine raced and he held it steadily between his legs. Karla sniffed the fumes. She put one hand on the engine casing and vibrated from head to toe. She did not feel like a grandmother yet.

"Papa! Listen!" Uli shouted.

"I hear you. I am not deaf."

"The bike is my little wings, understand? Straight up and away!"

"I understand."

"Come for a ride, Papa?"

"What?"

"Oh never mind. Some other time, perhaps. *Tschüss!* Grandpa! Grandma!" And off he roared, laughing. They watched till he was out of sight.

"Perhaps I will," Franz Josef murmured, fingering his bowtie. "Only let him ask me again."

Each After Its Kind

I was on a back road in Missouri daydreaming about California when a storm blew up. I didn't pull over and shut the windows. I kept on driving. The cornfields turned emerald-green. A violet-black bank of clouds boiled up the sky, slivered with lightning. In the intervals between thunder claps, there was an immense hush over everything. I was as alone as the first man.

It was my first trip out west. The trunk and back seat of the Valiant were packed with tools, books, some camping gear—everything I needed to begin my life anew. I had time to spare, not much money, lots of hope.

Suddenly a sheet of rain swept across the highway. I switched on my wipers and lights and slowed to 20. The fields and sky were now the same murky shade of grey, and I could barely make out the road. Water splashed my shoulders and face, a relief after the long sultry afternoon. I thought about my gear in the back seat.

A moment later a lightning bolt shot down like a long white finger about a hundred yards in front of me, bringing intense color back into the world. It lit up a man in overalls who was standing at the side of the road with one thumb stuck out. For a split second it looked as if the bolt were jumping out of the top of his head. Then a sharp volley of thunder ricocheted around inside the car. I pulled over.

He clambered in and put an empty gasoline can on the seat between us.

"Bless you brother," he said. "I'm bound for the Esso Station at Four Corners? You going that far?"

"I suspect I am," I said. "Would you mind rolling up those windows?"

He was a tall, stooped man. He twisted and flapped bony arms till the job was done.

"You moving somewhere Mister?"

"Frisco," I said. He didn't react at all. Obviously it was a name that didn't resonate for him as it did for me. Where was I coming from, he wanted to know. I explained that I had been living in Florida but originally came from Yonkers, New York. He said that he had lived in Polk County all his life and would stay there till the Lord directed otherwise, and did I have a calling to be moving on?

"I have itchy feet," I said and when he made no response, added, "It could be an indirect calling."

"He moves in mysterious ways."

An uncomfortable silence fell between us. I concentrated on the road. The man began to whistle softly, a tune unfamiliar to me, probably a hymn. When I looked over at him, he was hunched forward staring at the floor. Lightning illuminated the car. His Adam's apple was enormous and it fluttered as he whistled. A drop of water hung from the end of his nose.

He broke off whistling and jerked back in the seat.

"Horsefeathers," he said. "We've sprung a leak."

"A leak?"

"You've got a hole under this mat the size of a baseball and the water's rising fast."

"Oh shit."

A check of the back floor by my passenger—jackknifed over the seat— revealed the tide was rising there too. Water was bouncing hard off the road and splashing up through holes in the floor. And I thought I had lucked out picking up a slant-six in West Palm Beach for three hundred bucks. This was not a Florida car; it was a snowbird with terminal body rust. I'd be lucky if the bottom didn't drop out from under me before I got to the Golden Gate.

There was no sign of the rain letting up. Then I remembered the plastic litter bags my mother had pressed upon me before I left West Palm, along with a bag of chicken sandwiches I'd eaten on day one and a wishbone. The wishbone was dangling from the rearview mirror next to the giant furry dice that came with the car and had persuaded me to buy it. I pulled a litter bag out of the glove compartment.

"Here you go, pal, start bailing out."

He stared at the bag. It had a picture of a mother and baby on it and said "Life of Georgia Insures the South."

"You can roll your window down half-way," I instructed him. "The wind's blowing in on my side. You can fill the bag and dump the water out."

He went at it like a windmill, arms flailing mightily. Soon he was singing "Onward Christian Soldiers," and I was chiming in on the chorus and thumping time on the steering wheel for the rest. That's when I decided his name must be Ichabod Crane.

And so we drove into Four Corners, Missouri, which is a cross roads with a gas station, a general store and a boarded up vegetable stand. An attendant in a rainslicker filled both the car and the empty can and insisted on Ichabod taking an extra can. He stared mournfully at the two cans.

"Where are you parked?" I asked.

"Half a mile from where you picked me up, down the road to my house."

"I'll drive you back."

"Lord bless you, it's out of your way."

"I'm an out-of-the-way kind of guy."

We drove into the gloomy east. The worst of the storm had passed, thunder and lightning fading away, rain falling steadily but not wildly. Neither of us spoke. Then the bright glare of an oncoming car silhouetted the dice and the wishbone.

"That was a White Leghorn Hybrid," Ichabod intoned solemnly.

"You seem to know something about poultry," I said.

"I'm in the poultry business. So was my Daddy and my Granddaddy." After a long pause, he asked me why I had hung a chicken wishbone from the rearview mirror.

"My mother hung it there for luck."

"Why, mine did something like it too. Wishbones all over the place just where she left them. But never thought to do the car."

Ichabod warmed up noticeably. He wanted to know what kind of work I did, and the answer—marine carpentry—seemed to please him.

"I build boats," I sighed. "And I buy a car that springs a leak."

"Never you mind about that," he said. "Jesus respects a man who works with his hands."

The road into his house was not paved. I could hear mud slapping up under the fenders, and I began to wonder how I'd get back out.

"There's my rig now," he said. We pulled up in front of an ancient flatbed.

"What a wonderful old truck," I marveled.

"Yes it is. Daddy bought her new in '48. I looked after her real good. Never let the fuel run out before though and it's the second time this month. It's a sign for certain."

He brooded over his gas cans, then he brightened and he spoke with face shyly averted in a formal Sunday-best tone. "It's a long drive to the nearest motel and the road is bad. You're welcome to stay the night with me. It's humble, but you don't look to be the fancy type."

I hesitated. Fancy I was not. I had slept in the front seat of the car the night before and was still stiff all over. A bed and a shower were tempting. Taking my silence for assent, he got out of the car and began emptying gas into the truck. I could see a plastic Jesus dangling from his rearview mirror.

"Will you follow me, then?" he called.

"Lead on," I said. I was wet, tired, hungry, a little curious. Maybe he was a little crazy, but then who among us isn't?

At the end of the road was a weatherbeaten wood frame house bordered on two sides by towering oaks and willows. A patina of neglect lay over land and buildings. I noticed a large barn partly caved-in behind the house, and off to one side, a low concrete bunker, about half the size of the old barn and windowless. It was the one discordant note in a theme of picturesque decay.

He ushered me through the front parlor where furniture was covered with sheets. "Just the way she left it," he said. And into the kitchen where the floor was covered with worn but spotless linoleum, the table with a blue oilcloth. He left me there and went upstairs to put on dry clothes. I sat at the table and looked around the room. The stove and the fridge were of the same vintage as the flatbed truck. A varnished plaque on the wall beside the table read "God

Bless this House," and on the nail from which the plaque hung perched a small wishbone. Orange rubber gloves were pinned to a wire above the sink. They reminded me of my ex-wife. I could see her standing at the kitchen sink and complaining about the unwashed cups and glasses she had to pick up in my wake.

Ichabod came back and put a kettle of water up to boil, then brought a loaf of bread and a flat of eggs out of the pantry and broke several of the eggs into a bowl. "Now these here shells crack real easy, do you see? They are as delicate as God made them. Just you wait until you taste them."

To my surprise that dour face began to glow as he prepared the eggs. He was not so grim-looking as I had thought. With those high bony cheeks and narrowed eyes, he had to be part-Indian. His skin was dark and well-muscled. He was lean, not skinny. About my age, 39 or 40. I examined my own city-bred arms, sunburnt and flabby, and the potbelly that had become as familiar as my nose. I wanted a cold beer, or at the very least a mint julep. My stomach rumbled noisily, my mind wandered. Was I still in the South or was I Out West yet?

My host set two platters on the table, heaped with lightly scrambled eggs and two thick slices of buttered bread. Also cups of strong coffee. He sat opposite me, bowed his head, recited a blessing. I chimed in on the amen and set to. Those were indeed exceptional eggs, rich and creamy, with only a pinch of salt and pepper added. The bread was moist with a crunchy crust. Baked by a neighbor lady in exchange for eggs. After my sincere compliments to the chef and the baker, we ate in devout silence. Then he wiped his mouth with a paper towel, sat back in his chair and looked me full in the face for the first time.

"Mister," he said. "I clean forgot to introduce myself. Never got your name neither."

"My memory's always better on a full stomach," I said. "Name's Harley Gentry."

"Harley Gentry," he repeated slowly. "Would you spell the last name?"

"G-e-n-t-r-y."

"Amazing."

"What is?"

"I am Harold Gordon, see? We have the same initials. H and G."

He was scrutinizing me closely, perhaps for additional resemblances.

"Tell me, Harold, if it's not a secret, how do you produce these delicious thin-shelled eggs?"

"A secret!" He laughed harshly. "I leave the hens alone. Let 'em scratch around in the yard, lay when and where they please, mate when they please."

"They're organic then."

He looked puzzled. He explained that about three years ago he had begun to dismantle and sell piece by piece all of the automated equipment that had been acquired by his father since the late forties and then by himself as a young man. He had known in his heart from boyhood on that it was ungodly to automate reproduction and tamper with His creation. He had always dreaded retrieving eggs from hens who were locked up on a patch of wire mesh under a light bulb day and night. They were likely to peck his fingers in sheer frustration.

"Why a wire mesh?" I inquired.

"So they don't sit in their own droppings and become unclean. Well if they're left to roam around that's not going to happen, is it? And if they're not overbred so they can lay thick eggs that won't crack before market, and lots of them, then they're not going to be sickly, and that's a fact. And the reason why they want the shells so thick is they brought in these egg conveyor belts, see. It sounded like a real good idea at first, you didn't risk getting your finger chewed off..."

I listened as he traced the history of poultry breeding since World War II, astonished not so much by the information as by his lucid commonsense approach.

"What changed your mind?" I asked.

He rolled his eyes ceilingward.

"Oh," I said.

Harold got up to clear the table and I helped him. He washed. I dried. Over the soapsuds he thanked me for my understanding, and I let go a wisecrack about chickens being man's best friend that flew right between his ears. He was somewhere else. He sighed deeply. Not everyone, it turned out, had been so understanding. His brothers in the Grange had snubbed him. His wife had left him. I noticed that he had not put on the rubber gloves to wash the dishes. They were probably hanging where his wife had left them.

"Maybe it was a good thing Daddy passed on when he did, the Lord forgive me saying so. Ma, now, she joined him not long after."

His wife had divorced him and had taken away his little girl, that was the hardest part. We were back at the table drinking a second cup of coffee and eating stale Oreos. "That is hard," I said seriously. I regretted all the wisecracks now, both spoken and unspoken. "My wife left me too," I offered. And did not add that it had been a great relief for both of us.

"Children?" he asked.

"A girl and a boy. They live in New Jersey."

"I knew it," he said softly. Once again that glow came over his face, a faraway look in his eyes. "It is hard, yes it is, but it has been decreed."

The only decree I know from is my divorce decree. I said nothing, not trusting myself to ask a simple question.

He hunched over the table, bringing his face closer to mine. "Three years ago the Lord singled me out," he whispered. "I was fishing on Pineknoll Lake when He took me by the hand and told me what to do. He caused the lake to shine and fish to leap. And He said the earth is corrupt and filled with violence, pollution and ungodliness, and the end of all flesh is come. He decreed that I collect unto myself all manner of fowl each after its kind, of fowls of the air by seven for they are clean ..."

He broke off abruptly. His eyes seemed to bore through the mask of polite interest I had assumed. "Come, I'll show you," he said.

He walked into the pantry and I followed a few cautious paces behind. There a door led to the backyard. It was still raining steadily, but gently, and it felt good to be outside. The air smelled sweet. My shoes sank in the mud and briefly I panicked, thinking about my Valiant. How the hell was I going to get out of here?

Harold unlocked a door on the concrete building I had noticed when we drove in. We went inside. It smelled like an old-fashioned barnyard. He switched on a dim red light. The bulbs were placed at intervals beneath the lowest tier of roosting stalls and the light did not seem to disturb the sleeping fowl. There were four tiers of doorless wire cubicles along each wall and a double row down the middle of the building. In each cubicle, two or three birds slept. I could see that the markings varied in each group.

We walked down the first aisle and Harold named the different breeds: Rhode Island Reds, Bantams, Sumatras, Andulasians, Dorkings, Wyandottes, Barred Rocks, Dominiques, Sultans, Hollands … and in a cubicle by herself a rare and homely avis called the Transylvania Naked Neck. There were cocks as well as hens, I noticed. He said he did not follow the common practice of feeding newly-hatched cockerels to the pigs. All these birds were free to come and go, and each one chose to be with its own kind. God's plan. I nodded and nodded. God, I was exhausted, and the litany of fowl was beginning to pale. On the second aisle there were a few ducks and geese, two turkeys. Harold regretted that this portion of the collection was incomplete. He needed a swan, but swans were expensive. "Yes," I yawned, "not to mention pheasant, squab, New Guinea water fowl, ostriches …" Harold's face sagged. He was incapable apparently of recognizing irony, and I, unable to survive for long without it.

"Where will you put your flocks when Armeggadon arrives?" I inquired. "Will you build an ark?"

He stared at me. In the red light his face glowed eerily. I remembered how pleased he had been by my line of work and hastened to say that this marine carpenter was not in the ark-building business. I didn't know a cubit from a rabbit.

"I won't be needing an ark, Hartley. Have you forgotten God's covenant to man? He set the rainbow in the sky as a promise that water shall no more destroy all flesh. He didn't mention fire though now, did He?"

"No, no. He didn't."

In the silence that followed, my skin goosepimpled. I giggled nervously. "Say, Harold, what do you think will happen to the other innocent beasts, you know, the lions and the lambs. Do you think other people have been delegated to collect them somewhere, each after its kind?"

"It may well be," he replied solemnly. "It's too big a job for one man anymore.

Back in the house he showed me to the den, where I would be sleeping. He put a sheet and blanket and pillow on the couch. Then he turned the TV on—a small black and white set—and sat in a lounge-rocker in front of it. The show was a sitcom about a white middleclass family that has adopted a black child. He got out of the chair and punched in another channel. This was a sit-crime. Someone was being machinegunned. Another channel. Skimpily clad go-go dancers. He turned the set off, nodded grimly at me. "And if that ain't bad enough, then there's the news."

I nodded back. My eyes were closing. I felt unconsciousness closing in, blotting me out while I was yet sitting. From far away I heard Harold's voice, insisting.

"Don't you never say any prayers H.G.?"

"I am not a praying man," I said, eyes still shut. "I am a laying down man." And I stretched out on the couch. He came over and covered me with the sheet.

"Well but you are a Christian?" he asked anxiously.

"No."

"No? A Catholic then?"

I forced open one eye and looked at him. "A Jew," I said.

"A Jew!"

I was awake again. He was examining me with unrestrained curiosity as if I were an exotic breed of rooster. Perhaps I was the first of my kind he had ever encountered. But no—it turned out he'd met one other, a Mr. Blatt, ran the feed store in Eudora, cheated his Daddy in a deal. A regular Shylock it seemed, hook nose, dark skin, kinky hair.

"But you're fairer than I am," he marvelled.

"My father is of Scotch and Irish descent," I explained.

"Then you're only half a Jew," he said sadly.

"No. I am a full Jew. It comes through your mother, see."

"Oh, I see." But he looked suspicious.

"Goodnight H.G.," I said firmly.

"Goodnight H.G."

He paused at the door. "I know He means you for a sign, but it's a puzzle to me yet."

"Jews and chickens go back a long way together," I mumbled and rolled over. Harold turned off the light.

I awoke at dawn to roosters crowing. They had been crowing at least since 2 a.m. because I woke briefly then and looked at my watch, fell asleep, dreamed... I almost never remember my dreams, but this one I'm sure I'm never going to forget. In it my daughter was a grown woman. She had fallen in love with a chicken-skinned man and planned to marry him. His skin was yellow, pimply all over, hung loose on the bones. I found him physically repulsive. Being a good liberal father, though, I felt obliged to accept him into the family. But then I also was repelled by the thought of the chicken-skinned grandchildren they were going to produce. I woke up feeling queasy.

Harold looked into the room.

"You sure do snore up a storm, Hartley," he said. "Just about shook the house down."

That was as close as the man ever came to a joke.

"Mind if I use the bathroom, Harold?"

"Make yourself at home. I'll have breakfast waiting."

There was a huge old tub with four clawed feet and a rubber hose for a shower. And the toilet was truly an antique; its chain hung from a tank suspended from the ceiling, and between the tank and the throne a turkey wishbone had been hung over a nail in the wall. His mother at least had had a sense of humor.

After showering I paused in the hallway between bathroom and kitchen to inspect the photos hanging there. In faded turn-of-the-century mezzotints, standing women and seated men stared grimly into the future. A young couple (his grandparents?) posed before a painted backdrop of the Eiffel Tower— World's Fair, St. Louis 1904. That small boy had to be Harold and the thin anxious-looking woman with marcelled hair beside him, his mother. He was holding a fishing pole and a large fish, and grinning at the camera. At the end of the collection: a fairly recent color portrait of Harold, his wife and daughter, all wearing blue-checked shirts, all scrubbed and tidy with starchy smiles.

He had been watching me quietly from the kitchen. "That last one was taken in Eudora," he whispered, though there was no one else around who could have heard him, "at the J. C. Penny's there."

Breakfast was ready. It was toast and soft-boiled eggs, fresh coffee. Those yolks really were superb. Harold watched me eat wistfully. Soon I'd be gone, like everyone else. And he hadn't figured it out yet. I had an idea though.

"Listen, Harold, you ought to move to California too."

"California!" he scoffed.

"Sure. You would be appreciated there. You could earn a decent living. Californians love to eat fertile eggs, free range chicken. The sun shines all year. Here you're a fish out of water, you've outgrown Four Corners. There, you'd fit right in."

"How do you know that? You never even been there."

"I've researched it carefully, and some of my best friends are Californians. Besides, you remember what Horace

Greeley said, don't you? Go west young man. Well, there's another H.G. for you." I stopped, seeing his face change. "Think about it," I said.

"Oh I will, I will." He folded his arms across his chest and stared out the kitchen window. "All my life," he began, broke off, sighed. I was embarrassed to see tears in his eyes.

"About time for me to go," I said.

We walked out into the yard. The rain had stopped before sunrise. The concrete bunker—or was it a fall-out shelter—glittered in the morning sun. Some of the chickens were outside scratching in the dirt, clucking. I saw with relief that my car was parked on high ground. Vapor steamed off the surface.

"So long, H.G.," he said.

"So long, H.G."

I got into the car. It turned over immediately. Great. I would not be stuck in No Corners, Missouri. I drove slowly off and at the first bend looked back. There was Harold, a gaunt scarecrow in front of an old grey house, pointing solemnly up at the sky where a perfectly formed rainbow arched. My scalp prickled. I stepped hard on the accelerator and the furry dice jiggled against the chicken wishbone.

Art Class at Harmony Villa

The new guy lowered himself into the hot tub where Gloria and I were sipping gin and tonics out of plastic glasses. He was pudgy with a bushy gray moustache. By now, all the women in Harmony Villa knew Leon was a widower.

"We were married fifty-two years," he told us. "Not a day goes by I don't miss her."

"I know it's difficult to lose someone you love," Gloria murmured.

I stared at her. Gloria had divorced three husbands, all still alive, and when her mother died, she was more relieved than grief-stricken.

She stood up and sat on the rim of the tub, plump arms glistening. In that black low-cut swimsuit and the dim light, she looked younger than sixty-five plus. She was on Medicare now, but I didn't know her exact age, though we'd been friends for thirty years. I sank into the water up to my chin.

"Where are you from, Leon?" she asked.

He glanced at her, then away.

We learned he had directed the art department in a Manhattan ad agency. Then he quit to freelance and finally had time for his lifelong passion, painting in water color and oil. He and his wife had moved to the Bay Area five years ago.

"You're an artist, how wonderful," Gloria enthused. "Why don't you teach an art class here?"

"Let me think about it." He contemplated the water's surface.

"You teach, I'll organize. I know there are artists in the building. Kate and I'll be your first students."

"Whoa, I couldn't paint the side of a barn."

"Anyone can learn to draw and paint," Leon smiled at me. "If they have the desire."

Gloria kicked my shin underwater.

"Alright, I'll try," I said reluctantly.

The art class met every Wednesday morning at two long tables set up end to end under the skylight in the Harmony Villa community room. Other residents sat nearby at smaller tables, playing cards, gossiping and complaining about their arthritis and bad knees, and sometimes they turned the big TV on for news or a football game or someone might play a CD on the boom box, anything from Benny Goodman to Elton John. Leon flipped tiny switches on the hearing aids he wore in each ear to tune out noise.

He walked around the tables inspecting our work and offering critiques. I could never resist another smudge of mustard yellow, a dash of indigo.

"Leave it alone, Kate," he told me. "It's finished. You mess with it, you'll ruin it."

Gloria put down her brush.

"Good work," Leon approved with a pat on the back and she all but purred.

Gloria and I volunteered at the hospital across the street. She worked the greeting station and I was in the gift shop a few yards away. When it wasn't busy, I'd step into the lobby so we could talk.

"Leon's paintings are in galleries everywhere," she told me. "San Francisco, New York, L.A. We're really lucky he's living here. He's such a darling man, isn't he?"

She was convinced Leon was the man for me. He couldn't be grieving his wife forever, and who, she reasoned, would be a better match for him than Kate McGowan.

"You're from Brooklyn, so you speak the same lingo, and you read the *New Yorker*. He's adorable. And you're still a looker."

"There's no there, there," I stage whispered.

Silence.

"No electricity."

"Oh, that will come, you just think about it."

I wondered about Leon after that. Could I conceivably be attracted to him? Or he to me?

When he leaned over to examine my painting, I smelled pipe tobacco and soap and felt the heat from his body. I noticed the gray and black hair curling on his forearms and springing up out of his unbuttoned shirt. I had always liked hairy men.

Like my ex, the love of my life, whose chest was a silky rug I would pillow my cheek on, that big hairball, and look where it got me.

Not long after my husband left me, I ran into Gloria at a spring street fair. Our children had attended the same schools, so we knew each other slightly then from PTA meetings. She was selling fudge brownies and passing out pamphlets for a new-age church.

"The brownies look delicious," I told her, drooping a little. "But I don't do religion."

"Take a brownie," she said. "My treat. They won't convert you to anything but sugar." And she laughed at her own joke, showing all her teeth, shiny and white like in a toothpaste ad.

When I hesitated, she put a brownie on a napkin and handed it to me. "Looks like you might need a pick-me-up," she said.

I took one bite. It was rich and buttery and redolent of past pleasures. I began to cry. I remember that her arms opened as if to embrace me.

"It's really very good," I managed to say.

Gloria and I wound up hiring sitters for the kids and drinking several pick-me-ups in a cocktail lounge later that night, and on many a night thereafter we cruised bars all over the North Bay. We were both divorcees with children still at home. We took our kids camping in the Sierras and to the San Francisco zoo, and, when no man was available, went to movies together. I invited her to plays and art openings—she'd never done either before. Within a few months, she was involved in amateur theater and had picked up an easel and a set of acrylics and brushes, and then persuaded me to take workshops with her, where, incidentally, we might meet "artistic guys." When she married again, I was her "best woman" — both times.

Leon's apartment was on the third floor, which meant plenty of sunshine. And pigeons. The pigeons hit the roof and upper balconies first. They arrived en masse not long after Leon did. I hated them, but Leon didn't mind at all. They reminded him of New York. He especially liked the newly hatched chicks.

"How can you stand that racket?" I asked. "They're flying rats."

"They're doves. Do you know they mate for life? That's a love song. My wife loved baby birds." And he cooed at them. "Hoo hoo who are you?"

I went over to his sliding glass doors and looked out at the deck of the balcony.

"You've got a layer of feathers and shit where they're nesting."

"Really? I hadn't noticed."

"It isn't healthy."

He shrugged. "Worse things have happened."

"Shit happens when you let your guard down, Leon."

He looked at me and clucked his tongue. "I'm of the glass half full school. How do you think I've survived this long with a bad heart, stone deaf and half blind?"

"What? What do you mean half blind?"

"I got cataracts. They're not operable yet. Everything looks murky. Dull. Flat."

"I can't believe it." I looked around the room whose walls were hung with luminous pastels, oils and watercolors, all by Leon. "How do you paint?"

He smiled serenely. He looked like a little Buddha. "How did Beethoven compose the Ninth? In his head."

He hauled out albums of photos, sketches and newspaper clippings. The brittle pages of the first album we leafed through were held together with rubber bands. Here were his juvenile cartoons, ink sketches, his first pastel.

"I never had any formal training," he said. "My uncle was an artist, too. It's in the family. They used to say I was born with a brush in my hand. Look at this, the first painting I sold before we got married, when Bess was my sweetheart. We were only 19. So my uncle bought a bottle of champagne and we all got tipsy celebrating."

I had a glimpse of a small watercolor of mountains and

a lake, but he was already moving on to the next album.

"Here are designs I did for the ad agency in Manhattan. I was the director of the art department, did I tell you? Andy Warhol was one of our contractors."

"No kidding."

"I still have some of his doodles somewhere. I sold two to pay Bessie's medical expenses."

"Did you like working there?"

"I loved it. It was good money with a good health plan. But those deadlines were killers. I never had time for my own work. It was Bess who talked me into quitting after thirty years, so I could paint full time. She gave me permission to be a starving artist." He laughed and patted his round belly. "The agency begged me to come back. Bess insisted I stick with it. She got a job that paid the bills."

Over the next several weeks, I examined every album and portfolio and heard the entire story of Leon's life— his childhood in upstate New York, his courtship and marriage, the accomplishments and credentials of their children and his artistic and professional careers. Some of it I heard several times. We all repeat ourselves as we grow older. But Leon, I came to realize, was enamored of his memories. Lucky man, he was in love with his own life.

"I've been blessed," he told me. "My only complaint is that Bessie went first."

"But that's selfish, Leon. Would you rather have had her suffer your loss?"

"Men are selfish brutes," he admitted.

Gloria was right. We did speak the same lingo. Whenever we ran into each other, he'd say, "How are you, dollink?" and plant a big wet kiss smack on my lips. I was genuinely fond of him, but though the gossips suspected otherwise, there was never anything more between us. Gloria kept pestering me to find out if we were an item yet.

"Not," I told her. "I'm not in the market anymore. Just drop it, kiddo."

"But he's sweet and so talented."

"He is still mourning his wife," I reminded her. "And he talks too much."

"Then he's a good match for you."

"Get off my case, for crying out loud. If you think he's so great, go date him yourself."

"Why are you so rude?" And Gloria flounced off.

She'd always been easily offended. Sometimes she didn't speak to me for days, even at the hospital or in art class. Once she'd recovered and we'd made up, it was like nothing had happened. I often asked myself why I put up with her. Bottom line, she cheered me up when I was down, and I suppose I did the same for her.

We could avoid each other, when need be, by sitting at opposite ends of the long table. Each artist set up her station and worked on her own painting or drawing. Leon also worked on small projects of his own or demonstrated techniques.

I enjoyed the class but I was not even a serious hobby artist. I never went home and painted like Gloria did, and I enjoyed the chit chat during our sessions, which she did not.

"Hush, I can't concentrate," she'd plead, but everyone ignored her.

Ethel Levine, who at 86 was the oldest member of our group, finally wearied of being shushed.

"Go back to your apartment and paint if you want it quiet," she snapped. This ain't the public library.

Gloria looked startled and a little wounded. She didn't come to art class again for two weeks. She tore up one of her paintings. "It was all wrong," she told me. "I ruined it."

She was busy with a new Bible study group, which periodically she'd pitch to me.

"You'll learn something every time we meet, I promise you, Kate. It's intellectually stimulating. A couple of cute guys just joined, too. But they may be a gay couple."

"Glor, jeez, you know I'm a born-again pagan."

"No problem," she said. "We are truly ecumenical."

Early in December, Gloria formed a committee to decorate a Christmas tree in the community room. Fewer people attended art classes and everyone was scurrying around, shopping and complaining about it, everyone but Leon, who seemed bewildered and depressed. Leon's son and only grandchild lived in Tahoe. He knew better than to attempt those mountain roads in winter in his clunker of a station wagon.

"They came and got Bess and me last year," he said, "but now they can't get away."

"Oy," said Ethel. "What a sad puss. You'll come to my daughter-in-law's when she makes latkes."

He cheered up a little.

Ethel had another idea. She had somehow wound up with two menorahs. She would donate one to Harmony Villa.

"And Leon, you can say the bruchah, right?"

"Can I ever." He beamed at us. "You're all invited."

"We don't have to be Jewish?" Gloria asked.

"No dollink. It's for everyone, just like that tree is. It's the festival of lights, a bright glowing light in the dark of winter."

"That's lovely," Gloria murmured. "So poetic."

On the first night of Hannuka, over a dozen people clustered around the piano, atop which perched Harmony Villa's new menorah. A few of the attendees were from Gloria's Bible group. A few were actually Jewish.

I was surprised that the menorah was electric and no candles would be lit. Instead little blue bulbs got turned on by hand.

"No one lights candles anymore," Ethel informed me. "Too messy. The house could burn down."

Leon explained the holiday is celebrated for eight days because of the oil lamp that, with only enough oil for one day, burned miraculously for eight, after a battle between the ancient Hebrews and some army, I can't remember which.

"We whopped those SOBs," Ethel whispered.

The prayer book Leon read from had yellowed, tattered pages. It had been a bar mitzvah gift from his grandfather, Reb Apfelzweig. Gloria touched it reverently.

Our holiday pot luck dinner took place a few days later in the community room. The tables were decorated with holly and pine sprigs. Gloria had taped a blue and white Happy Hannuka banner on the wall behind the menorah. The long serving table was laden with sliced turkey and ham, casseroles, salads, yams, potatoes, stuffing and gravy. I wore my red velveteen top and Christmas tree earrings. Gloria looked lovely in a forest-green suede pants suit and a pearl choker, her bright blonde hair arranged in a new pixie cut.

She saved me a seat opposite her and Leon. His smile was radiant. I think it was the first time he didn't mention his wife at least once in the course of the evening.

He took one of my hands and one of Gloria's. "I'm really very happy that I live here. I am fortunate to have you as my friends."

"Let's drink to that," I said, and poured out a cabernet for each of us.

Into her second round, Gloria put her head close to his and said, "Leon, I want to ask you something personal."

"Ask away." He raised his glass to her.

"When did you know you had to be an artist? Absolutely *had* to be," she repeated a little louder, in case he hadn't heard.

"Always. I was always drawing as a kid. I never wanted to be anything else."

I yawned.

"Say, did I tell you I knew Andy Warhol?"

"Yes," I said.

"No," said Gloria, big eyed.

"He free-lanced for my agency."

"For real?"

"Excuse me, lovely people." I pushed back my chair and stood looking down at them. "I'm going out to chew gum."

They nodded absently. I went into the pool enclosure and sat on a deck chair. It was a cold clear night and steam billowed out of the hot tub. Screw the holly jolly party, I thought. It's a glorious silent night out here. If only I had a cigarette, but I'd given that up, forever. Through the windows, I could see a blurred green streak that was Gloria leaning into Leon and wondered what that bleached-blonde flake thought she was up to, because nothing could possibly come of it. She was a Christian Republican and he, a Jewish Democrat. And what if she did snag him? A bad idea for Leon, considering the way Gloria went through boyfriends.

That winter, Leon, having neglected to get a flu shot, fell gravely ill, and his acolytes brought him food and comfort.

"He needs a woman to take care of him," Gloria said. "He certainly isn't taking care of himself. He's totally dehydrated."

I checked on him, too. He'd given Gloria an extra key, so he wouldn't have to get out of bed to answer the door. She shared it with me and the other women in the art class.

He looked wan and exhausted, propped up on pillows in bed. "Gloria made a pot of chicken soup for me," he announced. "Imagine that."

"Is it good?"

"Good enough for the job. She put tomatoes in it and I think spaghetti."

We both laughed. He had a rackety cough I didn't like. I fetched his cough medicine.

"I'll be fine," he said weakly. "Everyone is so helpful. Now listen, Katie, I don't want the class to stop on my account."

"What? How do we do it without you?"

"You just do. You've been doing it all along."

He was right. Gloria and I made sure everyone showed up whenever possible and we carried on without him. When Leon was well enough to go out again, he was tickled with our progress.

"You don't need me anymore," he said.

"Oh yes we do," we chorused.

Our group was flourishing and people from outside Harmony Villa got wind of the class and joined us, including a couple who lived on a ranch outside of town. They invited us all out there for an afternoon of plein air painting. We took photographs and came back with material for weeks to come.

Gloria suggested we do the wine country next and agreed to organize our field trip. One clear morning in early spring, several of us piled into her SUV with our painting supplies and picnic lunches. Leon rode shotgun. "Look at that, will ya!" he kept saying. He had never seen mustard growing in the ground.

Gloria drove carefully, her lips curved in a demure smile. She parked the car and Leon bounced out.

In the tasting room he was more interested in the labels than the wine.

"This is very well designed," he said, examining the bottle. "I guess they do it with computers now. We used to do it all by hand. I created an original type face myself for a series of ads for Motorola, and I also designed the logo. All in pen and ink with color washes."

"Fantastic," said the server. "And what should I pour you next?"

Leon flushed. "I'll take whatever the lady's having." He pointed to Gloria.

After the tasting I sat opposite Leon and Gloria at a small picnic table, apart from the others. He took both her hands in his and looked into her eyes, and then turned to me.

"Our best friend," he said. "You should be the first to know."

"Oh oh," I said.

"We're an item," he said.

"We're so in love," Gloria whispered.

"Wow, I had no idea." I looked at her closely and her cheeks reddened.

"We had to be sure first," she said.

"Then I'm the first to congratulate you." I put on a bright smile, but I was thinking, if you hurt him, I'll murder you.

"It's like a miracle," Leon said. "Like electricity turning on. We're incredibly happy."

"We're truly blessed," she said.

After that, Leon and Gloria did everything together from grocery shopping to bingo games. They walked around the building holding hands and went out to the I-Hop for the senior special breakfast, it was reported, at 7 in the morning. They painted oil portraits of each other painting, and Gloria had them framed.

For the rest of us, little had changed. We met every Wednesday and practiced our art. There were now two couples instead of one in the group plus the usual gaggle of widows and divorcees. A few may have envied Gloria. Most were pleased for Leon's sake. A kind of glow emanated from them that made us all a little wistful and uneasy.

Ethel had serious doubts.

"It'll never fly," she said. "Gloria's from another planet."

She could be right, I worried. What about their divergent religious and political views? And would Gloria stick it out? She had never been big on commitment. I couldn't say anything to her about it; she could be prickly. But the next chance I had to talk with Leon alone, I asked him, "What if Gloria wants you to be a Jew for Jesus?"

He seemed more amused than offended. "Don't you think we've been over that ground? We're not a couple of kids. We respect each other's beliefs and opinions."

"But she's a Republican."

He laughed. "She's not happy with Dubya. We're not as far apart politically as you might imagine. Gloria is passionate about ideas. I respect that, too."

"That's great," I said lamely.

"We're adults, dollink. We can take care of ourselves."

In the summer as the presidential campaign overheated, Leon and I came to art class wearing large Obama-Biden buttons. Gloria hadn't made up her mind. She still admired

McCain, but agreed Sarah Palin was our worst nightmare. She definitely didn't want another Clinton in the White House.

"I don't know if America is ready for an Obama yet," she drawled. "Or if he's ready for us."

About a week after the Democratic convention, I ran into Leon coming out of the elevator. His round face creased in smiles when he saw me.

"Gloria came out for Obama," he announced. "It's remarkable, when you consider she was raised in Little Rock. It gives me such hope, I can't tell you."

Gloria told me herself, with the radiant certitude of a convert. "Barak means blessing. It has the same root as 'bruchah' as in 'baruch atah adenoid.'"

"Adenoid? That can't be right."

"Whatever, it's marvelous. He is destined to bring us all together, black and white and all the colors of the rainbow."

Late in August Leon took the bus to Tahoe for a two-week vacation. He'd hoped Gloria would drive him up to meet his son and his family. His ramshackle stationwagon had expired in a parking lot fender bender, which was good because he really couldn't see well enough to drive. Gloria was driving him to appointments and taking him shopping.

"Another time," she told him. "That wouldn't be much of a vacation for me."

She was going instead to the annual adult summer camp of the New Life Christian Fellowship, a Bible camp in the woods near Occidental, where she could enroll in art seminars and political discussion groups. "I'll wear my Obama button," she promised. "That ought to liven things up."

"You give 'em hell, tiger," Leon said.

He boarded the bus and blew kisses out the window at us. Gloria and I waved goodbye until the bus was out of sight.

"He asked me to marry him," she said abruptly.

"What did you say?"

"I love him, but it would be a huge change. I need to think it over."

"It's not like you haven't done it before."

"True, but I never did it like he did it. Not till death did they part."

"You did say you wanted to take care of him."

She sighed. "He's not exactly robust."

"So just keep it boyfriend, girlfriend. What's the problem with that?"

"I really need this time off," she said. "I need space to think."

Leon looked terrific when he got off the bus, suntanned and relaxed, wearing Bermuda shorts, for Pete's sake.

"Nice legs, Leon."

"Thank you, dollink. Where's my sweetie?" He peered around at cars parked in the nearby lot.

"She's still in Occidental. She says she'll be home tomorrow."

"I thought it ended yesterday."

"She volunteered for some job that had to be wrapped up."

He nodded. "She's a very responsible person."

"She did sound a little stressed over the phone."

"Too bad. She'd have had a better time in Tahoe."

He was wrong about that.

Gloria phoned me again that night. She was home early.

"Don't tell Leon I'm back. I have to talk to you right away."

She was sitting near the window in shadows, her apartment lit only by night lights.

"I parked on the other side and didn't bring anything in," she whispered.

"What's with all the secrecy?"

"I can't face him tonight. I need one more night."

"For what?"

She took a couple of deep breaths, in, out, in, out. Maybe she took yoga at Bible camp?

"I met another man," she said.

"Good grief." I pulled a chair up to the window and let her talk.

Calvin was a full-blooded Lakota and a lay preacher. He was her age, maybe younger. Not as talented as Leon, but "gentle, wise and beautiful." They had spiritual values in common. He was the only other camper voting for Obama. Over the two weeks they'd been drawn irresistibly to each other.

"Let me get this straight. You're not in love with Leon anymore?"

"I didn't say that. I love them both."

"You can't have them both. Hello! This isn't 1968. It's 2008."

"What will I do?" She actually wrung her hands.

"Decide!" I said.

"I can't."

I was angry now. "Leon isn't a toy you put aside because you're bored. He's a dear soul who loves you. What you're doing is childish and cruel."

"You're horrible," she sniffled. She turned away and stared out the window. "I hate this place," she said. "It's a senior ghetto."

In a few days everyone had heard the news. Gloria dropped from sight. Maybe she ran off with the new boyfriend, people speculated. Leon stayed away from art class. Sometimes I'd see him listlessly sorting his mail on the bench outside the mail room. He looked pasty skinned and mournful, worse than when he'd first moved in. I'd give him a quick hug and invite him to call anytime, and he'd shrug and say, "Thank you, dollink," and never call.

The art group members were outraged, especially Ethel.

"She broke his heart," she declared. "I'll never forgive her for that."

Eventually Leon came back to the class, but he'd lost his pizzazz.

That was when management decided to put netting up over all the third floor balconies. Maintenance cleaned the pigeon shit and feathers off with a power hose. Leon really missed the pigeons. The pigeons migrated to the second floor.

It took the removal of one cataract to cheer him up a little. I drove him to and from ophthalmology appointments and the surgery. Afterward he said, "It's good to have the world brighten up again." And after a moment's pause: "It's just murky inside my head now, like things got turned inside out."

"Leon, you've got to pull yourself together. Good gosh, man, were you never dumped before in your life?"

"No," he said in a small voice.

"Then it was about time you were, don't you think?"

"Huh," he said. He seemed almost pleased with the notion.

I never told him I was getting the occasional email from Gloria. Why pour salt in a wound that was slowly healing? She was on the road now with her new swain, visiting reservations in Montana and Wyoming. How could Leon compete with that? She asked me to water her plants. "How is Leon doing?" she wrote. "Is he eating well? I worry about him being alone too much." I responded with any news I deemed appropriate. After a few more exchanges, she admitted she was often lonely herself, when Calvin went off hunting or drinking with his buddies.

Leon was ill again in November, even though he got a flu shot. It began with a bad cold and cough. We were watching election returns on the big TV downstairs and he was so overjoyed he wept. "I never dreamed I'd live to see the day," he said. Then he started coughing and couldn't stop. I took him right over to the hospital.

His son drove down from Tahoe and his daughter flew out from Chicago. I emailed Gloria that Leon had double pneumonia. Maybe that was a mistake. But I figured, if this got any more serious, she would want to know. And wouldn't Leon want her to know?

His children disagreed. They wanted him to rest quietly. An emotional scene could sabotage his recovery.

Gloria called me in tears. She was back in her apartment. She had already tried to visit Leon and been turned away. His room was opposite the nursing station, and they all knew who Gloria was and had been instructed not to let her into his room.

"That's the reward you get for being good," she said bitterly.

"It's possible he may not want to see you," I said. "He never talks about you. It's like he's sealed off that memory to protect himself."

"Oh no," she moaned. "If I could just see him once and tell him I love him and I'm sorry."

"His kids think he lost the will to live when you left him."

"Do you?"

I sighed. "He did go downhill fast, but then he was starting to pull out of it. And now? I don't think he's fighting. It may be his time to go."

"Then at least I should be able to say good-bye."

"For whose sake?" I asked. "Yours or his?"

"Why are you so mean?" She hung up.

I visited Leon almost every day and I could see he was failing. I said nothing about Gloria, but held his hand and told him "we all" missed him and loved him.

"You're an angel," he rasped through the oxygen mask. "If only Bessie could've met you."

"We'd have been best friends."

"I'll be with her soon."

"Ah Leon, for crying out loud."

He managed a small smile. "You don't buy it, huh?"

"Doesn't matter what I think."

"Only one way to find out."

I nodded, unable to speak.

"One thing I do know," he went on with difficulty. "I'll meet the great Creator himself. The chief *Macher* of this beautiful, screwed up world. We're his masterpiece. You and me. Everyone."

"Everyone?" I manage.

"So he made a few mistakes." Then he laughed and then he had a coughing fit and I had to buzz the nurse.

I had classes and errands the next day and when I managed to get over to the hospital the day after, his bed was stripped. I couldn't believe no one had told me. I asked the nurse on duty when he had passed. "Yesterday," she said. "I'm sorry, dear."

Did his kids just pack him up and ship him to wherever Bess is buried? They must be having their own private memorial service somewhere. But they should have known their father was well loved and we were his family too at Harmony Villa.

I dialed his son's cell phone. He was back in Tahoe and he sounded cool and distant, where he had been warm before.

"Leon was a dear friend to many people," I said. "We'd hoped to have some closure."

"So did his girlfriend, apparently."

"Gloria?"

"We saw her in the hospital yesterday. When she saw us, she turned and walked in the opposite direction. And when we went into Dad's room, he wasn't breathing."

"But he was dying, you knew that."

"I really don't want to discuss this," he said.

I could have said, but didn't, where were you when he needed you? If you loved him so much why didn't you visit more often?

I was too angry to phone or email Gloria. How could she have been so pig headed and selfish?

"Let's do our own memorial," I suggested to the art group. There were murmurs of assent. But it came to nothing. We were still meeting every week and, in a sense, that was Leon's ongoing memorial. One problem with having a service was that Gloria might attend, and no one wanted anything to do with her. Also, I think we all felt unmoored. I wanted Leon's son and daughter and grandson to come back and tell us their memories, but that was never going to happen.

The menorah with its little blue lights was back on top of the piano. I went the first night out of respect for Leon to listen to Ethel recite the prayers. She made a small plate of potato pancakes to cheer us up. But I was downhearted and left early.

Two days later Ethel spotted me going into the mail room and pushed her walker over briskly.

"Wait'll you hear what happened," she said.

Gloria came to the menorah lighting on the second night. It was just Ethel and Gloria, no one else.

"So she brings this big framed painting of Leon to put next to the menorah, that portrait she made of him herself. It's not half bad. And then she starts blubbering. So I tell her, 'the painting's okay, but get your sad puss out of here. It's not appropriate. When my Alvin died, *aleva sholom*, I didn't go out in public and carry on like this. And you're not even his widow. Stop your blubbering, if you want to stay and respect the holiday. Or go to your room and cry.'"

"What did she do?"

"She grabbed the painting and scrammed." Ethel nodded triumphantly. "I sure told her."

"Boy, you sure did."

"I hate her," Ethel spat out. "She killed him."

"She didn't kill him. He had pneumonia and a bad heart."

"If she'd stuck with him, he'd have made it." And she sailed haughtily away, the walker clacking along.

I rang the bell and banged on Gloria's door. I was thinking: Ethel was too cruel.

"I know you're in there. I'm not going away."

Finally she opened the door. Her hair was tied back with a red bandana. There were dark circles under her eyes.

Packing cartons were heaped all over the floor and on counters and chairs.

"You're moving?"

"Duh."

"Where to?"

"Not far. Sit down somewhere."

I looked around but there were no vacant chairs.

"What happened to Calvin?"

"That's finished. He was a big mistake."

"I know you went to the hospital, Glor. I haven't told anyone here and I won't. Tell me, what happened."

She stared at the floor. I raised my voice.

"Tell me or I'm going to hate you forever and a day, I swear."

"I had to see him," she said finally. "As soon as the nurse turned her back, I slipped into his room. He was sleeping with the oxygen mask on his face, and I sat in a chair by the bed and waited. Then he opened his eyes and saw me, and he smiled the sweetest smile behind that mask, and I told him I would always love him, in this life and the next. He said something I couldn't make out and closed his eyes and I think that's when it happened, because his chest kind of fell down and I couldn't hear breathing. But he was still smiling, Kate. Then I saw the flat line on the monitor. I ran out of the room to get a nurse, and I saw his son and daughter and panicked.

"You don't know what he said?"

"Sounded like zagazooned. Must be Yiddish."

"His kids were plenty pissed."

"They were wrong to keep me away. He was waiting to see me before he could move on."

"No way to know."

"For ye of little faith."

That was the last straw. I hated her when she got sanctimonious.

"I think you broke his heart and maybe that's why he died," I spat out.

She drew back as if I'd slapped her.

"Oh God no, you don't mean that. It was his time. You said so yourself."

"He certainly was heart broken. Anyone could see it, even if you were blind, you'd know it. What did you expect would happen to him? That he'd pick himself up and find someone new?"

She opened her mouth, shut it. Her eyes flooded.

"What I can't understand is how you could have hurt him like that. I thought you had a heart. You're heartless."

"I made a bad decision," she said, and her voice quavered like an old woman's. "I never wanted to hurt him. You've got to believe me."

She looked so truly miserable, I relented. I felt like opening my arms to her. But it was too soon for hugs.

"When do we stop making mistakes?" she asked.

"Even God makes mistakes," I told her. "Leon said so."

Lucky Lady

The houseboat's small and needs some work, but the price is right. Elated, Johnny phones his girlfriend to tell her he just bought a house for 400 bills and slip rentals are cheap at the boatyard, so he's moving in. Peggy wants to see it right away.

"It's a pigsty" he says. "I gotta clean it up first."

"I'll take before and after pictures," she pleads.

"Naah, what for?" Before she can answer, he's saying good-bye, gotta run, see you later. Give her an inch, she'll move in on top of him.

He hurries back to the dock to take another look. It isn't much — one room with a galley and a head, the boards a weathered grey. The name peeling off the prow is "Lucky Lady." This lady has seen better days. But so have the other ladies in his life — all Lucky Lady needs is fresh paint and a bucket of ammonia to degrease the interior.

He's ten minutes late picking up his mother. Twice a week he takes her shopping, twice a week he takes her to the beach. It's a shopping day, but she's waiting outside the apartment building with her picnic basket and deck chair, dressed in the flowered sundress and straw hat she wears to the beach.

"Ma, what are you doing out here?"

"I'm waiting for the bus, wise guy."

He takes her arm, picks up the basket, the deck chair. "Let's go inside."

"Inside? What for?"

"We're going shopping, right? You won't need all this stuff."

"Oh." She sags against him, deflated, sticky skinned. "It's not a beach day?"

"It's Wednesday, it's a grocery day."

She blinks rapidly, then flashes her lopsided grin. "Pretty funny, huh Gio?"

"Yeah, you're a card alright." He notices uneasily she has lipstick on her teeth. That crooked smile, the watery pale blue eyes, will she fall apart when he tells her he's moving out?

"I'll get my shopping list," she says, and holding herself extra straight marches inside the building, Johnny behind her hauling chair and basket.

"Ma, listen," he calls, "I got an idea."

She fumbles in her purse for the key. "Jeepers, where did the stupid thing go?" Her voice is querulous.

She's on the edge, he thinks, and hesitates. "Let's go to the beach right now," he says, with more enthusiasm than he feels.

"I found it," she announces triumphantly. "See, the big ring you gave me. It works."

"You can go shopping tomorrow," he persists.

She puts the key in the lock and turns it before answering.

"You don't have to humor me," she says. "That's a terrible thing, to forget an entire day."

"I'll get into my trunks," he says and hurries into his bedroom. There he strips quickly and puts the sweaty clothing in a hamper. The room is the smallest in the apartment and, except for a large spray of bright red tissue paper carnations on the bureau, the most spartan; the few things he owns, tucked away in drawers or closet. His mother could use the extra space. Her china and furniture and crystal vases, the afghans she crocheted, his father's bowling trophies and photographs of five generations fill all the available space in living-dining room, kitchenette and master bedroom; her clothing spills out of two closets. The flowers she makes herself spring from the vases, splashing bold color everywhere.

He hurries out in his swim trunks to find his mother seated at the dining table drawing perpendicular lines on a large sheet of paper with a ruler and crayons. At the top she has printed the days of the week and "1964" in square black letters.

"It's a calendar for any month," she explains. "to put on the front door so I can see it when I go out."

"Great idea," he says. "You doing this now?"

"I'm getting it started." She winks at him. "In case I forget."

Under the shade of a palm tree, Annemarie is knitting a sweater. She is propped up on the padded beach lounger Johnny bought her. It's so comfortable she could snooze.

He isn't working tonight. But, he reminded her, he has to be home before five to shower and shave for a date with that woman, a very common type, which means he won't come home until tomorrow.

"You're not swimming to Cuba today?" she cracks. "Only to Key West," he says, and takes off — splashing, diving, swimming like Johnny Weismuller. His father was also a terrific swimmer. Johnny has his father's shoulders and arms.

She recalls her husband's calloused hands, how he crushed walnuts in his fist or carefully lifted a child. She'll never get over losing the old rooster, she thinks. What business had he going first? If it wasn't a sin, she'd have followed him to the grave.

So she tells her new friends in the parish: She had one foot in the Pearly Gate when her son brought her to Miami to start life over. She doesn't mention that Johnny works in a tavern around the corner from St. Gabriels.

"He almost won the Golden Gloves," she brags. "Before the war, he was a champion bantam weight, Gentleman John. You can't imagine a gentler boy or man. I've got three daughters, each one bossier than the next, want me to come to them, you gotta be kidding."

Nor does she mention he's divorced and running around with yet another floozie. If he was serious about that woman he'd marry her, and they would have their own house. But what he said on the drive over to Matheson Hammock was "I need more privacy. I always wanted a boat. Cheaper than another apartment over the long run. You can stay here. Nothing will change except you won't see my mug every single morning. I'll be ten minutes away."

She understands that he is helping her in slow stages deeper, further into her widowhood.

Peggy Malloy is large-boned with shoulders as broad as Johnny's. Although shorter, she outweighs him by 20 pounds. He has always been fond of ample women.

She washes lettuce in the sink while he chops onions at the table with the knife he just sharpened for her. "Was your mother surprised?" she asks casually.

Her back is turned to him. He looks thoughtfully at the swell of her buttocks beneath the loose muumuu.

"I'd say she was surprised I bought a boat all of a sudden. Yeah, she thought it was for fishing or maybe sailing. I don't think she's surprised I'm moving out though."

"Really?" Peggy turns to look at him. "But you never mentioned it before, did you?"

He shrugs. "I'd try, but she'd get this hurt look. Or else—" He hesitates. "This knowing look, you know. Like I'm some kind of playboy."

They both laugh.

"So then she says, what about this studio apartment down the hall, somebody's moving out, she heard. It would be more comfortable for me. And she could take a one-bedroom. Like she'd been thinking about it."

"Shorter apron strings," Peggy murmurs. He hears her but says nothing. She comes over to the table and pours them each another glass of chilled white wine over ice cubes.

"Here's to your new home," she says brightly. They click glasses, drink.

It is still sweltering hot at twilight. A small rotating fan stirs the air in the kitchen. Johnny has taken off his shirt. His narrow chest is delicately muscled, golden brown, almost hairless. He has draped a towel over his white bermuda shorts to protect them while he helps prepare the dinner.

Peggy's muumuu is supported by an elastic band, that — loosened in the wash — has slipped halfway down her plump breasts and lodged there precariously. The fabric is Kelly green, her favorite color. She wears the muumuu constantly around the house and garden. There are small dark stains all over the front that she hopes blend with the floral design.

They work quietly and efficiently together as if they have been doing this for many years, when in fact their affair began less than a year ago, just before he brought his mother down from Cleveland. Johnny knows what to do in a kitchen. He was a short order cook and salad prep chef before he tended bar.

I love you, Peggy thinks. She knows better than to say it aloud. She drinks the rest of her wine quickly.

"How big is it?" she asks suddenly.

"Depends what you do with it, angel."

"No silly, the boat." She takes a small knife and begins slicing green beans at an angle, the way he showed her. The blade cuts cleanly, swiftly. He has been sharpening all her dull knives with two stones, one a week.

"It's smaller than your bedroom, but bigger than mine," he says, "including the galley."

"Gee, that's kind of small."

"Yeah, I don't need much."

"I'd sure like to see it," she says eagerly. "I don't care if it's messy. I could help you clean it up."

"I'm going to fix it up myself," he replies firmly. She struggles to stay cheerful.

"Okay, I get it, first you have to piss in all four corners."

"Something like that." He beams at her. Her spirits lift. "I'll check the charcoal," he says, and goes out the back door.

She pours herself more wine and slices beans furiously. He loves me, he loves me not. Then the knife slips.

To her surprise, blood spurts over the board and the beans.

When Johnny returns she is running cold water on her thumb and squeezing it below the cut. A trail of blood dots the floor between table and sink.

"I'm down for the count," she says gaily. "But still kicking."

"Let me see the boo boo." He stands close to her and takes the injured thumb carefully in his hand. "Jesus, those knives are sharp, didn't I say?"

"You did. You warned me."

She feels both comforted and foolish. His strong and wiry arms are busy around her, doing everything right.

Her thumb is wrapped in gauze and elevated on a mound of pillows. Johnny lies with his head on her lap facing the TV. They drink coffee laced with brandy.

In Dodge City, tough but goldenhearted Kitty bosses the cowboys who hang out in her saloon — a single working girl who never gets her man, not even once a week; Sheriff Matt is no romantic cowboy.

Poor Kitty, Peggy thinks, celibate *and* childless.

Her boys lived at home till Johnny showed up, then they were out the door. "Did I scare them off?" he joked. Buster landed all the way in California and Clark, though only a hundred and twenty miles west in Naples, may as well have moved to China; he has his own life, a girlfriend Peggy has yet to meet. The boys are green-eyed and square-jawed like Peggy. But they have Alan's lanky build. Snapshots of them as children and young men are tacked haphazardly on all the walls of her small house, the "higgeldy peggeldy" house, Johnny calls it.

Alan used to call it "a goddamn pigsty, Moonbean McSwine," and that's when he was in a good mood; meaning she was messy but sexy. She doesn't want to remember the bad moods. It was over a long time ago. The wedding photos are in a shoebox in a closet.

She has no photo of Johnny. "My mug'd crack the lens," he tells her. "You got plenty of pictures here already."

Above the TV hang two large photographs framed in black — one of John F. Kennedy; the other, a wedding portrait of her mother and father, whom she had buried within six months of each other. Her Dad went last in the spring, and by fall of the same year, the brilliant young President also lay stone cold bloody dead — not even her own age, and possibly a distant cousin. There were Fitzgeralds on her mother's side.

The day they buried Jack Kennedy, she felt half-dead herself. Her boss, Adele, blotted tears, put on more mascara, wept again. So unlike Adele, a woman of steel. Finally, the two women hung a black cloth in the shop window over the closed-lip, smiling manikins with their Jackie bouffants. They walked down the street to St. Gabe's for the memorial mass. Peggy waited in line to light a candle and Adele made her way to the main altar.

Among the guttering candles, Peggy could find no space for the three she'd bought. She tried to enter the nave but it was packed to the doors. The organ boomed. The music, stately and swollen, would have solaced her mother, irritated her father. She could not bear to hear another requiem, and went outside, clutching the candles.

She would have liked a drink but it was not yet noon. The sun looked bloated in a flat blue sky. A chill breeze came off the bay.

At the far end of the lawn Peggy noticed a large banyan with many trunks and viny branches tangling downward, rooting, forming new trunks. She hurried down the stairs against the crowd and over the grass to the tree. It was peaceful walking among the trunks, like being inside the tree. Looking upward in amazement at its intricate structure and shiny oval leaves, she tripped on a root. The candles flew out of her hand, she fell forward and wound up on her knees in the loamy soil, surprised but not hurt.

There was a mossy alcove between the roots. In it someone had placed sea shells, dried petals, and a tiny plastic doll. Bits of melted wax. She too could light candles here, why not? But she had no matches. That was when she burst into tears.

"You alright, Peggy?" she heard, and looked up to see Johnny Hiyadol standing outside the banyan.

"I'm fine," she gulped, wiping her eyes.

His name wasn't really Hiyadol. Adele called him that, though not to his face, because he greeted every woman who sat at the bar where he worked with the same line. "Hiya, doll," he'd say.

He was a short skinny guy with a long nose and thick black hair that had a touch of grey in it. She scarcely knew him then. He took out a pack of cigarettes and offered her one.

"I don't smoke," she said. "But I could use a light." She held up the candles.

He smiled and, stepping in through the trunks, handed her a matchbook. "The Grove Pub," the cover said. She couldn't light a match, her hands were trembling so. "Let me help," he said, kneeling beside her.

They sat quietly for a while before the spluttering candles, shielding them from the breeze with their bodies, and Johnny smoked his cigarette. Then he said, "I saw you come out of church. Guess you didn't hear me say hi."

"I didn't see you."

"Then I saw you take a fall, else I wouldn't have bothered you."

"You're not bothering me."

"Let's get a cup of coffee," he suggested.

She shook her head. "I can't leave the candles burning."

His smile deepened. "I think it's a portable altar."

"Oh, of course it is," she laughed, and blew out the flames.

They went to the Florida Pharmacy, across the street from Adele's of Coconut Grove, and ordered lunch, and Peggy set the candle stubs up in the ashtray. Over tunafish salad sandwiches, they talked about their dead. Johnny's father had died last winter. He was worried about his mother. Was it Peggy herself who planted the idea of rescuing Mrs. Filipello? She told him she thought that her own father had died of grief. Some people could not be left alone.

They were still drinking coffee and talking two hours later when Adele popped in to fill a prescription. She eyed them with obvious curiosity. Adele looked glamorous in a black chemise and pillbox hat, her blonde hair in a French twist.

"I have a splitting headache," she sighed. "To hell with the shop. I'm going straight to bed and watch funeral reruns on TV."

Peggy was startled. The funeral had slipped her mind.

Johnny yawns. "What d'you say, kiddo? Bedtime?"

"You bet." She stands up too quickly. The room tilts and spins, then steadies.

In the bedroom he embraces her, his body hard against her soft skin. She is grateful that he doesn't mind the fatty rolls around her waist and thighs. The more there is to love, he said once, as close as he ever came to saying how he felt. The muumuu drops to her hips, then to the floor.

Peggy falls back on the bed in a swoon of alcohol and love. The bandaged hand flops uselessly.

"Why don't you just lie back tonight," he murmurs.

"You bet," she says and shuts her eyes. Even now, at 40 plus, she can't think about what is actually happening between her legs. Instead she thinks about a pond in a jungle. The water is lapped to a froth, becomes a whirlpool, sucks her into pleasure as profound as grace, and spits her out again, shaken. Where did a former altar boy learn such tricks? From how many other ladies?

Over their morning coffee he seems distracted.

"You're thinking about the boat, huh?" she asks.

He smiles. "You're a great pal," he says, surprising her. "I've been thinking, I shouldn't look a gift horse in the mouth. You want to pitch in, why not?"

"Gee thanks," she says.

"It's just that I'm used to living alone. It's been tough the last year. I want you to understand that, if I get a little prickly. Not take it personal."

"I'm not moving into your damn boat."

"Damn straight you're not."

They both laugh guardedly.

"I've been thinking too," Peggy ventures. "In case the boat gets too cramped for you, if you want to keep anything here, or sometimes just hang out, the little bedroom isn't being used for anything but storage since Clark moved out."

"I'm still helping Ma with rent, remember? I got a whole room there."

"Yeah, I know. Only I think maybe you'd like to hang out here sometimes instead of there. She'd never know."

"We'll see how things work out," he says.

Peggy can't look at him. She says into her cup of coffee, "Your one-night-a-week-pal, that's what I am."

"Ah, Peg." He leans over the table and pats one shoulder. She twists away. He sighs. "I can't make any promises. My first duty is to Ma. Hey, look at me, will you? I really do care for you, you know. You're my angel lady."

"You love me?" she asks in a small voice.

He hesitates. "Yes," he says. "It's hard for me to say it."

"Me too," she says through sudden tears. She could live on this crumb forever.

Peggy and Adele met at Burdines when they worked in the Junior Miss department. Both women were going through bad divorces then and had teenagers to raise. Otherwise they had little in common. Adele isn't the type to settle for crumbs; she made off with a fat alimony settlement. Then she bought the dress shop in the Grove and hired Peggy.

"So he loves you one night a week, so?" Adele says, and without pausing for an answer, sweeps on. "Your problem is you're too nice for your own good. I can't tell you how many times I've refrained from taking advantage of you myself. What do you see in that little runt anyway?"

Her jewelry clanks, she talks with her hands. Peggy tunes her out. After all, Adele doesn't have a steady boyfriend. Johnny says she's too overbearing.

"Don't hang out at the Pub every night," Adele advises. "Give him something to wonder about."

They are closing up the shop. Usually they go around the corner to the Pub for a couple of beers.

"C'mon, let's do something different!" Adele checks herself out in the long mirror, smooths her dress, a simple black A-line. Her hair is up in a severe but elegant chignon. She freshens her lipstick. Peggy watches wistfully. Adele is slender, sharp-nosed, wide mouthed, not a beauty, yet somehow beautiful. She hustles Peggy into her car, a red MG convertible, and Peggy says a silent prayer, because Adele always drives too fast.

They go to a lounge where happy-hour well drinks are 11 cents for ladies only, paintings instead of dartboards hang on the walls and the barmaids wear skin-tight gold lamé pants and skimpy halters. The room is full of sleazy replicas of her ex-husband looking for fresh meat at 11 cents a chop. It makes her queasy. She and Adele crowd up to the bar and Adele orders two Beefeater martinis. "Screw the cheap booze," she says. "We're celebrating."

"What are we celebrating?" Peggy is mystified.

"The anniversary of my last period," Adele announces. "Sex minus anxiety. Cheers!"

They click glasses and Peggy gulps the martini, embarrassed to be blushing. But it's too noisy for anyone to have overheard. She wonders not for the first time how old Adele really is. Didn't she say she was 39 when she got knocked up and flew to Stockholm to have an abortion, Peggy counts, three Christmases ago?

A heavy-jowled man in a pinstriped suit buys them well drinks. He and Adele seem to hit it off. Peggy takes the gin and tonic and moves to the wall, where her back feels safer. She drinks three more gin and tonics, which somehow keep appearing in her hand and eats an entire bowl of cheese popcorn, also free.

A man who ordered drinks for every woman in the house starts cursing the barmaids, and they have to call the cops finally, because the lounge is too classy for a bouncer. She thinks wistfully of the Grove Pub, a beer and wine joint with a pool table. Johnny would have had the turkey out in two seconds by the scruff of the neck.

Listen Adele, Peggy says to herself, because she would have to shout to be heard and anyway she would never say in a public place: that little runt is the best lover I've ever had. Oh, says the Adele in her head, oh really? So, how many have you had?

Lucky Lady gets a new white coat inside and out, the exterior trimmed with Kelly green. He finds a small can of the green that Peggy likes on sale, a lucky sign. It means a lot to her and is no skin off his back. It means she gets to piss in one of the corners. She paints the trim while he scours out the cabin.

The boat has been up on the ways for a month and photographed by Peggy at every stage. When the last coat dries, they bring a bottle of champagne over to the yard and launch her. They putt-putt in the boxy little boat over to the marina past a row of sleek sailboats. Peggy is dolled up in a low-cut green sundress with spaghetti straps and a floppy wide-brimmed straw hat. She pours champagne. She waves at the people on the dock, and they wave back.

Johnny feels defiantly foolish. He knows his rig looks like an old top hat under sail. But it is all his. He steers her gingerly back to the slip and hooks up the powerline. The next morning he moves in.

Peggy meets him at the dock. He told her he didn't need her help moving out, meaning that might upset his mother, who wouldn't talk about the boat all month unless he brought it up, and then fussed around him while he moved his boxes. He doesn't need help on this end either. It makes Peggy feel useful.

They carry a few cartons on the boat, a tool box, the laundry hamper, a radio. "That's all?" She seems surprised.

"It's all I need."

"You're storing stuff in your old room?"

"I didn't bring the paper flowers is all. They'd take up half the boat."

Peggy looks around the small room as if seeing it for the first time. She examines the plain pine table, two chairs, some shelving, a single cot fastened to one wall. She sits on the bed.

"It's awful lumpy." Then she lies on her side, back against the wall. That leaves a strip of mattress maybe 18 inches wide. "Tight fit," she says.

Johnny shifts from foot to foot. "There's plenty of room in yours."

"You don't want me staying here overnight?"

"I'm not saying that. I got nothing against tight fits, now and then. Let's check it out."

He slides into place beside her, one arm under his head, the other around her waist. Peggy giggles. She is sticky to the touch. He hasn't planned on anything but, what the hell, a matinee. She is plump and yielding as ever, especially backed up against the cabin wall, and she wears an accommodating dress. They are confined by the narrow cot and abutting wall to a minimum of motion. Her skin tastes salty.

She is crying. She does that sometimes, out of pleasure, she says.

"Bon voyage," Peggy blows him a kiss, after planting a long Frenchie on his mouth and practically floating out of the car. "Till tomorrow," she calls.

What a hot dame, he thinks. Not a mean bone in her body. One in a million that Peggy. Maybe it's time he settles down? At the very thought his back stiffens. He can't imagine living with any woman again month after month, year after year. He tries to picture it with Peg sometimes, to force his mind not to go blank. It just isn't very interesting. Someone's always home waiting for you, something always needs fixing. What is the point? He likes quiet, clean rooms, privacy. He's better off making house calls.

His mother's apartment is a few blocks away from the Pub. Sometimes she walks by on the way to St. Gabe's. She waves but she never comes in. Adeles of Coconut Grove is around the corner. His mother never goes in there either. The dresses are for young girls, she says.

He phones her from the bar before 5 just to say hello, how are you, and remember, don't wait up for me.

"Since when do I wait up for you?" she sniffs.

"Just kidding, ma. Look, I'll see you in the morning, okay?"

"How come? It's not one of our days."

"I was thinking I'd take you to breakfast, then we'd go look at the boat now it's all fixed up."

"Wait a minute, I'll check my calendar."

After a long pause, she comes back on the line. "I'm free," she says.

Johnny's room is emptier than usual. She'll leave it that way. He might change his mind. The boat could sink.

The flowers that won't fit in his boat are a startling crimson against the white walls. A small pain flutters in her chest, heartburn, from eating too much at dinner, *his* share of the pasta. How can she cook for one?

She wants to give him something for the boat. The flowers are too big? She will make small ones, very small, a perfect miniature bouquet, with a nautical theme, that can be attached to a wall. It won't be easy working small, her fingers are too arthritic to hold the scissors long.

She's going to miss him most of all in the kitchen. Lifting up pot lids to sniff. Teasing. Oh, she feels weepy and worn down from the heat. She should go to bed early, sleep off the blues.

Sleeping alone she's used to. She slept on a cot in the spare room because Joe coughed so loud. Afterward, their bedroom smelled of his dying and she didn't move back in. She'd wake up every two hours listening for his cough.

Now she can't sleep at all. She gets up once to check the double lock on the front door. Every hour or so her bladder feels full and she goes to the bathroom but sometimes nothing comes out. The night wears on. Every board that creaks could be a burglar. The heartburn fingers and pinches her chest. Somewhere a dog howls.

It is 3 a.m. when the pain expands delicately, filling her entire chest. She lies very still. It passes. She sits up and switches on the light. The pain returns, more insistent this time. Her heart beat speeds up, her breath grows short. He'll find her stone cold in the morning, she thinks, poor Johnny. He'll be sorry he has no phone on that boat.

It isn't so bad a pain really. But it's not going away. Her skin is clammy with sweat. Aren't cold sweats the beginning of the end? On the phone next to her bed a list of emergency numbers is taped, too fuzzy to read. She dials the operator.

Johnny calls Peggy at the shop to explain why he can't have dinner with her.

"She'll be fine," he says. "Her heart's real strong. It's a hiatal hernia, like a really bad heartburn is all. On top of that she gets an anxiety attack, which feels like a heart attack but it's in her head, see. So off she goes in an ambulance in the middle of the night. Yeah, I'm taking her home pretty soon, but I don't know, maybe I better not leave till she's asleep."

"Maybe you better stay with her tonight," Peggy says.

"Yeah, you're right, I better."

"Okay, well, see you."

"Right. Thanks, angel."

And hangs up.

Adele yawns and says, "He stood you up, huh?"

Peggy shrugs. There are still two hours till closing. She wishes Adele would go to the bank or the wholesalers. The clock ticks loudly and no one comes into the shop. Adele paints her long nails purple and reads the business section of the *Herald*. Peggy stares at her own nails, ragged and bitten. She hates Adele suddenly and intensely. But the feeling passes. Really, she pities Adele because she has forgotten how to love. She's turned sleek and cold, like a shark, always on the prowl.

Johnny dreams he's strapped to the bow of a motor launch sailing out to sea with no one at the helm. He awakes with a start on the bed in his old room. Through the wall he hears his mother's uneven snores. Later he serves her tea and toast in bed.

"I'm alright," Annemarie says. "Go to your boat, for Pete's sake. I'm not an invalid."

He has a new plan. It was a mistake to change things so quickly. Three nights he'll sleep here; three nights on the boat. Or sometimes two nights at Peg's (he doesn't mention this to his mother). A little something for everyone. After Ma gets used to being on her own, he'll cut her back to two nights, then one, then none.

She gets out of bed to mark the three nights on her calendar with a green crayon. The beach days are blue; shopping is red. Every square has a color in it; some have two.

Peggy tells Adele, "I'm playing it cool."

Adele shrugs. "You're not getting any younger. Tell him to shit or get off the pot."

"That's ridiculous. Anyway, what makes you such a big expert?" Peggy's voice goes up a notch.

Adele does not respond. She is checking off the contents of a large box. Two women come into the shop just then and Peggy turns to greet them pleasantly. Adele pushes the carton into the stockroom and comes out with her handbag. She nods at Peggy, her mouth in a tight line and goes out the door. Moments later the red MG roars past.

To hell with her, Peggy thinks. Queen Adele.

Adele phones an hour later to say she will not be back and Peggy should close up herself. Her telephone voice is throaty and soft like Jackie Kennedy's. She never *sounds* angry. She is probably lolling around her pool drinking a martini. Peggy thinks she hears a man's voice, though it could be the TV. It could be someone Adele has picked up. She likes to cruise the whitecollar bars and bring guys home for "happy hour water sports," she calls it.

Maybe being thin makes it possible to be casual, like trying on a new dress every day because you look good in the latest fashion.

Six weeks later Peggy is in the Florida Pharmacy eating a sandwich at the lunch counter when Johnny's mother comes in to get a prescription filled. Apparently Mrs. F. doesn't see her; she heads directly for the prescription pickup. Business is brisk at the Pharmacy. People come in for lunch from the galleries, the boatyard, and shops. The two women find themselves waiting in line together at the only cash register.

"How are you, Mrs. Filipello?" Peggy asks.

"Couldn't be better, Mrs. Mullins."

"It's Malloy. You can call me Peggy, though."

"Mrs. Malloy." The older woman fidgets with her pocketbook. After a pause, Peggy says cheerfully, "I haven't seen you in quite a while."

"I keep busy."

"But I saw the floral arrangement you made for Johnny's boat. It's just beautiful."

"Oh?" Annemarie looks quickly, sharply at her rival.

"Really," Peggy says. "The details are wonderful. It can't have been easy to work on that scale. The sea shells are the perfect touch."

"You're right," Annemarie unbends a little. "It wasn't at all easy. But I've only got the one son."

They are out on the sidewalk now in the heat and the fumes from bumper to bumper traffic. Through the cars and across the street, Peggy sees Adele watching through the shop window.

"He brags about you," Peggy says softly.

"What?"

"Johnny brags about you." She raises her voice.

"I heard you the first time. I didn't believe it."

"But it's true. You're lucky, you know. I have two sons who haven't phoned me in two months."

"Oh they're still boys," Annemarie offers. "It's a stage they go through."

Peggy nods, pretending agreement. She would never want her sons to feel obliged to call her. "I have to get back to work now." she says. "It was real nice talking with you, Mrs. Filipello."

"Likewise, Mrs. Malloy."

"See you soon, I hope." Peggy steps off the curb and stops short. Cars are rolling nonstop through the intersection. The traffic signals are broken. Behind her she hears Johnny's mother, spluttering, "What is this, the

Indianapolis Speedway?" Then Mrs. F. steps into the street with her arm forward, palm out. "STOP," she hollers.

"Stop!" Peggy screams, and jumps after her. Brakes squeal on both sides. Traffic parts and the two women march across Grand Avenue as if through the Red Sea, Mrs. F. in no hurry, with her arm straight out. Behind them come two young women with several children.

"Well it's no wonder he's proud of you," Peggy calls out, her parting shot, for Mrs. F. has already waved good-bye and is sailing off down the sidewalk, chin in the air.

"I can't believe it," Johnny says, hanging up the phone. He leans on the bar where Peggy and Adele are sitting.

"Peg, she wants to have you over for dinner."

"Why not?" Peggy says. "It's perfectly natural, isn't it?"

"Yeah, I guess." He hurries off to fill an order.

"How come Johnny looks so nervous?" Adele asks.

Peggy watches Johnny in the back-bar mirror, mixing a wine cooler, chit-chatting. His long nose bobs as he talks. Her funny valentine. "Jeez, Adele, don't you remember what it feels like?"

"What?"

"You know, love. Being in love."

"Yeah, I remember. It isn't worth the aggravation. It's like religion. You're a true believer. Or you're not. I never was, not really."

Johnny comes back. "Out of the blue. Invite your nice lady friend over, she says. That nice Mrs. Malloy."

"Is it code green for tonight?" asks Peggy. They are in stage two of what Adele calls Operation Apron Strings Withdrawal.

"Yeah, green." He looks at the two women quizzically. They smile.

Johnny's feet fly over the duckboards. He dashes out to bus the tables. He doesn't slow down, even after Peggy and Adele leave the Pub.

The dinner gets crayoned into Annemarie's calendar during stage three, which means — on paper anyway — that Johnny has rescheduled to one night a week at his mother's apartment.

But in November when she catches a flu, he drops by frequently to fix pots of soup and clean up before going to work, then checks on her again after work, so naturally he flops in his old room. Peggy has a bouquet of mixed flowers delivered with a note: Be well. Looking forward to seeing you soon. Peggy Malloy.

"So thoughtful of her," says Annemarie. She is sitting up in bed but has a low grade fever.

"Yeah," Johnny says uneasily. "You need a few more flowers around here."

"Fresh flowers," she rallies. "That's something special. Men never think about it. Your father, not once, may he rest in peace."

Johnny buttons his lip, nods. His old man Joe, poor guy, never had much peace in his life, worked himself straight into the grave. He looked peaceful in his coffin though. That's when people send you flowers.

"Soon as I'm back on my feet," his mother says, "we'll have a nice dinner together."

"Something to look forward to, huh?" Then he thinks, there's no getting around it, why resist?

"Ma, how about I make a dinner on my boat, for just the three of us?"

She beams. She's going to put it down in purple.

Peggy wakes up on her couch, hot and sweaty, the lights still on and TV flickering. Her blanket is twisted on the floor. She turns off the set and cranks a jalousie window open. The breeze cools her skin.

Wide awake and hungry she rummages in the refrigerator and finds a jar of peanut butter. When she was pregnant, she ate peanut butter by the tablespoon. She looks for a spoon.

She settles back on the couch with the blanket pulled up to her chin. Now she's chilly and can't get back to sleep. Peanut butter sticks to the roof of her mouth. What if I'm pregnant, she muses. We don't always take precautions, do we? Like that time on the boat? She counts backwards. A crazy idea, she tells herself. But yet, what if? She did miss her last period. And she lies quietly with hand on belly picturing Johnny leaning over a crib. "Hiya, doll," he says. It's a girl with green eyes and fuzzy black hair. She always wanted a girl.

Mrs. F. would be all over the kid.

What would Adele say? You're old enough to be a grandmother.

A slow flush creeps up her face and neck. It flames up suddenly in her face, heat radiates down her chest, her arms and legs. In a few moments she is drenched in sweat. Oh my God, she thinks, the Change, and she lies there panting a little, too astonished to be disappointed. What will happen to me now, she thinks.

Johnny sees Peg's big white Chevy lumbering down Aviation Avenue toward the marina, hears it too. The muffler's loose that Clark is supposed to come in from Naples to fix. But yesterday she let him know she washed and polished the car and vacuumed the inside.

He sees the two women picking their way carefully through the yard to the dock — one short, one tall — both broad-hipped and wearing colorful dresses, dark glasses and straw hats. His mother is talking with both hands. Peggy is carrying a bulky wicker basket. He can hear them laughing all the way down at the end of the dock where he's been waiting, with his captain's cap on, the hibachi ready to fire up.

The sound of their laughter is what gets to him. Not just that Peggy sounds extra loud, a little too high-pitched — she's nervous, that he understands. But it never crossed his mind till now they had anything in common, that they might ever share a joke.

"Johnny!" they shout with one voice.

For a moment he sees himself casting off and sailing away while they stand on the dock wailing, "Johnny! Johnny?"

"Ahoy!" he shouts, tips his hat. They are all smiles, hooray we're having a picnic.

"Welcome aboard, ladies."

"It's just like you," his mother pronounces, after inspecting the boat. This is her first visit. She's pleased to see the flower and seashell bouquet on the wall above the table. She notes the narrowness of the bed.

They go out on the dock. Peggy has her camera. She asks a passerby to snap all three of them arm-in-arm in front of Lucky Lady.

The morning was sunny, but now the sky is overcast, flecked with heat lightning. A mild breeze blows in across the bay. Johnny brings out his two folding chairs and a third he borrowed from the Pub, and Peggy unpacks her basket. Crackers, smoked clams, salami, prosciuto, mandarin oranges. She takes out a bottle of Chianti, hesitates. Johnny uncorks it with his Swiss army knife.

"Ma, will you join us?"

"I'll have a little," she says, with her lopsided grin. "It's a special occasion."

He fills two glasses and half of the third, avoiding her gaze.

"To special occasions," he says. They click glasses.

His mother sips, makes a wry face. "It's very strong, isn't it?"

"Jesus, that's plain old Dago Red," Johnny snorts. "My old man would've loved it."

"You see how he talks to me?" She leans toward Peggy confidentially. "His father never used that word."

"Which one?" Peggy asks, genuinely puzzled.

An uncomfortable silence follows. Peggy's face turns bright pink and her forehead is damp. "I mean the D-word or the J-word?" she ventures.

"Oh it's not important." Annemarie smiles, but not as kindly as before, it seems to Peggy, who takes another drink of the D-word wine. And another.

Johnny doesn't exactly relax. He feels a bit relieved though. It's the palsywalsy scenario he can't handle. Tension he is used to.

Emergencies he can deal with.

Just as he puts the steaks on the grill, down comes the rain. A sudden squall, no mere sprinkler. Sky and water are the same gunmetal grey, smudging the horizon. He ushers his guests inside the boat, carries in their chairs and goes back out with an umbrella for the hibachi. Thunder rumbles in the distance, lightning fingers the pier.

"It's not worth getting killed for a steak!" his mother calls.

"You're right, Ma," he says. He finishes cooking in the galley, flipping stations on the radio. Nothing but Christmas carols. Too bad he can't afford a marine radio with a weather band.

"It just doesn't seem like Christmas to me," Annemarie sighs.

"Do you miss the snow?" Peggy asks.

"Not in the slightest. It's cold and dirty, you can't even take a walk. Slip once and your bones are broken. Snow," she snorts, "you can have it."

Peggy falls silent. Rain pelts the tin roof, Lucky Lady rocks in light swells.

In the galley Johnny whistles and mashes potatoes with butter and ricotta, the way his mother taught him. He brings out platters heaped with potatoes and steaks, a big bowl of salad. The two women look at him hungrily, not at the food. He opens a half gallon of wine.

"So what's missing from a Florida Christmas, if not the snow?" His voice booms oddly in the small cabin. His mother pauses, fork in midair. Her eyes cloud over.

"Oh," says Peggy softly. "It isn't Florida, is it? It's family." She glances at Johnny. "I mean, the parts that are missing."

"Parts are missing," Annemarie repeats somberly. She stares at her plate. "Pop liked a good steak, remember?"

"Sure I remember. Steak medium rare and a glass of Chianti. Hey, chin up, pal. He would want us to enjoy ourselves, right?"

"Let's drink to Pop!" Peggy sings out. The glasses click again. "To my Pop, too," she adds weepy-eyed. She pours everyone more wine.

Annemarie softens. "You lost both your parents, didn't you dear?

"Within months of each other."

"You were orphaned!"

The women eye one another approvingly.

After the meal Johnny serves coffee and the cannoli his mother made that morning. He and Peggy spike their coffee with brandy but Annemarie declines. "You're trying to get me tight," she tells them archly.

"My God, they're heavenly," Peggy rhapsodizes, her mouth full of the flaky pastry, and gesturing with one arm, she knocks over her coffee mug. The hot liquid splashes on her dress. She stares helplessly at her lap, the ugly brown stain. She feels the heat seeping into her legs and expanding, gushing upward to her arms, her chest, her head.

"Cold water will get it out," Annemarie suggests.

Peggy looks up to see Johnny mopping the puddle.

"You have a wonderful son, Mrs. Filipello," she says.

"Oh, this boy of mine," Annemarie giggles, and for a moment can't go on. She is a bit tipsy herself. "This boy caused me no end of trouble, can you believe it? Before he became a perfect gentleman, he was a young scamp. Bad Johnny Pancake, this one."

"He certainly is a gentleman," says Peggy gazing fondly at him. "I don't know about a pancake."

"Now ladies!" Johnny begins. But his protest is cut short by a sudden crack of thunder followed by a complete blackout. Lights wink out all over the shore as far as they can see through rainstreaked windows. He lights the kerosene lantern and hangs it from a hook in the center of the cabin, where it sways gently. Their shadows move up and down on the cabin walls.

"How romantic," Peggy says.

"Are we safe?" Annemarie asks. "Phoo what a smell."

"Kerosene's safe," Johnny assures her. Safer than electricity, he thinks, and casually goes over to the fuse box and disconnects the line. But he isn't fooling anyone.

"I can't stand the unpredictable weather," his mother's voice goes up a notch and Johnny braces. "One moment sunny, the next thing you know, a hurricane. We should have ground under our feet in an electrical storm." She is gripping the edge of the table, which is teetering now. "I don't feel so good all of a sudden," she says. "Maybe I'm seasick, huh?"

"Yeah," he says. "You better lie down." He and Peggy both jump up to help her to the cot.

"Not for long, Gio. I want to go home."

"Had a glass of beer about an hour ago," he teases. "And it went right to your head."

"I mean it!" She looks ready to cry.

Peggy hiccoughs. "I'll drive my car right up to the dock," she volunteers.

"Not without wings on it you can't," he says. "You go out the way you came in. Ma, we'll bundle you up real good, you'll have two pairs of arms to lean on, and we'll just have to slog through the rain to my car. Or stay here where it's dry. It's as safe as anywhere else. The entire hull is lined with rubber at the water line."

His mother's mouth is set in a tight crooked line, her eyes shut. He knows what she's thinking. It's all his fault, he's bad Johnny Pancake again, the boy who jumps out of the skillet where he belongs and rolls off on his own, causing no end of trouble.

They wrap her in two sweaters and a poncho and get off the boat in a gusty rain. Down the pier they sway three abreast, not yet on solid ground. Annemarie clings to both their arms and takes slow careful steps.

Once they're off the pier Peggy starts singing: "'O'er land or sea or foam, wherever we may roam, you will always hear us singing this song, show us the way to go home.' C'mon. Everybody sing. We'll get there sooner."

"That's ridiculous," Annemarie sniffs and Peggy shuts up.

"Watch your step here," Johnny cautions. Both women seem unsteady on their feet. "You still got your sea-legs," he adds.

The boatyard is a dark obstacle course that he knows his way through by day or night, though usually it's lit by the odd lamp. Rain streams down their faces and into their shoes. The ground is puddled and mucky. But the thunder is fading away along with the threat of electrocution.

His car is within sight, perhaps a hundred yards away when Peggy stumbles. Her feet slip in the mud and shoot out in front of her. In an instant she has landed on her behind and Annemarie, still gripping Peggy's arm, is toppling over as well. Johnny holds on with all his strength and manages to right his mother before she falls.

"You alright?" Johnny looms over Peg, with his mother clasped firmly in one arm.

"Wha' happened?" Peggy gasps. Then she giggles. She isn't hurt apparently. "The old banana peel joke, y'know, funny." But no one else is laughing.

"I'll get Ma to the car. I'll be right back," Johnny says.

"No wait." She tries to get up, slips again. "Oh shit."

"I'll be right back," he says again.

"Shit shit shit," Peggy mumbles. "Moonbeam McSwine, oh Christ."

Johnny gets his mother bundled into the car at last. She sneezes violently, then settles down and glares.

He goes back for Peggy, who is crying now. "I feel just awful," she whimpers.

"Take it easy, now. You think anything's broken?"

"No."

"C'mon then, alley oop." He pulls her up and she leans heavily against him. Her breath smells stale and winey.

"Oh no," she groans again.

"C'mon, let's go," he urges. She twists away and leans over to vomit, not quietly, but as though something's being torn out of her. He'll have to clean that up later, he thinks, annoyed.

"The banana peel joke isn't funny," his mother declares. "Not when you're 80 plus years old. If you hadn't held on tight I'd have broken a few. That woman drinks too much."

Annemarie is fine the next day, not even a cough. But she's gone back to carping about trashy women who drink in bars.

"Wait a minute," Johnny defends the absent Peggy, though he himself is not too pleased with her at the moment. He had driven her home and helped her to the door, and when she lifted her face to him, turned away. "When'll I see you?" he heard her sniffle. "I'll call you," he said and hurried back to the car without turning around.

"Yesterday she was that nice Mrs. Malloy. Then she had one drink too many, sometimes it happens when she's nervous. Then she got seasick. That makes her not nice? You got seasick too."

"She got sick from too much wine, I was watching."

"You weren't exactly abstaining yourself."

Annemarie ignores that and insists, "She isn't nice enough for you."

"She is nice enough for me," he says flatly.

"Then why don't you marry her?" Triumphant.

"I'm not the marrying kind."

"You never met the right girl. And you won't, in a tavern."

"I met her in church," he says.

"Alright." She looks incredulous but relents a little. "Okay, so she's nice. But she's got a drinking problem, you can't deny it. I feel sorry for the girl. She can't have had an easy life."

So his girlfriend's a drunk and his mother's an emotional basket case. They both cling to him like leeches. He feels sorry for himself, poor old Johnny Pancake, back in the skillet.

The next three days he goes to work, he goes home to his boat and he doesn't phone either one of his ladies. He enjoys the solitude, the trim little cabin. He could live like this for the rest of his life, he thinks. He imagines sailing off to the Bahamas, solo.

Ma calls him at work, and he takes her shopping. It's too wet and cold now for the beach. He's polite but that's it; he's annoyed with her as well. She could have tried harder.

On the fourth day after the dinner party he begins to worry about Peggy. It's unlike her not to call or stop by after work. It's his Wednesday off. He walks up from the boatyard to Adele's, thinking to surprise her. Only Adele is in the shop.

"Peggy's taking some vacation time," she says coolly.

"Where'd she go?"

"She didn't say."

They stare at each other.

"I'm not the enemy," he says. "I'm her friend."

"You could have fooled me."

"What is this horseshit, Adele? I never say boo to her, I treat her like a lady."

"You hurt her."

"I hurt her!" He throws up his hands. "She hurt herself. She got fall-down stinking drunk. Or didn't she tell you?"

"Whose fault is that?" Adele bristles. "Her boyfriend keeps her at arm's length, he pours her drinks. Stay in your corner. Bottoms up."

"She drinks whether I'm there or not. She hangs out with you, you're some influence."

"We manage," Adele says stiffly. "We do our work. We raised our kids."

Johnny takes a deep breath.

"Funny she didn't mention a vacation to me," he says. Adele shrugs.

"Okay," he says. "You're her friend. You tell me, what am I supposed to do now? Send her flowers or what?"

"Flowers?" Her penciled eyebrows jump up.

"Yeah. Look, if I hurt her, it wasn't on purpose. Maybe I was standoffish, okay. So, how do I make up to her?"

"Maybe flowers." Adele smiles.

He continues. "If you happen to hear from her, you could tell her I'm sorry."

"Anything else?" she prods.

"Anything else is none of your business."

What else is there, he thinks, and he sees himself in another sleeker boat, sails billowing, heading for some tropical island, just himself and the boat.

Peggy is vacationing in her son's apartment in Naples, a small one-bedroom with kitchenette. I need a little getaway, she tells him, and he offers her his bed. She insists on the couch.

Her first night there, Clark treats her to dinner at the pizza parlor where his girlfriend works. Sharon is a thin, quiet girl with long dark hair, no make-up and horn-rimmed glasses. Peggy feels old and awkward around her. The next night Clark stays over at Sharon's and she doesn't see him for a day and a half.

It rains without let-up and she slogs back and forth along the empty beach. If she caught a bad cold would

Johnny come over and fix her soup? Was it her fault she got sick on his old crate? She didn't have more to drink than usual, the water was rough, the ground slippery. She could have hurt herself, so why the cold shoulder? Tears and rain stream down her cheeks. Is he simply tired of her? Is it all over? Is she alone again, and maybe forever? A wild keening moan wells up — she hears the sound astonished. Herself, carrying on as if he'd gone and died.

She has calmed down, she thinks, by the time Clark comes home from the garage. He has called meanwhile to check on her and she has fixed his favorite dinner, breaded pork chops and collard greens.

"We could have invited Sharon," she says. But Sharon works dinner shifts except the night before when she was off.

"You could both sleep here," Peggy suggests. "It wouldn't bother me, and it's your place."

"Sharon would be embarrassed." He stares at his plate, pushes the collards into a mound on one side. It's Buster likes the collards, Peggy remembers, not Clark. And her skin flushes up again. The heat is so sudden and violent she can't speak.

"How's Johnny?" Clark asks, still not looking at her.

Tears fill her eyes.

"Mom, what, what's going on?" he stutters. "Maybe I can help?"

Peggy shakes her head. "I'm too embarrassed," she manages at last.

Alone on Wednesday night, she watches *Gunsmoke*. Iron woman Kitty works the stick and slugs down hard liquor. Peggy has rationed herself to one wine cooler per evening, half soda, and she sips it slowly. The phone rings. She jumps off the couch.

It's only Adele.

Adele tells her Johnny was looking for her. "He's worried, he's sorry, he's your friend, he says. And he's getting you flowers."

Peggy is quiet.

"I didn't tell him where you are, I kept my word. Do you want me to?"

"No," says Peggy. "Let him worry a little longer."

"Now you're talking," Adele laughs.

In the morning, Peggy packs her suitcase.

"Take care of yourself, mom," Clark says. He seems concerned, but also relieved that she's leaving. At least he's fixed the muffler on her car.

The Chevy purrs along Tamiami Trail under dark clouds. The road is straight with little oncoming traffic. She is hopeful for the first time in days. Nothing will faze her now, she decides, not the sudden thunder and lightning playing over the swamp, nor the hot flashes in their wake. She drives on and on through miles of dense mangrove forest, its aerial roots as tangled and mysterious as her future.

A Devil of a Girl

Molly remembers twenty people at dinner every night, counting the boarders.

Rose makes a sour face. "There couldn't have been," she says. "The table wasn't big enough."

"We pushed two tables together. The cloth didn't cover the ends, remember? I see it plain as day."

"You haven't seen that tablecloth in fifty years."

As always Rose has the last word. She is the older sister by two years and this is her apartment, a tiny efficiency in southwest Miami. Her late husband Max slept in the twin bed Molly sleeps in now. Molly has lived with Rose since she flew down for the funeral over a year ago and Rose insisted that she stay. A divorcee without children, where else could Molly live comfortably on so meager a pension? And besides, Rose had never lived alone in her life.

The other apartments, many no larger than theirs, are occupied by big Cuban families who spill out into the center courtyard and onto the sidewalk evenings. The sisters watch from their porch.

"They could try to speak English once in a while," Rose grumbles. "They don't even make the effort."

"Ma didn't speak English," Molly reminds her. "Unless she had no choice."

"She didn't yell at us," says Rose, and turns her hearing aid down.

Did they ever really get along? Throughout childhood they had to double up on one bed. All six sisters slept in the same room, five brothers in another, and Rose bossed everyone. She never knew how to have fun, Molly thinks.

Molly was the first girl in the family to bob her hair and paint her lips, the only one in their generation to marry a gentile. Look where that got you, Rose's face seems to say, Rose and the framed photographs of her children, grandchildren and one great grand, arranged in a circle around the golden anniversary portrait of herself and Max on the wall above the TV.

A young mother wheels her baby around the courtyard, and Molly, leaning over the porch rail, coos, *"Buenas dias boobelah."*

"Señora, habla español?"

"No, I only *habla buenas dias, gracias.* I'm too old for more than that." The woman laughs. Every evening she offers another word *en español,* which Molly repeats and then forgets.

Rose attends a Hadassah luncheon every two weeks. Molly went once and dozed off during the speeches. Even the food was boring. Now she looks forward to some privacy while Big Sis is away. She turns the TV off the moment Rose is out the door. Rose leaves the set on even when no one is watching because it reminds her of Max, who watched it all day long when he was ill. The recliner has a sweat stain where he rested his head. Molly is content to sit in the recliner and read murder mysteries and sip iced tea while the fan stirs warm air around her. If the heat is oppressive she'll walk a few blocks to the air-conditioned branch library.

She wears a flowered dress and straw hat for these outings, and walks with a cane, as her knees are arthritic.

The librarian is a handsome, courteous young fellow. He is sweeter to her than to Rose, who sometimes comes to the library looking for Molly, not for books.

Between home and library Molly passes a white stucco building with narrow frosted windows she can't see through. Its massive wooden door is recessed in an arched entrance under a neon cocktail sign. One afternoon she steps into the shade of the entry to catch her breath.

The door swings open. Smoky air drifts out and cools her skin, reminding her of something. Oh, but what? A man in suit and tie is leaving. He smiles politely and holds the door ajar.

"Thank you," she smiles back and steps past him into a dark and quiet room. The door clicks shut behind her.

She stays still until her eyes adjust.

"Good afternoon, madam." The bartender ducks under the counter and waddles toward her, a portly man of middle years. "May I see you to a table?" He offers his arm and escorts her to a small booth and then strikes a match to what looks like Aladdin's lamp.

His face is jowly and solemn in the dim light. "What's your pleasure?" he asks.

"A Manhattan straight up," she says. "A good stiff one, please."

The wall next to her booth is hung with a Persian carpet. Behind the bar where her drink is being prepared she sees a giant hookah, a scimitar and other exotic artifacts. She is the only customer. He serves the drink in a long-stemmed glass with a small bowl of peanuts and a napkin. The glass is inscribed "Rubiyat Room."

"This is a beautiful room," she says. "Where did all these things come from?"

"My father had an import business," he replies.

Molly learns his name, Hugo. Although his father traveled the world, Hugo has not left Florida since World War II, when he was stationed in the South Pacific. The Rubiyat Room was opened by Hugo Senior during the boom years as a dinner club with a speakeasy in the storage shed, after which he took off to Istanbul, for starters. Until Hugo was old enough to take it on, his mother had managed the lounge. "They're both gone now," he concludes gravely.

Molly murmurs sympathy. She sips delicately from a fluted rim. The first drops sting her tongue, they fire up her heart. It has been quite a while since she felt this good. The best part is that never in a thousand and one nights will Rose think to look for her here.

She takes out her glasses and holds the napkin to the lamp to read the verse printed on it.

> A Jug of Wine, a Loaf of Bread—and Thou
> Beside me singing in the Wilderness—
> O, Wilderness were Paradise enow!

"My husband once gave me an exquisite perfume called Paradise Enow," she confides. "And a pair of silk harem pajamas."

Hugo nods encouragingly.

"Mr. McLean traveled far and wide on business," she explains. "But I stayed put. Like you." She does not mention that after twenty years of marriage McLean ran off with a younger woman. And left me singing in the wilderness, she thinks. Then wonders what happened to those silk pajamas.

She wore the outfit for days on end, traipsing about the steam-heated apartment in billowing pale peach trousers and scanty top. She didn't have to work then;

she read magazines and novels by the score, and nibbled the chocolate bon bons her husband mailed from New York, Chicago, Atlanta. "To sweeten you up," he wrote. "For the Queen of Hearts, from your ever loving Jack." At night she had the double bed to herself and plenty of time to fret. Was he never coming home? She could well imagine what he might be up to, but not what kept him away. Why had he married her in the first place? Not for money, she never had any. He did love her madly once, or so he'd said. An orphan, he loved her big family as well; twenty people at table, what could be jollier?

The new boarder looked a little like her brothers — tall and broad shouldered with dark thick hair. Except his hair was straight, not wavy, his skin fair and his green eyes looked intently, swiftly, secretly into her own. No one else noticed. They all thought Jack McLean was a capital fellow. He clowned with the boys as if he had grown up among them. Her brothers — all baseball fanatics — would toss boiled potatoes to each other down the long table rather than pass the plate, and McLean had an excellent aim. He had picked up a smattering of Yiddish too. "Danke shayn," he would say. Or with a sweep of his arm, indicating all of the sisters, "Hello shayne madels, wie gehts?" Her younger sisters giggled and blushed. But she knew who he really meant. Everyone said Molly was the prettiest.

After she eloped with the "Irisher," he was never again welcome at that table. The rift with her parents took several years to heal. And as it turned out, it was the idea of a family that McLean enjoyed, not the ongoing reality of it. There would be none of that Rabinowitz congestion in his own home. But he was terrific with the kids when they visited later on; her young nieces and nephews adored their Uncle Jack, the girls especially.

Hugo reminds her of an undertaker, such doleful eyes. He seats himself with a bowl of lemons and cutting board at a nearby table. With a small, sharp knife he peels the rinds into perfectly lemon-shaped spirals. She watches spellbound the gleaming blade and deft pudgy fingers.

"My husband sold chef's knives for a while," she remarks. "He was skilled with his hands."

"You must miss him a great deal," Hugo murmurs.

"Not in the slightest," she says.

Hugo smiles. Or is it a nervous tic? A moment later his face is funereal again.

"It was long ago," Molly adds, and wonders if McLean is still alive. If he is still with what's her name, or did he drink himself into the grave? To think, for many years she was convinced she would never get over the loss. She had given up so much for him, she couldn't give up the habit of loving too. And why had she been devoted to the man, knowing all that long, long time he was a two-faced liar and a cheat?

She remembers why. Memory seeps back in as if the intervening decades were layers and layers of thick cotton, she can almost feel his fingers glide around her waist — they are dancing in a smoke-filled speakeasy somewhere — Cleveland — and that shock of pleasure, his eyes green as fire taking her in. Oh to be desired is a fine thing, it is damp satin peeling off and the slap of skin on skin in the dawn light, at least she had that once.

Then what happened? She got older. He moved in with a woman half his age. It was not the end of her life. There were other men afterward, discreet affairs, but no great flame leaping. Flannel nightgowns.

Hugo brings her the bill on a small bronze dish. It's very reasonable, considering the peanuts. She leaves a good tip.

"Would you by any chance have a mint?" He does, of course.

"Stop by again, Mrs. McLean," he urges.

"Oh I will."

She opens the door cautiously, leaning on the cane, and sticks her head out into blinding daylight. No one in sight. Good. She walks slowly, humming to herself. Her back is straight, her head held high. All the Rabinowitz girls have beautiful posture, she thinks. Oh but Molly, you're a devil of a girl. And she laughs aloud.

In the courtyard children are playing tag. They screech and push each other, whirling like dervishes. The darlings, she thinks, and her eyes fill with tears. If only she hadn't let McLean talk her into those "miscarriages."

Molly unlocks the door. She is bushed, but can't rest until she brushes her dentures and rinses her mouth. At last she sinks into the recliner.

Rose wakes her up when she turns the TV back on.

"The door was unlocked," Rose says. "We could've been robbed."

"I could've been raped."

Rose ignores this. "I brought home leftovers." She eyes the recliner. "I'm pretty tired myself."

Molly gets up. "I'll fix you tea," she says softly and goes into the kitchenette. How she pities her sister, whose chief pleasure now is making off with leftover cold cuts.

"And thou beside me," she whispers to the kettle.

Flamingo

Just as she'd drifted into sleep, a thump startled Alice awake. And another. A series of creaky thumps above her, like a box spring mattress being jumped on. She heard a woman moaning, faintly at first, then louder.

Alice rarely saw her neighbors. Once in a while she spotted a stooped, gray figure emerging from one of the louvered doors or moving at a snail's pace down the long damp corridor.

It was funny at first to think of some dear old thing getting off when she herself, scarcely 24, wasn't getting any. But it happened often enough that she began to be annoyed. She considered banging on the ceiling with the broom.

"Shut up!" she yelled one night. There was no response.

The apartment had been quiet when she moved in, the only noise a dim thrum of traffic from the boulevard a few blocks away. It was a high-ceilinged studio with kitchenette in a decaying building that in the boom years of the 1920s had been a posh hotel. A double row of royal palms led from the front entrance past the buckled remains of a tennis court down a weedy lawn to Biscayne Bay. In the halls, plaster hung from the ceiling exposing bare board.

A stairway on the second floor led to the flat graveled roof, where there were a few dilapidated lounge chairs on a wooden platform and a sweeping view of the bay. When it wasn't raining, she'd climb to the roof with a cup of coffee to watch the sun come up.

She had watched those lush glorious sunrises from the porch of her former boyfriend for almost a year. Now some other woman was making him coffee.

Rain or shine, Alice worked on her thesis every morning at a small formica table facing a wall. Afternoons she had a clerical job in a campus office. Most evenings she studied in the library. At night she lay awake worrying that her thesis—Eros in Early 18th Century Europe—was too flimsy and she would disgrace herself on the comps. The daybed was lumpy and narrow. A jalousie window adjacent to the bed opened to the back end of the parking lot and occasionally beams of light swept over her.

Some nights, the moaning from the apartment above, unaccompanied by thumps, sounded as though her neighbor were in pain or suffering dry heaves. Perhaps Alice had misinterpreted. She listened closely but could not discern anything other than a woman moaning. The boyfriend could be the silent type. Or the woman could be masturbating. Compulsively. She alternated between indignation and pity.

In October the nights were given over to howling wind and torrential rain. The walls seemed to sweat, the windows rattled. Once she realized the building had survived much worse, she was able to sleep. Now it was a sharp clap of thunder that scattered her dreams. Her room turned bright as day for a heartbeat. She lay awake listening until the thunder faded. Her neighbor would be listening too, she thought, subdued by the storm's power. All her elderly neighbors must be listening, each on a narrow bed bathed in sudden fierce light.

The storms rolled in over Miami for three weeks without a break. Alice plodded on through the gloom, feeling half drowned and, at times, unbearably sad. When the sun came out at last, she raced up to the roof. It was mostly underwater except for the raised platform with its twisted lounge chairs. So intent was she on the brilliant blue sheen over sky and bay, she didn't notice at once she wasn't alone. A bulky woman in a pink chenille robe was balanced precariously on one of the battered chairs watching Alice navigate the puddles.

"Ahoy!" she called cheerily. "Welcome aboard."

"Good morning," Alice replied. "Lovely day, isn't it?"

"The most beautiful day of my life," the woman boomed.

They smiled at each other. The woman had crooked, stained teeth in a face once plumply handsome. Tangled gray hair fell below her shoulders. Her name was Sabrina.

"Alice, huh? You look like Alice in Wonderland. I always liked the name. My first daughter was Alice. She died in a car crash, and she was the good one. The other one won't talk to me, Adele. She married up. I bet you're a good one."

"Good enough," Alice said. "Have you lived here long?"

"Couple of months. Don't get out much, been a little indisposed. This is as good as it gets, I tell you. It's one hell of a view. The sky, the boats, the birds. Did you see that flamingo?"

"No. Where?" She looked around, puzzled.

"Down on the lawn on the bay side. I've been watching it all morning from my room. It looks lost or hurt. It's not even full grown. Take a look-see."

Alice waded over to the raised stucco barrier that enclosed the roof and leaned over it. In the long grass between the palms, almost hidden by debris blown in by the storm, a small pink and white flamingo was preening itself. The bird stretched its neck and emitted a series of nasal honks. It spread iridescent wings, and then sank back. She thought either a wing might be damaged or one of the stick-like legs. Shouldn't it be standing on one leg? Where was its flock?

"I don't know what to do," Sabrina fretted. "I talked to the manager. I begged him to keep his awful cat inside. So the son of a bitch says, 'If it croaks, I'll stuff and mount it.'"

"Maybe I can find someone at the university to help. I'll check around this afternoon."

"The sooner the better."

Sabrina watched the girl splash back to the deck. "Your apartment leak?" she asked.

"No, it's on the first floor."

"I got pots all over the place, have to use an umbrella when I'm on the can. Nothing can be done till the rainy season's over, he tells me. But guess what. They're never going to fix the roof on this dump, and that's a fact."

"What do you mean?"

"Look around, what do you see?"

Alice looked at the tall glassy condos that flanked their derelict home.

"Prime real estate," Sabrina sighed. "Enjoy it while you can, that's my motto."

"Maybe you could move downstairs," Alice suggested.

"And give up my view? Not on your life. I'll get more pots." She laughed and spluttered, then began coughing hoarsely.

"I better go back and dry out," she said. She had taken off her slippers, which were soaked. The bare feet were swollen with protruding veins.

"Can I help you?" Alice offered.

Sabrina got up slowly leaning on a cane. She looked at the small pond between the platform and door. "Maybe so," she said. "Pride goeth before a fall."

Sabrina lived in the apartment above hers. Of course she does, Alice thought, strangely pleased.

The room was even more sparsely furnished than her own, with only the day bed, a small card table, two folding chairs and one plastic bucket. There was no TV or book shelf, nor were there curtains on the one window. It could have been a nun's cell, if not for the walls, which were covered almost completely with photos, drawings and travel posters.

"Would you like a cup of tea, dear?"

Alice hesitated. "I can't stay long. I have to go to work."

Sabrina made her way around the bucket to the kitchenette, her cane clacking on the linoleum. "You'll need a strong cup of tea to keep your batteries charged."

Alice was drawn to a series of black and white photographs of a shapely blonde woman in a flowered dress. Some were nude portraits. Many of the sketches taped to the wall were of the same woman, surely Sabrina in her youth.

"Who did these? They're quite good."

"Oh, the love of my life. A terrific artist, full of himself he was, and married to someone else. I had a few of his paintings once, oils. They'd be worth a mint now."

Sabrina put two steaming mugs on the table and a package of ginger snaps. Alice was hungry. She ate and drank gratefully.

"I used to have such pretty tea cups," Sabrina sighed. "But I gave them away. Travel light, that's my motto."

"This is like kind of a cool wall paper." Alice admired travel posters for Paris, Buenos Aires, Tangiers, Crete.

"Are they places you've been to?"

"No, honey. They're places I'd like to go to."

"So would I."

"Don't wait too long," Sabrina cautioned. "Time bites you in the butt, I guarantee it."

Alice looked at her watch. "It'll bite me now if I stay much longer."

"Don't forget about that flamingo." Sabrina fished a crumpled card out of a pocket. "Let me know what happens, okay?"

"I live below you, by the way," Alice said as she went out the door.

"Do you? How nice. I've never heard a peep from downstairs, but I tell you the guy next door snores all night long. He's got emphysema, poor soul."

Alice made a half-hearted attempt that afternoon to find an avian or wildlife expert on campus. Her boss was no help. He dumped a box of transcripts on her desk to file by 5 o'clock. No one wanted to talk to her about one storm-injured flamingo.

Before leaving, she phoned Sabrina.

"It's too late anyway," Sabrina said wearily. "That damn cat got it or maybe a raccoon."

"Is it… did it?"

"It's dead, honey. Probably was a goner, to begin with, all alone like that. Sure was a pretty little thing."

Alice came home earlier than usual and went out to the lawn. There was no sign of the flamingo or its violent demise. She looked up at Sabrina's window, but it was dark. I'll call her tomorrow, she thought, fingering the card in her pocket. But the next day she was busy and she forgot about the card.

Now that she knew who was making the nocturnal sounds, they no longer disturbed her. It was like the traffic on Biscayne Boulevard; she didn't hear it.

She planned on visiting her new friend once the ordeal of thesis and exams was behind her. But by then she was exhausted, and put it off.

Alice rediscovered the card while doing her laundry. "Sabrina Smith, Artists Model," she read. The phone number had been crossed out and penned in several times. She called Sabrina that afternoon. But the line was disconnected.

It was quiet at night, she realized uneasily, and had been for several days. She went upstairs and knocked on Sabrina's door. No answer. She came back an hour later and knocked again. "Sabrina," she called. "Are you alright?"

The door to the next apartment opened and a grizzled, burly man stepped out.

"She's gone," he said, his voice raspy and faint.

"Gone where?"

He stared at her from bleary eyes. "Gone to her maker. She passed last week. You a friend?"

She nodded, unable to speak.

"Sorry to break it to you so sudden like. Sabrina was one hell of a woman. They threw away the mold."

Alice climbed heavily to the roof and sat in a lounge chair. It must be the lost opportunity that weighed on her, the stories she'd never hear over cups of tea. A wave of nostalgia for the old hotel and the life still flickering in it swept over her, as if it had already been demolished and the tenants displaced, a bewildering presentiment of more loss yet to come.

A flock of geese gabbled up from the bay and wheeled above her head. If only she'd been able to save the damn flamingo.

Pluto's Cave

A ndrea is seated on the other side of the chapel, between Uncle Ed and a red-headed woman. She's wearing a black leather jacket and skinny pants, and her buzz-cut blonde hair shows dark at the roots. Her friend is also dressed in black leather.

My mother elbows me and hisses in my ear, "No respect."

"At least it's black," I say.

I saw my cousin's motorcycle in the parking lot, which means she didn't drive her father to the funeral. The old man is slumped in his wheelchair, shoulders trembling. His familiar tuft of hair, white now, crests above a shriveled frame. Andrea ignores him. She's staring at photos of her mother, my aunt Sophie, arranged on a low table before the lectern.

Behind Andrea and Ed sits the youngest of my mother's many sisters, Aunt Nadine, straight backed and regal in a gray silk suit. She puts a hand on Ed's shoulder and says something which seems to calm him. Andrea half turns in her seat toward Nadine and, seeing us watching, raises a hand in greeting, her mouth set in a grim line.

Andrea was three months old when Aunt Sophie placed her on my lap for the annual family Christmas portrait. The photo shows me with a goofy smile, squeezed between the boy cousins on a sofa. The baby grabbed the end of my braid and wouldn't let go, her bright dark eyes questioning me, or so I thought.

I could never tell that baby what I knew.

How I'd seen Grandmother make Aunt Nadine sign that paper. How Nadine's fingers with their tapered pink nails were shaking as she signed. Aunt Sophie and Uncle Ed signed, too. Grandmother commanded from her rocker in a black widow's dress and black cotton stockings rolled up at the knee, arms folded over her chest.

"Hey you, little big ears," she barked, looking straight at where I was crouched behind the sofa. My mother hustled me out to the porch and squatted with both hands on my shoulders. Her pale blue eyes bored into mine.

"Francine, I want you to promise you will never tell a soul about this. For the sake of the child."

My parents and I lived with Grandmother in the Shasta Valley on what was left of the family ranch. From the front porch, pastures and scrub oak stretched to the horizon where the giant mountain towered snowcapped year around. Our nearest neighbors were three miles closer to town.

Nadine had lived at home when I was small. After high school she roomed with Aunt Sophie and Uncle Ed in Sacramento until she got herself in trouble. Sophie and Ed couldn't have a baby. The way my mother explained it, the baby was Nadine's gift to them.

The summer before the baby was born, Nadine came home, to my great joy, for I loved her most of all the aunts. I scarcely knew the others then. Nadine was tall and slender, small boned, her hair long and dark. I was a chunky, seven-year-old towhead. I thought she was as beautiful as a storybook princess. Only now the princess had a belly that was round and firm as a small watermelon. She let me touch it when the baby kicked.

She brought one suitcase with her and a framed photograph of her boyfriend, who had been in Italy for over a year defending democracy from the fascists and did not know about the baby. I was too young then to puzzle out these details. But I learned another secret later that summer. Either my mother told me, or, more likely, I over-heard this as well. Nadine had been seduced by another soldier on leave, who was killed by the Nazis.

Early in September Uncle Ed and Aunt Sophie visited for two days. They had come to take Nadine back to Sacramento, so the baby could be born in a hospital. Nadine and I came out to the porch when we heard the car rattling up the road. Ed unfolded himself from the coupe, tall and lanky in a creased suit, his hair windblown and sticking up like a rooster's comb. They had driven directly from the school where Ed taught and he still had chalk on his hands. Sophie, a head shorter, seemed to be wilting in her flowered cotton dress. She tried not to look at Nadine's belly.

The next morning everyone sat around the kitchen table for a long time, instead of jumping up to wash the dishes or go to work. My father didn't bolt his food and read the newspaper as he usually did. He lingered and talked with his brother-in-law about the war winding down at last. We had a special breakfast of blackberry pancakes and sunnyside-up eggs, and Nadine made me a cup of coffee-flavored hot milk

"This is like paradise," Ed beamed at us. "You never breathe air so fresh in the city."

"It's too darn hot for paradise," Grandmother sniffed.

Ed had been raised on the mountain and he missed it every day, he said. Then he looked at me and winked. "Why so glum, Miss Francie? You going to miss your auntie?" I frowned and did not reply.

Nadine also looked glum, I thought. Surely she didn't want to leave our mountain paradise.

"I know where we can cool off," Uncle Ed went on. "Who's for heading out to Pluto's Cave?"

"Count me in," Nadine said eagerly.

"Me too," I said, though I had no idea what or where this was.

My father looked at me. "You ought to see the lava tubes, Frannie," he said. "I never have time to take you."

Grandmother and Mother were appalled. It would be dangerous for Nadine to traipse down a lava tube in her condition. But Nadine insisted. "I'm not a child. I can take care of myself."

Grandmother raised her eyebrows and tightened her lips. Aunt Sophie murmured, "Only be careful enough for two, Nadie."

"You come too, Sophie," her husband urged.

"You've lured me to that cave one time too many, Edward Fromm. I promised to help mother with the canning."

"All the girls were meant to do the canning," Grandmother said sharply.

"I'll help tomorrow, Mother, cross my heart." Nadine jumped up from the table and bused and washed the dishes, and I dried them. Grandmother shook her head and sniffed.

Off we three went in Uncle Ed's 1938 Ford coupe, me in the rumble seat.

"The cave is like being on another planet," he told me. "That's not a bad idea," Nadine said.

The road seemed to go on forever. When I fussed, Uncle Ed told me I couldn't expect Pluto to be right around the corner. "It's like going to the smallest, farthest away planet in our solar system, toots," he said. Finally he pulled over and parked next to a telephone pole with a small hand-lettered sign nailed to it: Pluto's Cave. A rough trail led through scrub oak to a stony, hole-pocked clearing. The holes were smaller, collapsed lava tubes, I learned. We had to walk even farther along a fire road and another trail to get to Pluto. But it was worth it, because it had a huge gaping entrance and it was in three parts like a weird truncated snake with its head sticking out of the ground.

It was chilly inside with dusty columns of light slanting down to the rock cluttered floor. The second section had a kind of skylight. The farther we walked down into the tube, the darker it got. We all had flashlights.

"Cool enough for you now?" Uncle Ed's deep voice echoed eerily. "It was boiling lava once." He explained that the cave was a hollow tube of lava that formed when the mountain erupted. "Millions of years ago, now just think about that." He said if I were patient I would find traces of that distant past in the rubble, and he had a small collection he'd started when he was about my age. We shone our flashlights into dark corners. A bat flapped out suddenly squealing, and I squealed even louder and, in a panic, dropped my flashlight and ran deeper into the cave.

When I looked back my aunt and uncle were talking about something, their heads close together, and I couldn't hear what they were saying. I remember feeling irked. Shouldn't the adults be comforting me? I ran around a bend, where it was so dark I couldn't see my own hands.

The tube was narrower here. I had to feel my way along the walls.

Somehow I wound up in a crevice or kind of chimney that sloped upward to the light, and I clambered along it and got stuck in a narrow passage with my shoulders and legs free, and my plump little belly wedged in between the walls. I screamed and sobbed.

I heard them shout my name and come toward me in a great hurry.

"Oh shit," Nadine said, and that echoed around the tubes, to my delight. Oh shit oh shit oh shit.

"Are you alright?" Uncle Ed asked her.

"You get Frannie," she said. "I'll wait here."

I learned later she had stumbled, and he caught her. Next he rescued me, popping me out of that tight spot like a cork from a bottle. He carried me whimpering back to where Nadine waited. I had scrapes on my knees and hands.

When the hullabaloo subsided, Nadine said the baby was kicking and Uncle Ed insisted she rest. We went back to the middle section and she settled herself on a flat rock under the skylight, one hand resting on her belly. "Baby born on Pluto," she said. "We'll all be in the news." We gazed at her so solemnly she burst out laughing and I couldn't help but join her. Her laughter seemed to bubble up inside me and bounce off the walls. Uncle Ed shook his head. "You girls, now wouldn't we be in a pickle."

"But Ed, you know all about biology, too," Nadine teased. My uncle looked very worried. He took her arm gently but firmly and escorted her back to the car while I raced ahead. Early the next morning Nadine left with her sister and brother-in-law for Sacramento. Andrea was born the day after that, two weeks ahead of schedule.

Until she was ten Andrea spent three weeks every summer on the ranch and after that she went to summer camps. Grandmother was partial to Andrea. I thought it was because she'd been named for Grandpa Andrew. I realize now she was Grandmother's baby's baby. A delicate, pretty infant in frothy pinks and lace. A whiny two year-old. Or a miniature cowgirl with plastic six-shooters terrorizing the goats on her summer visits. It didn't matter how she behaved. Grandmother adored her.

Aunt Sophie dressed her daughter like a princess, but Andrea had other ideas early on. She wanted jeans and cowboy boots, not frilly dresses; and horse riding lessons, not ballet or tap. When she was 14 they gave her an electric guitar and a drum set and soundproofed the garage. She got a Harley for her 16th birthday. When she was 18 she mounted it and took off for L.A. with the guitar and didn't come home again, unless she was flat busted and Aunt Nadine, who had settled there, couldn't or wouldn't bail her out.

What I knew and had promised my mother never to tell seemed in time like a dream, increasingly remote, yet never entirely forgotten. It was something I always had that Andrea did not.

Sophie's pastor is a broad shouldered, florid man with a deep bass voice. When we shake hands he looks me straight in the eye and makes sure he's got my name right. He seems to have known my aunt well.

"Jesus has been at the center of Sophie's life for many years," he informs me. Apparently, after Andrea left home for good, Sophie all but moved into the Reformed Baptist Living Christ Church.

Uncle Ed believes in science, in the wonder and beauty

of the natural world and the cosmos, as he often told us on starry summer nights. He'd bring his telescope to the ranch and set it up on the front lawn. We'd look at the surface of the moon and incomprehensibly remote milky nebulae and once we arose at dawn to gaze at the morning star, Andrea and Ed and I, but not Sophie, whose health was always delicate.

Members of Sophie's church step up to the lectern to share their memories of her, perhaps a dozen congregants in all. Some read notes, other speak spontaneously. She was active in church programs for years and much loved.

There is an awkward pause when the pastor looks over at the first few rows. My mother shifts uneasily beside me. Ed, half paralyzed from a stroke, can't talk. Andrea is too stunned. And I? What do I really know about my aunt? I stare at the photos on the table. Her toothy smile unsettles me. Aunt Sophie was a little too eager to please, too affectionate, and too easily hurt. Her sisters have more backbone, each one feistier than the next, as if my grandparents had only been practicing on their first born.

It is Nadine who rises to speak for all of us. She adjusts the microphone to her height, puts on reading glasses and opens a notebook. She is still slender, her gray hair shoulder length, her skin tanned and creased around the eyes and neck.

"Sophie was both sister and mother to me," she begins. "She was a courageous and generous woman whose chief joy was her family, especially her daughter Andrea, and Ed, her husband of over 50 years."

Ed strains forward in his chair.

"It was summer 51 years ago when he took her on their first date up to Pluto's Cave." Nadine is explaining what this is to the uninitiated flatlanders when Ed sputters, "Ssss" and holds up two fingers.

"Second date. Sorry Ed. Sophie always said it was colder than Hades in that cave. And that Ed did his best to keep her warm."

Laughter ripples through the chapel. My mother frowns and braces herself for more. She doesn't know, but might suspect, that I found my way back up to Pluto's Cave with my first boyfriend. She has no doubt heard that half of Shasta County lost its virginity up there on scratchy army blankets. I don't mean Sophie. Oh no, our Sophie's courting was in another, more innocent era, before beer cans, condoms and graffiti littered the million-year-old lava tube.

Nadine, having veered a little too close to wildness for Mother's comfort, returns to the official family screed. Ed and Sophie married and moved to Sacramento, where Ed taught high school physics and Sophie worked as a secretary until about four months before Andrea was born.

"Sophie nurtured and supported her daughter in whatever choices Andrea made," Nadine goes on. "She was in the front row at every high school musical performance. And in recent years she welcomed Andrea's partner Willow into the family.

"Unfortunately, my sister endured multiple, episodic illnesses, none of them severe enough to subdue her spirit until the very end." Nadine takes off the glasses and her voice breaks a little. "Rest in peace, dear sister." She crosses over to Andrea and hugs her and sits next to her and Willow.

My mother clears her throat. Her eyes are damp.

The pastor concludes by suggesting donations to any of three research foundations in Sophie's name. There are cards on the table at the rear. Everyone is invited to return to the church social hall after the burial and continue the celebration of Sophie's life.

Outside the chapel Andrea scowls at her motorcycle. The engine seized up in the heat and won't start.

"We can hike there," Willow suggests. "It's only a mile."

"What, and miss the second act? You two ride with me," I direct. My mother gets in the limo with her two older sisters and their husbands. Uncle Ed rides in Aunt Nadine's car. Andrea and Willow load the wheelchair into the trunk.

We drive at a crawl in a long procession behind the hearse, air conditioning on high. I look back as we top a small rise. There are a half dozen cars full of relatives and the rest are friends or members of Sophie's church. Tailing at the very end like a caboose is a small red car with one driver.

"Your aunt's eulogy was so touching," Willow says.

"You know, Mom didn't like that cave," Andrea interrupts. "She was afraid of it. And Daddy knew it, too."

"I'm not surprised," I say. "It's beautiful, but scary."

"You told me once if I wasn't good I'd go straight to hell down a lava tube."

"I don't remember saying that."

"You sure as hell did."

Aunt Sophie's casket is elevated on sawhorses next to a large green tarp that covers the grave and a mound of earth. Some hundred yards away two men lean against a picket fence, shovels in hand. The casket is heaped with floral wreaths.

A woman in a gray pants suit approaches us. She's carrying a clipboard and a bouquet of long-stemmed yellow roses. She presents Andrea with a rose and checks off her name. "It's to place on the casket," she informs us. Ed and the four remaining sisters get roses, and now anyone else who wants to participate. So I take one.

The mourners are clustered in a semi-circle on the grass around the pastor, who also holds a yellow rose. There are a few folding chairs near the casket for the elderly and infirm. Andrea and Willow station themselves behind Ed and I thread my way through to my mother, murmuring greetings to those I know by name — my aunts and cousins and their spouses. I can't keep track of all the children. The last time I saw so many of them was at Grandmother's funeral fifteen years before. People I don't recognize are still parking their cars and streaming toward the grave site.

A woman climbs out of the red sports car. She is plump with short cropped gray hair and wears a business suit. She looks familiar but I can't place her.

The pastor launches into a homily, which mercifully he keeps short while the sun beats down on us. The air is sultry and still. Uncle Ed is straining to say something. Andrea drops to her knees beside the chair and takes his hand. He manages a half smile for her somehow, then seems to forget what it was he wanted to say.

"Rejoice in life everlasting," the pastor intones. "Sophie is going home to the place Jesus has prepared for us all." He puts his rose on the casket.

Nadine comes over and pushes the wheelchair forward and helps Ed place his rose. The other aunts and their husbands follow. I come along with my mother. "Happy trails, Aunt Sophie," I murmur and Mother goes, "Tsk tsk." "I mean it," I say, and walk over to where Andrea hunkers with Willow beside her, two aging Goth princesses. I put an arm around Andrea.

The ladies of the church who are Sophie's friends come up next one by one. Some of them bend over the casket and kiss it.

"This isn't saying goodbye," Andrea mutters. "I never got to say goodbye. This isn't her."

"Honey, you need to do this," Willow urges. "You need closure."

"Pretend she's listening," I say.

Andrea nods and takes a deep breath. She gets up and strides forward looking like a black avenging angel. People make way. She places the rose carefully so that its stems and petals touch the casket's surface and for a moment, sways there at the foot, holding onto the sides. Suddenly Andrea throws herself forward face down on the flowers, thorns and all, and she embraces the casket with both arms.

"Holy smokes," Willow breathes.

In a minute, Andrea gets up and her face seems softer, though a bit scratched. She goes over to her father and Nadine and hugs them both.

People start for their cars. But Andrea and Nadine have decided they will stay with Ed to watch the actual burial. "You go ahead with Fran," Andrea tells Willow.

We get in my car and I drive uphill to turn around. I look back at the burial site where the workers have already converged. Nadine and Andrea have pulled up two folding chairs and are sitting on each side of Ed, their heads bent toward him, listening.

Tables are laden with cakes and cookies and bunches of grapes. There are two large bowls of fruit punch and canisters of coffee and hot water for tea.

"I'll need a shot of something stronger after this," Willow says.

"Stick with me, kiddo."

She laughs, her eyes scrunching up. I like her. I think she's been a good influence on Andrea. They've been together four years. Before that, Andrea was a part-time lap dancer and played lead guitar in an all-girl punk band in Santa Monica, which maybe she still does, but she has a better day job now.

"Andrea and I want a baby," she confides.

"Which one of you?" Willow isn't as young as she looks from a distance and Andrea is 45.

"We'll only be able to afford one of us. I'm younger, but I have the career track job. What do you think her Dad will say?"

"He'll be thrilled," I assure her. "He could use some good news."

The woman in the business suit greets me. "Hello Fran, it's been many years." She notices my hesitation. "Lillian Markham. I had your daughter in junior English. And your son took debate. How are they doing?"

"They're doing great. They're fine. Lillian, how kind of you to come."

She smiles sweetly. I remember that smile. My son had a crush on Mrs. Markham. She had an hourglass figure then and wore cashmere sweater sets. She was also an excellent teacher, funny and innovative. Uncle Ed taught in that same school for years.

"I'd hoped to speak to Ed," she murmurs, looking around.

I explain why he's late. "I'm sure he'll be pleased to see you again," I say.

I'd last seen her in Santa Cruz perhaps a dozen years ago. I had a temp job staffing a booth at a health fair in one of the hotels. There was also a National Teachers of Science conference in town, so it wasn't a surprise to spot Uncle Ed in a café window. I was about to cross the street and go into the café when I realized that Lillian Markham was seated opposite him. Why was she at a science teachers' conference, I wondered. Then he leaned across the table and took her hands in his. This could have meant anything, but they were regarding one another so intently that I backed away. I never knew any of the details, the beginning or end or the curve of that liaison, if such it was. I never told anyone what I suspected. Uncle Ed did not have a reputation for philandering. But Sophie was so often ill and he was still a vital man.

I go outside the church social hall to wait for Nadine to drive up, thinking Uncle Ed might appreciate a heads up.

The car is already parked and Andrea is pushing her father in the wheelchair at a furious clip across the lot, with Nadine in her wake. It's like watching a sudden summer storm loom up.

Andrea glares at me as she charges into the vestibule.

"What happened?" I ask Nadine, but she doesn't answer and hurries on inside.

The crowd parts before them, leaving a clear path for Lillian Markham, who manages to be stationed where Andrea parks the wheelchair.

"Ed, I am so very sorry," she begins. Ed looks at her. His mouth twists, then he drops his head and bawls.

Nadine rushes up to comfort her brother-in-law. I see my mother staring, her mouth agape.

Andrea backs off. Willow is at her side in a heartbeat, and they both go out to where I'm standing.

"Why didn't you tell me?" Andrea demands.

"Tell you what?" Willow looks at us bewildered.

"Aunt Nadine is my birth mother."

"No shit."

"Fran fricking knew all along."

"I was only a kid." I protest. "All I really remember is Mother saying I'd fry in hell if I told anyone. I never even talked to Nadine about it. I'm kind of shocked she told you or said I knew anything about it. Right there at the grave."

Andrea bites her lip. "She didn't want to. Daddy pleaded with her. He kept saying 'tell, tell her.'"

"Why are you so pissed, sweetie" Willow says. "You have two fabulous mothers now. And one's alive and well, and you love her, too."

"I'm pissed because I've been lied to all my life. I'm over 40 and now I don't know who I am."

"Of course you do," Willow soothes. And then reconsiders. "Oh, you mean biologically? Did she say who the father was?"

"Some soldier who died in the war."

"That's what I remember hearing," I say.

"Whose name was Jones? Like, give me a fricking break. Jones, hah! Sure, it was. She's dicking me around."

We fall silent and turn to look at Ed, still weeping, and the two women bent over him.

"Poor Daddy," Andrea sighs. "He's totally unglued."

"See, Ed *is* your dad," I say. "Doesn't matter who knocked Nadine up. He and Sophie are your parents. Like you and Willow will be parents."

"Willow told you?" Andrea brightens.

Willow nods, distracted. She peers at Ed through narrowed eyes. He is quiet now. Nadine is fiddling with the tufted hair and Lillian is smiling her dazzling smile.

Then Willow blurts out, "This is going to sound crazy, but maybe Ed's your birth father, Andrea."

"What are you saying? That is so gross." Andrea is furious again.

"Forget I mentioned it."

Willow glances at me, but I make my face bland.

It has never once crossed my mind, but I think she's right. I can imagine how and why it happened.

Did Sophie know? Does my mother? Lillian? I'm never going to ask. Some secrets are too messy to tamper with.

The summer I turned 15, Uncle Ed woke Andrea and me before dawn so we could watch the morning star come up through his telescope. Groggily we followed him into the dark yard, trailing our nightgowns in the wet grass.

It was critical to stay totally still while peering into the lens. "If this contraption moves by a hair we'll be halfway across the solar system," he warned us. He braced Andrea with one arm while she had her turn. But she managed to bump it afterward, and he patiently readjusted the settings.

"So what," she pouted. "It's not as good as Mars. Anyway, I'm hungry." And she stalked back into the house.

"Okay toots, it's ready now."

I stepped carefully up to the lens and Uncle Ed stood behind me and put his hands on my arms to steady me.

Venus swam up glowing from the lower quadrant of an indigo sky. "Oh," I gasped.

Even more astonishing was the warm glow on my skin where my uncle's big hands held me firmly. I felt his breath on the back of my neck.

"You see it all?"

"Yes."

"Don't move now."

I couldn't move to save my life. That warm glow floated like a balloon down my spine to between my legs and lingered even after he gently pulled me away and went back to tinkering with the scope.

I'm certain he never had an inkling he was the first man to stir me. I was deeply embarrassed and unusually quiet.

After a while, Uncle Ed, his voice hushed, said, "It's awe inspiring, isn't it, Frannie?"

Breaking Up

My father had been moodier than usual since he quit smoking, giving up a 35-year, three-pack-a-day habit. His bursitis was flaring up too, and he didn't sleep well. It hadn't helped that, before I got my own car, he was picking me up from my job in the diner at one in the morning, twice a week.

The other two nights Jack Blitz brought me home from work. Jack was in med school and the only guy I'd ever dated that my father liked. My mother liked Jack too, but then she liked anyone who was nice to her, and Jack was a friendly guy.

"I had a boyfriend named Leo Blitzstein once," she told me. "A lot of people shorten their last names. Maybe they're related. They look alike. He was very nice too."

"So what happened to Leo?" I asked.

"I didn't love him. He didn't make me tingle like your Daddy did when he kissed me."

Daddy and I had talked about my buying a car and looked at ads in the paper, and then one night after work there he was with Jack in the diner parking lot next to a 1959 Chevy Biscayne. It was big and black with sweeping white tail fins.

"Surprise!" My father tossed me a set of keys. He peered into my face expectantly.

I managed a smile.

"Norm got a real sweet deal for you," Jack said. "Only $50 down."

They were protecting me, I knew, from the hard-boiled ways of used car salesmen. Still, it was my first car and I hadn't even chosen the color.

"I really do like black and white," I told them. "It's so dramatic."

Driving the car was a challenge, as I was accustomed to the power steering in my father's car. "Gangway," I cried. "Here comes the QE-2."

"Avast ye landlubbers," Daddy shouted at a couple of startled strangers in passing. He began to hum the only sea chanty he knew.

Jack sat between us on the front seat and joined in on the chorus. "Yo ho ho and a bottle of rum." He put one hand on my thigh, his fingers tapping the beat. I quickly removed it.

Not long after I got the car, I quit my job and broke up with Jack, and later that evening, drove home sucking a mint to mask cigarette smoke and alcohol. The house was dark. I found my mother half asleep on the couch in the Florida room. She sat up blinking.

"I dozed off waiting for you," she said. "You forgot, didn't you?"

She was wearing her hospital volunteer's uniform. One night a week she worked in the gift shop at South Miami General. But she couldn't drive and I had promised to take her there before my shift.

"Oh god, I'm sorry, Mom. Why didn't Daddy take you?"

"It's his poker night. He didn't have time, he said. He got really mad at you."

In the dim light she looked younger than 45, her slender neck dark against the pink nylon dress. I had a uniform on too, the black skirt and white blouse of a waitress. I kicked off my shoes and socks.

"I'm not going to the hospital anymore," she said.

"How come?"

"Norm doesn't want me working at night. He doesn't like me volunteering there. I could pick up germs. We could all get sick. He says he's sick and tired of driving me back and forth." She paused to let this sink in.

I hung my head, but I was more irritated than ashamed.

"He says why should I work and not get paid. So then I tell him I'll get a real job. But he's against that too."

"I don't get it," I said. "You used to work."

"None of my sisters had to. None of our friends' wives work. He's got his pride."

"But I'm working. Both my sisters are working."

"You girls aren't married yet."

"Mom, that won't make any difference. It's ridiculous."

"I know it is. You can't tell him anything." She looked at her watch. "Are you off work early?"

"I quit the job," I said. "The manager's so horrible, I couldn't stand it another minute. And the tips are lousy. I can work in a cocktail lounge as soon as I'm 21 and make really good money."

"A cocktail lounge," she repeated doubtfully. "Your father won't like that."

"He'll get used to it."

"He has to understand you're not his little girl anymore," she said, smiling at me.

This was encouraging.

"There's something else I've got to tell you, Mom."

"Yes, dear?"

"I broke up with Jack. I quit the job *and* the boyfriend."

"Oh no, Rita, what a shame. He's such a nice boy."

"He doesn't turn me on, Mom. No tingles."

Jack was smart and zany and rode a Harley. His cottage was piled everywhere with paper, books, LPs, dirty clothes, unwashed dishes, rotting food and pot roaches. He smoked dope morning, noon and night, and never missed a beat as I did under the influence. Almost every conversation was a monologue, during which he supplied me with a great deal of practical information ranging from hangover fix-its to vinegar douches.

This was a Coconut Grove beatnik pad. I liked the candles in the chianti bottles and the chaotic disorder so different from my own home. Jack played music for me I'd never heard before. Coltrane, Monk. *Sketches of Spain* — music that made me long for something that wasn't happening.

His face was wide and freckled with flat cheeks and eyes that narrowed to slits when he laughed. He often laughed at his own jokes. Was it the wild snigger, the frequent lectures, or the pale sticky skin and sparse hair on his chest—too much like my father's—that explained the lack of some essential chemistry between us? When he penetrated me, I thought about scalpels scraping in and out. Smoking dope did not enhance the experience. Nor did his telling me one night that I had a strong odor. That was when I got the vinegar douche lecture. I was embarrassed at first, then puzzled. What about the way his apartment smelled?

The most aroused I got was riding behind him on the Harley. I'd fasten the helmet, hitch the waitress skirt thigh high and, after he'd revved the motor, swing one leg over the seat, and off we'd roar, with me hugging him from behind, frightened and exhilarated, for how could I trust machine or man; but oh those powerful vibrations between my legs as we rushed through the air.

When Jack brought me home from work, he'd cut the motor a block away and coast in. "Don't want to wake the old man," he'd say, and I'd hop off. Still straddling the cycle, he'd plaster wet kisses all over my face, his tongue lapping around like a big friendly dog's. "Jack's going home to jack off," he'd say cheerfully when I broke away. Then he'd roar off on the bike.

So that was the odor in his apartment, I realized. The unwashed sheets, the congealed semen. The entire two rooms needed a vinegar douche.

I couldn't tell my mother that. Instead I told her Jack was a know-it-all. When I said I just wanted to be friends, he'd shrugged. "Them's the breaks," he'd said. I'd have ended it sooner had I known how easy it would be.

"He may be hiding his true feelings," my mother suggested.

"He doesn't know how to have feelings."

She nodded thoughtfully.

Two cars went by in succession, their headlights sweeping across the dark living room and spotlighting the throw rug at our feet, a fiery red and gold oval shag. "You like the rug, don't you?" she asked.

It was a new rug that had appeared on the terrazzo floor not long after I got my car.

"I told you I did," I snapped. I didn't want to talk about a rug.

"I love that rug," my mother murmured. "As soon as I saw it, I had to have it."

I nodded, but my attention wandered. I was figuring what I'd have to earn to afford my own apartment. So much for car payments, tuition, food, and $75 a month for a studio apartment.

"It wasn't cheap," Mom said. "He thinks I saved the money out of my allowance. But he doesn't know everything."

I studied the rug. The shag was thick and brilliant against an otherwise subdued color scheme. I had no idea what such things cost.

"How did you pay for it?"

"Promise you won't tell a soul."

"Cross my heart," I swore.

"I sold my blood," she whispered.

"Wow," I managed. My mother was thin, small boned, often tired. A strong wind could blow her away. How could she have blood to spare?

"I went seven times," she continued, gazing at the rug. "I had to take two buses. The first time I almost fainted. I begged them to let me try again."

"Oh Mom!" I blinked back unexpected tears. "That's awful."

"But sweetie, it wasn't awful. They were very kind. They gave me orange juice and let me rest. I have one of the rarer types, B negative. It will save someone's life some day." She looked pleased. "I'll donate it the next time. The hospital has blood drives, you know."

"I've got to make more money," I said.

"What else could I do? Your father won't let me work. My allowance just barely covers the bills." She put a hand on mine. "But the money you give me does help."

I shrugged. It was a pittance.

"It's a beautiful rug," I told her.

She cheered up. "He would never have agreed to buy it. I did it all on my own. Was he ever surprised!"

"Good for you," I said uneasily.

"He treats me like a child."

"I know," I sighed. This was familiar ground. But when I looked at the concentric circles of red shag — blood red — I felt a little dizzy.

When I was younger I'd get up at dawn to go fishing with Daddy off the Rickenbacker Causeway. I had to be dragged from bed grumbling, but then the morning air was cool and fresh and charged somehow with his excitement. After stopping for bait we drove over the first bridge span to a sandy parking strip. "Alright sportin' life," he'd tease. "Today we land the kookamonga." He'd bounce along the narrow catwalk, whistling and hauling an ice chest on one shoulder, while I carried the poles. His shoulders were broad and strong. I was proud of him then. He caught lots of fish. He could make me laugh when I didn't want to. He could also juggle apples and oranges and do head stands.

My mother had never fished off the causeway. She didn't like the taste of fish, although she'd learned to fry it to perfection. She would not have enjoyed sitting for hours on the catwalk, legs dangling way up over Biscayne Bay — she was acrophobic. I felt a bit shaky myself, always on the brink of danger, yet safe because my father would save me if I fell into the bay. "Isn't this the life?" he'd gloat. It was the only time I could remember him sitting still.

He taught my sisters and me how to fish and swim and also how to drive. But not his wife. I think they tried a driving lesson once a long while back and had given up. "Your mother is too nervous to drive," he'd say.

His jokes embarrassed me now. And I wished he wouldn't stand on his head; it was bad for his heart. The doctor said he should avoid getting angry. We had to be careful not to irritate him.

We couldn't discuss politics anymore. The last time we argued about something, Nixon or Vietnam, I had to back off when his face got abruptly salmon red. Why, when we both mistrusted authority and he had never voted anyway, was he so upset? Because I'd dared to disagree with him.

My mother was stroking the rug with a bare foot. At least the rug won't be leaving, I thought. I could pack everything I owned in the Chevy and move in one trip.

Mom cleared her throat. "I want to talk to you about something."

She hesitated and I waited, puzzled. What was left after seven pints of blood?

"I'm thinking about divorcing your father," she whispered to the rug.

I was too shocked to respond.

"I've never told anyone about this," she said. "Your father has not been able to — you're old enough to understand — we have not made love in a long, long time."

Why is she telling *me*, I thought. What about a shrink? Of course, my father would never consent. Therapy was for crazy people with money.

"How long a time?" I asked, finally.

"I don't know, ten, maybe twelve years. When we were first married, the first ten years, that was like paradise. Then everything changed, I don't know why."

"Mom, he does love you. I'm sure he does."

She shook her head in frustration. "He taught me everything I know about love. Now when he's in a good mood, he pecks me on the cheek. You know what he's like in a bad mood."

"Have you ever talked to him about it?"

"Are you kidding?"

"How can you go from not ever talking to asking for a divorce?"

"I can't talk to him."

She looked like she might cry. I'd never seen her cry. I said whatever came into my head, in a rush.

"All I know is it's not like breaking up with some guy you go with for a couple of months, I mean like Jack. I never was in love with Jack. But you and Daddy were really in love, right? He's just got some problem that needs fixing."

"I did speak to a pharmacist a few years back," she reflected. "He gave me something, and I told Norm they were vitamins. It seemed to help for a while. But he didn't want to spend the money. So then I thought, maybe he's seeing another woman."

"Oh no," I cried. "I can't believe it."

"I don't know what to believe anymore," she said. "I shouldn't have told you about that."

You shouldn't have told me any of this, I thought. What would my father do if she told him she wanted a divorce? I imagined his rage. Or a bitter sulk. "If you leave it could destroy him," I said finally.

"He's too tough," my mother protested. But she looked worried.

"Where would you live?"

"Here? He could get an apartment. Unless you want to live with him instead of me?"

"That won't be an issue before too long," I said.

"I know," she said.

Is that what she was waiting for, the empty nest?

"He can't support two households," I told her. "He can barely manage this one."

She sat up straighter. "I can get a job, a real job."

I bit my lip. My mother had never had to manage on her own. I stared at the patterns in the rug, as if the future could be read there. But it was only a rug.

"I can work as a cashier," she insisted. "There might be an opening at the hospital."

We heard a car drive up then and stop. Lights flashed on and off, on and off. His signal. We got to our feet and stood side by side, our bare feet in the shag. I gave my mother a quick tight hug. She felt both delicate and wiry. *How could he not love her?* It was inconceivable.

His sandals squeaked on the steps. The door burst open.

"Hey, what are you cats doing in the dark," he drawled. He switched on the overhead light in the living room and came toward us with a hop and skip, jangling the change in his pockets. He wore checkered bermudas and a white t-shirt. His face—still good looking—was creased with laughter.

"I took those guys to the cleaners," he exulted. "I'm taking y'all out to eat tomorrow. Whaddya say we drive down to Marathon Key to the all-you-can-eat shrimp place. Is it a date?"

We nodded, dazed.

"My two best girls," he beamed.

Boondocks

Everyone in the bar was looking at Nick's girl. At her mini-skirted dress and long shapely legs. Rita was a little wild tonight, he thought uneasily. But he had never seen her dance before.

Only Rita could do the hully gully with Jack Wallace and still manage to move gracefully over the sticky floor. Jack was about as drunk as usual, a big bony truck-driving man wearing the frilled shirt he'd just been married in. His bride, Carol Sue, perched on a stool watching. She couldn't do the hully gully because the big toe on her left foot got stepped on in a fight last week, plus she was six months pregnant.

Carol Sue had pitched her bouquet at Rita so hard it came apart against her arm — held up not to catch the flowers but to shield herself. They'd left the petals scattered outside the town hall and driven in a horn-blaring procession of three cars and a truck cab the hundred yards or so back to Jackson's Lounge to celebrate, all drinks on Nick, who managed the bar. He helped the night girl pour out the first round himself. Rita had offered to pitch in, but she'd already worked a full shift. He gave her a handful of red quarters for the jukebox and told her to get the party rolling.

Nick was spiffed up in a maroon satin vest and string tie, and his elevated, spit-polished boots clicked rapidly over the duck boards. He was not a drinking man, but for this occasion he had driven into nearby Miami Springs to buy a bottle of Strega, not available at Jackson's. He thought Rita would be impressed by the foreign-sounding liqueur, and he had a sweet tooth. *Cara mia mine,* he sang, rubbing lemon peels around the rims, and keeping one eye on his cara mia. His fingers ached a little. It was going to rain tonight.

Carol Sue thumped her empty glass on the bar and he refilled it promptly.

"Your girlfriend looks about fifteen in that dress," she said, eyes narrowed. She took a deep drag on her cigarette. Nick shrugged. Maybe that's why he felt older than his years.

Carol Sue sat up straighter and patted her hair. It was piled up in a bright blonde beehive. "I need me a knife," she announced. He stared at her alarmed and she huffed at him, "To cut the damn cake."

Rita had put the wedding cake and paper plates on the pool table in a narrow room off the main lounge. There was a battered upright piano in one corner behind stacks of empty cartons and folding chairs. Nick set the two glasses of Strega on top of the piano and with one finger plunked out the wedding march. It was out of tune, but only he would notice that.

Rita sat close to him. He smelled the shampoo she had washed her hair with that afternoon. She'd put it up in a French twist that emphasized the fine lines of her face. But the twist was loosening, so she removed the pins, and waves of red-gold hair cascaded over her shoulders, glinting in the light from the bulb that dangled over the pool table.

The newlyweds were stuffing cake into each other's mouths and laughing so hard they almost fell down. Rita jumped up to get a folding chair for Carol Sue.

"Won't you have a seat?" she asked softly.

"I ain't no cripple," Carol Sue replied.

Rita put the chair aside, flustered. She busied herself cutting the cake and Nick came over to help serve.

Carol Sue eyed them. "So when you lovebirds gonna tie the knot?" she drawled.

Rita smiled politely and said nothing.

After a small silence, Carol Sue snorted, "Will you look at Nick, he's red as a beet."

He would have liked to push her face right in the cake. To his relief, the wedding party staggered back into the lounge to dance, the bride somehow accommodating her injured foot to the beat.

"Down in the boondocks," she shouted. *"That's the part of town I was born in."*

No class, Nick thought.

"I'll play you something real pretty," he said to Rita, drawing her back to the piano.

"I thought you couldn't anymore," she said.

"I could for you."

He flexed his fingers, then ran through *Heartbreak Hotel* for starters. Rita put an arm around his waist, and he knew he was love's fool. He looked at her quickly. She was watching his hands. He pounded on the stained keys as though they were responsible for the arthritis that had stiffened his joints. He was only 29. He played the next song savagely, *Only the Lonely.* But stopped after several bars. What was the use? Rita was startled.

"That was powerful," she said.

She took both of his hands in hers and held them to her cheek for a moment, rough skin against smooth.

"How did you wear your hair, Nick? When you had the band. Were there groupies?" She seemed excited. "I'd have got up front and said, back off girls, he's mine."

Nick laughed. Those were the days alright. Nick Valenti and his Valiants. He wore his hair then like he did now. Black and curly, no pompadour, nothing special, small side burns. And the girls went for that, he guessed. Only he was losing it now. He bent his head to show her.

"It was your eyes," she declared. "Not your hair. Your warm, alive brown eyes."

Nick whooped. "Ah, that means I'm full of shit, up to my eyeballs. It runs in the family, see."

"A congenital condition," she smiled.

"Yeah, that's exactly what I meant to say." He picked out a few notes with one finger. "Congenital."

With a sigh she put her head on his shoulder, and he moved his mouth and nose over the top of her hair and looked down the strip of green felt to the partially demolished cake, with its confectionary couple lying on their sides, staring stiffly at one another.

The jukebox music was slow and weepy now, Patsy Cline crying *baby, baby, the whole night through,* one of Rita's favorites. He got up from the bench, carrying her with him, and they glided alongside the pool table cheek to cheek. He put one hand through her long hair and the other on her hip. He loved holding her while the short shiny dress slid over the curve of her hips. She moved her fingers through his hair and when he kissed her, put her tongue in his mouth. They didn't teach her that in college, he thought.

She had told him that working here was an education in itself. She'd never listened to country music before, or realized there were people who could drink 24 hours a day and not fall off their stools. Jackson's was a truck stop outside the Miami city limits in the town of Paradise Glades, which consisted mainly of bar, gas pumps, motel and town hall on a highway leading into the Everglades. Its few permanent residents lived in dilapidated trailers along a canal. Nick had a sparsely furnished room in the motel.

He was not supposed to get involved with employees, but had fallen for her hard, almost at once. She had responded to his tentative overtures with surprising passion. He'd do anything to keep her.

"Let's cut out of here for a few days," he said. "I'll take you to the Bahamas."

"What would I tell my parents?"

She had to go home every night. He imagined a two-story house in South Miami, a stucco *Father Knows Best* house with palm trees. Her father sold life insurance.

"Tell them I love you," he murmured. They were swaying in one spot and he couldn't see her face. She said nothing, just pressed herself against him. All a man can do is try, he thought.

He whispered his dream in her ear. He wanted to support her while she finished school. Then she could teach and he'd go to college. To become a lawyer. Meanwhile they would rent a small house with a garden. He left out the part about children.

Rita mumbled, "You shouldn't ask me that. It's not rational."

"Rational?" He pulled back to look at her. She was hard to figure out sometimes, warmhearted yet throwing out words like a man puts up his fists. His fingers hurt intermittently, in time to the music.

She said, "It's only been three weeks, Nick. How can you ask me to live with you after three weeks? Not to mention getting married."

"Alright love," he said, "I'll ask you again next week."

She told him he was hopeless. But he was encouraged by the way her full lower lip curved in a smile, though her eyes remained thoughtful. They kissed, a long searching kiss that shivered what hair was left on his head.

The entire wedding party plus a few paying customers drank to the health of the bride and groom. They toasted the mother of the bride and the mother of the groom — wherever they were — and after that the mayor, Hon. George Jackson. Mr. Jackson said he would perform another ceremony anytime, name the date.

Rita switched to gin and tonic. "Strega doesn't go with cake," she explained, and Nick finished her glass. She was dancing with the groom again in a clownish fashion. *"I've got a tiger by the tail, it's plain to see,"* she mouthed the words and winked at Nick. He beat time on the rim of the padded bar. He couldn't make out what kind of dance that was. Neither could Jack apparently. Jack sat down on the floor and said he needed another drink. Dancing made him thirsty. Nick had to help Carol Sue pull him over to a booth. They propped him up on the seat and shut off the Black Label lamp, and when Nick went back to his stool someone else was sitting on it. He recognized the man but couldn't recall his name. He had a bumpy nose and thick lips with a burned out cigar hanging from the corner of his mouth.

"Nicholas," he began and the cigar dropped from his lips. He paused bewildered.

Nick slapped him on the back. "How's the building trade?" he asked.

"Yeah," said the man.

Meanwhile the mayor was whirling Rita around the dance floor.

"Nicholas, zit true?" the man went on. "That your girl, Nick?"

Nick nodded. They watched her dance, her mane of hair swinging about the mottled pate of Mr. Jackson.

"She's got class," Nick said. "I learn a new word every day. Sometimes two."

The man grunted and put his arm around Nick's shoulder. "Looks like good ass," he said. "Hey. Don't mean anything bad, Nick. Was a compliment."

Nick asked him to let go of his shoulder, and he did.

"Nicholas," he began again.

"Careful, pal."

"One liddle thing. How come she's here? With all that class."

Nick leaned carefully on the padding. "Must be some-thing bracing in the air," he said. "Like me."

"Oh," said the man, and drained his glass. He thought about it. Then he poked Nick in the chest. "You said one time. Pal. You said. Don't mix pleasure with business."

Nick poked him back.

"That's my business," he said.

"It's bad for business. Damn your eyes."

Nick waited.

"See. You hire a pretty girl. A redhead. See, I mean, real pretty, Nick. And then she says, Nick, I'm *his*. Hands off. Not good for business, see?"

"It's none of your business."

"Yeah." The man licked his lips and he looked around the room. "Yeah. Every man-jack here. Like some of that."

That's it, Nick thought. He watched the man's blurry face fall away from his fist. He was about to kick him in the head, when Carol Sue pulled him back. He asked her if she wanted her other toe stepped on. She helped him pull the man to the side door. They dumped him in the parking lot. Carol Sue limped back in, but Nick leaned on the side of the building for a while and took several deep breaths. A fine drizzle cooled his face. Heat lightning flashed over the Glades.

The door opened and George Jackson weaved out.

"Night Nicholas," he said. He slapped Nick on the back. "You've got a good woman, boy."

"Goodnight, Mr. Jackson."

Nick watched him back away and stumble over the inert figure and pick himself up as if in a series of stills.

Carol Sue hobbled back out with Jack leaning on one arm. She had a large pocketbook on the other.

"We'll take off now," she said.

Jack put out his hand and shook Nick's hard and thanked him for everything. For the party. The loan. Everything. Nick said it was his pleasure.

"We'll leave," Carol Sue said, "soon as you give us the car key."

"Oh sure." He fished it from his pocket.

A white Grand Prix slid by, hardly audible, with the mayor in it.

"Your turn next, Nicholas," he called.

He found Rita alone in a booth and slid in beside her. She was tearing a straw into small pieces on the table.

"I'm sorry if the fight upset you," he said, rubbing his knuckles.

"I thought your job was stopping fights," she said.

"I'm off duty, babe. Besides, the asshole insulted you."

"I see. You were defending me."

"Damn straight I was."

"My hero," she said flatly, and he bristled a little.

"Anyway, I'm quitting," she blurted out.

"Quitting?" He peered at her intently. "You're not quitting me, are you love?"

She blinked, hesitated. "I'm quitting the job, not you," she said. "I can make more money somewhere else. So could you. You're too good for this place."

"No, I'm not," he said. "But maybe you are."

She frowned. "The tips are lousy here. You know that. I did better waiting tables. But now I've got bartending experience."

He didn't want to think about her no longer working here. He would miss seeing her every day, terribly. And if she got a job in another bar, how could he protect her?

"Party's over," he said. She looked so sad then, he had to do something, anything, to make her smile again.

He swooped her up and carried her out of the lounge and up the motel staircase to his room, and somehow opened the door and got her onto the bed. They were both laughing.

He undressed her eagerly, though his fingers were stiff. The drapes were closed but the neon light outside still turned the walls alternately red and blue. Rain began to pelt the window. She would have to drive home in a storm.

The puzzled way she watched him made his heart contract. When he came, and afterward, he held her so hard that the next day she complained of a wrenched muscle in her back.

Body Parts

Nora found the prosthetic leg in a puddle behind the university's medical school, not far from where she'd parked her car. There had been a brief, fierce storm while she was in her classes and she wondered if the leg had tumbled through the air from somewhere or been deliberately abandoned. Though dented and cracked, it might still be functional, and she felt something ought to be done with it. But when she attempted to give the leg to medical school staff, she was rebuffed.

She took it home, thinking to install it in her bedroom as found art. Its cartoonish pink plastic skin amused her. And yet it was mysterious. Who had discarded it and why?

Her parents were not amused.

"It's filthy," her mother said.

"I'll clean it up," Nora offered.

"Get it out of here now," her father said. "We don't need somebody else's garbage."

She couldn't explain why she'd felt compelled to rescue the leg from that puddle and was loath to consign it now to the trash. So she carried it out of the house and placed it gently in the trunk of her car.

And then, before too long, she forgot about it entirely. The leg migrated to the rear of the compartment and disappeared behind stacks of magazines, text books and camping gear.

Nora didn't think about the leg again until several months later, after she'd met Joey Fontana. By then, she was slinging cocktails in the Tiki lounge in North Miami Beach under the tutelage of Connie O'Leary, who was ten years older with freckled, sun-leathered skin and a cloud of dark teased hair, in which she pinned fresh jasmine blossoms every night.

She and Connie wore flowered sarongs slit up one side and bras covered in the same fabric, that plumped up their breasts, especially when they leaned over the bar. "Aloha," they chorused when customers entered the lounge.

Sometimes after work, Nora stopped for a nightcap at the nearby club where Joey Fontana sang and played piano. She felt comfortable in the Casablanca because other women came into the piano bar alone.

"You better stay away from the Caz," Connie warned.

"Why? I like it."

"Because, sweetpea, it's a hooker pickup joint."

"You're kidding, right?"

Connie raised both eyebrows, said nothing.

Nora clapped a hand to her forehead. "I'm an idiot."

Connie knew all about it, being in that line of work, herself. A single working mother, she couldn't earn enough at the Tiki to cover the rent and feed her kids. They only got three bucks a shift and had to split the measly tips.

"Joey watches out for me at the Caz," Nora said weakly.

"Joey's got a big thing for you."

She shrugged. "I guess."

"You're not interested?"

"No! He's like older than my father."

Connie laughed. "So why're you leading him on?"

"I'm not! He's nice to me, I'm nice to him."

"As if three kids weren't enough," Connie muttered.

Joey wore dark suits with a ruffled shirt and cummerbund, the costume for his gig. He was broad shouldered and barrel chested, and carried himself with dignity, Nora thought. He didn't slouch like a lot of old guys did. He walked with his head held high and a barely perceptible limp. His hair was shoe-polish black; heavy lidded eyes the color of strong coffee.

The other guys ogled her breasts and left quarter tips. Joey didn't ogle and he was a good tipper. He seemed to take a genuine interest in her, asked about her classes at the university, her family, her plans for the future.

"How'd you wind up working here, kiddo?" he asked.

She explained it was the only bar tending job she could get with no experience. She just had to be twenty-one and look good in a bikini.

"So I borrowed a bikini for the interview."

"You don't have a bikini?"

"I like to swim," she said. "Bikinis aren't practical."

A few days later he came into the lounge with a flat white box. Inside wrapped in tissue was a cream and blue striped bikini, exactly her size.

Nora hesitated. She looked over at Connie, who was buttering up someone else. Joey was watching her expectantly. "Thank you," she said. "I suppose every girl should have one."

"Especially this girl," he said.

Nora no longer stopped by the Caz after work. But Joey was often at the Tiki for cocktail hour. She told him she had to write papers and study for exams. It took a half-hour to drive home in the dead of night. All of this was true, though Nora never thought twice about staying up all night cramming for exams.

"Thatta girl," Joey approved. "Nose to the grindstone."

She went to the back bar to mix his drink and when she returned, he asked "So when can I take you to dinner?"

"I told you how busy I am."

"When you're not so busy. After your exams, as a reward. Someplace classy, like the Fontainebleau."

"Joey, I'm always busy."

"I see." His face tightened. "No time for a pal?"

"My boyfriend's the jealous type," she said desperately.

In fact, her boyfriend was too cool and too stoned to care what she did.

Joey smiled suddenly. He had perfectly straight white teeth.

Dentures, Nora thought.

"Can't say I blame the lucky fellow," Joey said.

Nora's boyfriend Arnie never invited her to dinner or asked about her plans for the future. Arnie wore dark sunglasses day and night, even in bed. He lived with three other hipsters in a long wood-frame cottage in Coconut Grove, whose rooms were smoky from cigarettes and pot and candles guttering in Chianti bottles. She was not in love with Arnie. She was fascinated by his long and graceful back.

"Would your boyfriend object if you came to my place for a swim before work?" Joey wasn't a quitter. "You could bring your books and study."

"Could I bring a girlfriend?"

Joey sighed. "Bring all your friends. Bring the boyfriend. I just want to see what the bikini looks like on you. Humor the old man, will you sport?"

She couldn't persuade any friend to drive twenty miles to Bay Harbor Island for a swim. Connie also declined, being truly busy herself, what with three kids and two plus jobs. There were dark circles under her eyes that makeup couldn't disguise.

"You don't have to worry about Joey. He's a gentleman," Connie assured her. "He's always been decent to me."

"Is he... did you?" Nora faltered.

"Oh no. No. Nothing like that. He knows my situation and he treats me with respect is all I'm saying."

Nora was still uneasy. "It's like I'd be doing him this weird favor. Which I don't want to do."

"You can always hot foot it out of there," Connie said dryly. "He'd never catch you."

"How d'you know that? He could be in training for the senior Olympics."

Connie stared at her in disbelief.

"You really don't know? He's only got one leg. The other one isn't real. I mean it's real, but it's man made."

Nora was shocked. "I didn't know. How would I know?"

"You got to admire the man," Connie went on. "He never complains."

Nora wiped the bar though it was clean. She knew Connie was watching her. Connie lowered her voice.

"He told me the girls really like his stump," she said with a sly grin, and then thought better of it. "Forget I said that."

"I didn't hear it," Nora said.

She drove past rows of shiny, late model cars looking for the condo's guest parking. Her battered Plymouth, needing a wash among other services, shuddered as she turned off the ignition.

Joey waved from a second floor landing. "Up here, sweetheart," he called and, poolside, heads turned to stare. She went up the stairs and into his apartment.

He was wearing white linen pants and a Hawaiian silk shirt, and he must have just shaved, because the after-shave lotion was so strong she wanted to sneeze. Nora had thrown on the denim shift she wore over her costume to and from work. She'd not bothered with makeup, since she was planning to swim. He examined her eagerly.

"You're lovely without makeup," he said.

"I look too young without it," she demurred, and turned from his gaze.

There was an upright piano in one corner of the room and a well stocked bar in another. Stacks of LPs, no books. A large burgundy velvet sofa with matching armchairs and on the walls, framed velvet paintings. She hated velvet paintings.

"What can I get you to drink?" he asked.

"Gin and tonic, please. Can I take it to the pool?"

"Absolutely. You can change in the bedroom." He pointed.

"I won't need to." She began to unzip the shift, then stopped, aware of him watching. "I'll take it off at the pool. I could use a towel, though."

Joey mixed the drinks and brought out one towel.

"Aren't you swimming?"

"I don't swim," he said curtly.

"I'm sorry." She flushed. How stupid, what was she thinking? She had not been thinking. But now she was thinking *stump*. What does it look like? What does it feel like?

"Why don't you swim?" She plunged on recklessly. "I'm sure you could. You do everything else so well."

"I don't like to expose myself. In public, that is."

They were standing in the middle of the room holding their drinks. She glanced at his legs, then looked him in the eye.

"I'd never have known if Connie didn't tell me. I don't even know which one is real and which isn't."

"I'll show you." He leaned over to roll up the cuff of the left trouser leg above the top of the white sock, revealing an unnaturally flesh colored calf. He rapped it with a knuckle. It sounded hollow. Then he straightened up and the cuff fell down.

Without pausing to think, Nora unzipped her shift and stepped out of it. She hoped he wouldn't stare.

"Thank you," he said simply. His eyes flickered lazily up, down, then away. He looked at his watch. "We'd better get down to the pool, sport. Don't want you late to work."

He turned and walked to the door with a peculiar rolling gait she'd not noticed before.

Nora climbed out of the pool and sank into the deck chair beside Joey's. She'd put her hair up in a knot and now it tumbled loose.

"You're a regular mermaid," he said.

"I could live in the water." She squinted at him, shading her eyes with one hand. "Would you swim if the pool were private?"

"Sure," he said. "I get in the pool in the wee smalls."

"Alone?"

"Sometimes." He looked at her closely. "Or with a special friend."

She fidgeted. *Stump?* she thought. *No.*

She opened the textbook she'd brought to study, read a few lines, closed it. The sun beat fiercely down, penetrating the umbrella. Joey kept wiping his face with a white hand-kerchief, monogrammed JF.

"I'm sorry," she said after a while. "I really don't like sunbathing."

"I don't like it either," he admitted.

They went back to his apartment. The cool air revived her.

"Another drink?" he asked.

"No, thanks. I should get ready for work."

"Wait," he said. "First, I got to say something."

She waited.

"I know I don't stand a chance with you," he began.

"Joey, please don't."

"Listen." He held up a hand. "I'm head over heels, but never mind. I'll survive. There's just one thing."

"One thing?"

"Yeah. It'll sound crazy."

"What is it?"

"I want to feel your breasts for like half a minute." He cupped his hands. "Your perfect breasts."

She crossed her arms over her chest. "I don't know if it's crazy, but it's not going to happen."

"Okay," he said, dejected.

When she came out of the bathroom with her sarong under the shift and her face made up, Joey was seated at the piano playing "Stardust," which he knew she liked.

"Forgive me?" he smiled.

"Of course," she said. "You're my pal."

He escorted her to her car. It was tilting oddly.

"That rear tire is flat," he observed.

"Oh shit."

"You got a spare and a jack?"

"I think so."

She hesitated, key in hand, remembering only then what else was in the trunk of her car. But it was too late, she had to open it. Joey found the jack and then removed some boxes to get at the spare tire. And there was the leg lying with its pink shiny knee slightly arched on a bed of mildewed paper.

"Oh shit," she said again.

"Why is that in your trunk?"

"I forgot it was there. I really did."

He regarded her sternly. "How can you forget there's a prosthetic leg in the trunk of your car?"

She frowned at the leg. If only she'd left it in the damn puddle.

"I'm too busy to remember every little thing," she said at last.

"Nora, is this your idea of a joke?"

"No," she protested. "I found it and tried to give it away, but no one wanted it."

"You couldn't have tried very hard."

She was deeply embarrassed and didn't know what else to say.

"I'm still crazy about you," he said quietly. "But I can't respect you now."

"Maybe you could do something with it?" she blurted out.

He turned away from her without answering and pulled the tire out of the trunk.

She only told Connie about the flat tire, that Joey had taken it off and put on the spare. How he wouldn't let her help, except that after he'd folded himself with difficulty to a seated position, he had to lean on her shoulder to get up again. Afterward, he never came into the Tiki again on her shift.

Years later Nora couldn't remember what she did with the leg. For a while, it was an ashtray holder in an apartment she shared with two friends. Then she lost track of it.

What she would not forget: The warm hand gripping her shoulder, the man's entire weight bearing down. And thinking, he might bruise her and how could she blame him.

Looking Up Miss Thompson's Skirt

Miss Thompson raps her ruler sharply on her desk to get our attention, she taps it as she waits for us to answer. She strokes it absentmindedly. If it weren't against the law in Canada, she would strap us all. Especially Dennis Moriarity. She would hang him from his thumbs if only she could. Moriarity is a skinny redheaded kid with a wild cowlick and Elvis Presley sideburns. No one calls him Dennis except Miss Thompson and maybe his mother.

"Right! You're wrong," Miss Thompson snaps.

"Wrong, I'm right!" says Moriarity high up in his nose, mocking her English accent. Miss Thompson grips the ruler in a clenched fist and stares at him in disbelief. "Dennis, you are a barbarian," she says, and she sends him to the principal, who is allowed to strap the hard cases.

I recite 144 lines from "Hiawatha's Sailing" for the memory work assignment. "Like a yellow leaf in Autumn, like a yellow water lily..." On and on and on... My classmates look astonished, then bored. Their eyes glaze over. Finally Hiawatha gets his canoe built, Miss Thompson gives me this tight little smile and an A-plus, and Moriarity tells everyone that Nora Moldoff is teacher's pet.

In the schoolyard Miss Thompson nods at me. I'm jumping rope with Judy Goldman and Corinna McNulty, and Miss T.

is walking from the sixth grade portable to the main building. She wears the same gray suit to school every day with a different blouse. Her bright yellow hair is pulled back in a knot.

Corinna snaps the rope and trips Judy. "Bet you anything she bleaches it," she says.

"Big deal if she does," Judy sniffs. Her hair is a black frizz that she plans to dye blonde and straighten when she's old enough.

Miss Thompson's eyebrows and eyelashes are blonde, I point out. Can she dye those too? Corinna thinks about it. She twists one long skinny braid around her finger. Her hair is waist-length and sometimes she chews on the ends. Her mother lets her keep pet mice and a mushroom farm under her bed. Corinna has an inventive mind.

The next day she brings five small pocket mirrors to school to balance on the toes of five kids, who will then be able to look up Miss Thompson's skirt and find out if her hair is bleached or not. The problem is Miss Thompson paces back and forth at the front of the room where the shortest kids sit, mostly girls, and none of the girls will do it, though they all want to know if Miss Thompson bleaches her hair. Because Corinna is tall, she sits toward the back next to a couple of hoody boys who failed sixth grade and are friends of one of her older brothers. Judy sits in the front row.

"I think it's nasty," Judy says primly.

"So is she," Corinna huffs.

They are always arguing. They argue even when they're turning ropes for Double Dutch, and I get tangled in the ropes. "Nora is out," Corinna says crossly, not looking at me. As if I'm to blame for something.

It turns out I occupy a strategic position. Little Marvin Blum, who sits in the first row near the door, took a mirror from Corinna and dropped it into his shirt pocket. All morning he kept his head down, and once he blushed when he noticed me looking at him. The next closest volunteer is Moriarity the Barbarian, in the desk to my left, already testing angles of reflection and sunlight factors. Three boys behind me were also happy to volunteer. But Miss Thompson rarely paces that far back and this morning she did not budge from the blackboard where she reconstructed from memory a genealogy of the kings and queens of England, which I secretly admired.

Corinna is disgusted. She would do it herself if she didn't sit so far back. Boys cannot be trusted, she explains on the way home from school. She knows because she has four brothers and no sisters. Judy disagrees, but Judy is an only child. I have two sisters, no brothers and absolutely no opinion on the matter.

"What about Marvin?" I ask.

"Him? He'll say whatever Moriarity says."

"What if we get caught?"

"You scared?"

"No, but..."

"But what? She won't like you anymore?"

"Alright," I say reluctantly. "I'll do it."

Corinna hands me a mirror.

I toss in bed half the night. It will be like spying with periscopes, I tell myself. Miss Thompson is an ogre. Canada stands up to the Crown. Our home and native land. By the deep sea shining water. I hear myself reciting "Hiawatha's Sailing," and wake in a panic. Am I going mental? Will I grow up to be another Miss Thompson — shut off in a world of musty verse, unloved, sour as a lemon, cold-hearted. Oh no.

But Miss Thompson was once eleven years old! I think about her with yellow braids and braces on her teeth, her pointy nose in a book. So what if she bleaches her hair now that she's old?

I drift into sleep again and see Moriarity smirking. Like the Cheshire cat's, his grin rises and floats free.

Last winter Moriarity chased the girls around the schoolyard. He caught all of us he could, even me. He threw me down in the snow and washed my face in it, and held me down though I kicked and screamed. When he let go I ran after him with a snowball.

When the snow melted he hunkered down against the school wall and watched us jump rope with those shifty eyes that seem to be looking under your clothes if you are a girl. Judy was jumping in her powder blue V-necked orlon sweater and new 30-triple-A bra, and Moriarity yelled, "They look good, Judy."

"Cretin!" she said. But she seemed pleased.

I went home, locked myself in the bathroom and hopped up and down before the mirror. Solid. The next day I made Corinna swear to tell me the moment my breasts begin to jiggle.

The morning air is warm and smells of summer. Fat junebugs are squashed all over the sidewalk. We move slowly trying to avoid them. My sisters turn cartwheels on someone's lawn, thick as a tufted carpet. When we moved to this suburb last year, it was all a muddy field.

From the top of the hill we look down at our school, a one-story red brick building, surrounded by white wooden shacks. It has one big yard for boys and girls — unlike the two separate playgrounds in our former school. But it is still divided. Jump ropes flash at one end of the yard, knots of boys play soccer at the other. "Double dare you," Ellie sings out. She and Sarah take off, racing each other downhill. I lope along mindful of Corinna's mirror sliding up and down in my back pocket. I think I detect a quiver in my chest. Before reaching the yard I slow to a sedate walk.

The windows in our portable are wide open and the air is still now and muggy. No one's whispering or passing notes. Even Moriarity is quiet. We are being drilled in grammar. Miss Thompson calls us up one by one in a random order to put diagrams on the blackboard. Not once does she rise from her chair where she is dictating sentences. Her clipped nasal voice makes me think of the Queen in Wonderland who uses her guards for croquet mallets. I no longer feel the least bit sorry for her. Even the chalkiness of her skin offends me. Does she never go outdoors?

Miss Thompson watches us suspiciously. She scratches periodically in the long grey ledger on her desk where our names and grades are recorded. The clock over the door ticks loudly. Chalk squeaks on the blackboard. Then a large noisy fly drifts into the room and circles it once, buzzing low over our heads and landing on Miss Thompson's desk. She glares at it. Carefully, she caps her pen and puts it aside. With both hands she raises the grade book and lowers it swiftly over the fly, wham, then delicately flicks its carcass to the floor with the tip of her ruler.

"Jolly good show, Miss T," Moriarity says, no longer able to restrain himself.

"Right. Up you go, Dennis."

He bebops up to the board. Cautiously I take the mirror from my pocket and place it on the toe of one shoe. No one notices. Everyone is watching Moriarity scraping chalk across the board.

I move my foot out into the aisle and back under the desk several times. In the mirror I see part of the ceiling reflected, but which part? I look up. Down. Up. Freshly painted anonymous green, with nothing to focus on.

"Nora?"

Miss Thompson is looking straight at me, not unkindly.

"Daydreaming again are you? Up you go now. Nora?"

The mirror clicks softly on the floor. I stand up, legs weak, palms sweaty. At the blackboard I drop the chalk, and I have to chase it across the floor to where Marvin Blum sits — with no mirror on his shoe. I look up at his round freckled cheeks and buck teeth, and I know he's going to chicken out.

Marvin won't look at me, not even at recess when he turns in his mirror. "Here," he says, thrusting it at Corinna. Corinna stares out over his head and off into space as if a Marvin Blum could not possibly exist. Then Marvin walks quickly off to where the younger boys are shooting marbles. "Coward," she scoffs.

I, however, have won her admiration, for taking a chance and surviving a close call. Miss Thompson admires me too, it seems, for my diagrams. "Well done," she'd said, her voice soft.

"It'll be a cinch," Corinna says. "You're the last person in the world she'd suspect."

Judy is gung ho too, now that the operation is underway. She and Corinna fuss over me, as if I'm a prize fighter and they're my managers and we're all getting ready for round two. Could be the real thing this time, not a test. Although we are sitting in the shade, I'm sweating. I look over at the marble games where Marvin has disappeared and wish I were there too. Is he a coward? Maybe not, if he can say no to Corinna. Maybe he knows he'd get caught. Some people are born to get caught. Or maybe he thinks it's wrong to look up someone's skirt, even Miss Thompson's.

Moriarity sidles over. His hair is greased down except for the cowlick, which is greased up. He tilts his mirror so that sunlight skitters across our faces and into our eyes.

"You wanna practice with me, Judy," he drawls.

"Practice on yourself," she says.

"I'm the one who needs practice," I say. "I don't see how you can do it without lots of practice. I think we should all practice for a week at least."

"Judy's the one with a skirt on," Moriarity interrupts me. He grins, showing all his teeth and gums like a chimpanzee.

"Get lost, creep," Judy snaps.

Moriarity walks off whistling. A long comb sticks out of the back pocket of his jeans. He goes over to where some boys are pitching nickels and combs his hair and stares at us.

"This mirror business is getting weird," I say. But Corinna ignores me.

"Why didn't I think of that myself," she murmurs, eying Judy's sundress.

Lunch hour after bolting down sandwiches we squeeze into one toilet stall in the girls' bathroom. I sit sideways on the toilet with the mirror balanced on one shoe, trying to look up Judy's skirt.

"Your legs are too close together," Corinna directs her.

"It's how she stands," Judy protests. She minces about the stall on tiptoe, arms stiffly at her side, nose in the air. "Right, you're wrong," she giggles.

"This is impossible," I complain.

"First you have to see the color of her panties," Corinna says. "See any pink yet?"

"Yeah. I saw pink for one second. What if all I ever see is Miss Thompson's panties for one second? I mean, what's it going to prove?"

"The hair sticks out at the edge," Corinna says impatiently. "My mother's does, even in a bathingsuit."

"Shhh," Judy whispers.

High heeled shoes are clicking across the floor. The sound echoes against the tiles.

We freeze in place. Corinna hunches over with her face close to mine. She has a faint mustache on her upper lip, I notice amazed. Her mother has got to be hairy all over, with that same mouse-blonde hair only more of it, hair that cascades out of her head and springs from between her legs.

I have never seen my mother's. Her bathing suit has a little skirt.

A door clicks shut.

Corinna slips out of the stall. Judy is right behind her. "Last one out is teacher's pet," she says.

In the afternoon we do mathematics at our desks. Miss Thompson walks slowly up and down the aisles, squinting through her glasses at our work. She is going to look at everyone's work, she says, and we are going to practice until everyone understands the Principle of the Thing. She looks significantly toward the back of the room. Behind me I hear loud whispers and shuffling. She glares. They quiet down. Judy turns to smile knowingly at me.

I concentrate on the math problems. I wish I could solve all my problems this precisely. It is so absorbing that I do not notice Miss Thompson approach till she is breathing on my hair. I have not yet put the mirror on my shoe. "Fine, fine," she murmurs, and sweeps on by.

Will she stop again at my desk? I hope not. But Corinna is watching my every move. So I get out the mirror and carefully lower it to my shoe.

Miss Thompson is moving up the row to my left where Moriarity is waiting for her. I see a mirror balanced precariously on the toe of his running shoe. He doesn't understand any of the problems, he claims. She bends over his desk, droning explanations, peppering him with questions. He props his forehead on his hand, shielding his eyes, and slouches so far over he is almost falling into the aisle.

"Sit up straight and pay attention to me," Miss Thompson says sharply.

"I *am* paying attention," he says, not moving.

"Dennis Moriarity!" she warns.

"Yes, ma'am?"

"Sit up now!" she snaps. She gives him an abrupt push on the shoulder that knocks his elbow off the desk. The mirror flips off his shoe and lands with a soft thud across the toe of one of Miss Thompson's pumps.

"What on earth," she begins, looking down, then all around the room. I follow her gaze. Marvin Blum is staring up in the air. Slivers of light are flicking across the ceiling. Miss Thompson looks up, then thoughtfully down again.

"Right," she says coldly. "Don't anyone move."

Now she prowls the aisles inspecting our shoes.

While she quickly pounces on three boys and collects their mirrors, I am sliding my mirror under my other shoe. I cover it with my foot — too fast, too hard. The glass shatters under the heel, a faint tinkly sound.

In the awful silence that follows, Miss Thompson holds out her hand without speaking. Her eyes are magnified by the thick lenses in her glasses. She seems to be staring right through me. I bend over quickly and retrieve the glass. Miss Thompson takes the shards from me and marches back to her desk and sits down. She examines the mirrors one by one before speaking. The four boys are to go to the principal's office with her at recess. Then she looks stonily at me.

"Nora, you will stay after school."

"But I have to take my sisters home," I whisper.

"Right. No buts about it." She raps her ruler on the desk.

"She does too," Corinna cries from the back of the room. "They're little kids. They can't go home alone."

"You speak when you're spoken to, Miss. As for the little sisters, they will wait outside this classroom. Nora, you will make that arrangement during recess."

The four boys are in the principal's office a long time. They come back one by one with smug faces. Moriarity looks especially pleased with himself. I can't stand the sight of him.

At recess Corinna and Judy are wild to know what Miss Thompson is going to do. There might be special cases when she can use the ruler, Corinna speculates. What am I going to say? I don't want to talk about it. I head for the small kids' part of the schoolyard to tell Ellie and Sarah they will have to wait for me after school. They are bowling with marbles. Ellie has a big collection of aggies in a purple Crown Royal bag with gold strings. I promise to trade her one Captain Marvel comic for three marbles.

Then I go over to where the boys are shooting marbles and win two more. I squeeze myself in against the wall of the building and yell, "One will get you three!" I win two and lose one. This cheers me up a little. But then along comes Marvin Blum. He still won't look me in the face; he just turns red and messes up his shots and loses two nice cats-eyes. I should be pleased to win but I feel worse than before. I have eight marbles. I arrange them in a circle and shout, "One will get you five."

"When you gonna grow up?"

It's Moriarity, leaning over me, blocking the sun.

"Leave me alone, cretin."

"Aren't you a little old for marbles?" he persists.

I don't answer.

"I'll try a shot," he says, stooping down. He picks up one of my marbles and draws it back for a shot.

"Hey, give that back!" I lunge for the hand with the marble in it, but he pushes me away and scoops up the remaining seven marbles, spins around and runs off toward the soccer field.

I jump up in a great burst of anger. I seem to fly over the ground. Or could he have slowed down on purpose, I wonder, just as I tackle him. He's laughing, holding up two clenched fists. I claw and kick him.

"You're losing your marbles," he roars.

I break away and whack with one fist at his stomach. To my surprise, and Moriarity's too, that knocks the air out of him. He grunts and drops the marbles. But my triumph is brief. There isn't even time to pick up the marbles. He grabs both my wrists and twists my arms back.

I can't see his face, nor can he see mine. I kick at his shin, a mistake; he presses my arms harder.

"Stop," I beg. "You're breaking my arms."

"Say uncle."

I struggle but can't shake loose. Moriarity is pressed close against my back, his breath warm on my hair. Except for the pain in my arms I like the way this feels. Tears come to my eyes but I squeeze them back.

"Uncle," I gulp. He releases my arms and I keep my face turned away.

"Don't cry," he says.

"I am not crying," I say fiercely. We both bend over to retrieve the marbles and this time I feel his breath on my face.

"It didn't hurt that much," he says, handing me the marbles.

I march away without another word.

"Aw, girls," I hear him say.

The rest of the afternoon I do not look up from my work. I sense rather than see Moriarity trying to get my attention. Miss Thompson pays no attention to me at all. I am sure that she despises me. When the 3:30 bell rings everyone bolts out the door and leaves me alone with her.

Slowly, deliberately, she writes in her ledger. Then she takes a lined note pad out of her drawer and writes on that. I sit up very straight and wait, surrounded by rows of empty desks.

Finally Miss Thompson raises her head.

"Come up here please," she says.

I stand before her trying to read the writing upside down. It must be to my parents. She is quiet a long time. When I dare look up I find her leaning forward with her face propped up in her hands. It is a tired face. She has taken off her glasses and is rubbing her eyes.

"Why did you do it, Nora?" she asks, still not looking at me.

I'm not going to say, to find out if your hair is bleached. I say nothing.

"Do you understand what you did?"

I say the first thing that comes into my head.

"We were sending secret messages with mirrors."

Now she looks at me incredulously. Without glasses on and at this close range, her eyes are unfocused, gentler, yet still penetrating.

"Secret messages," she repeats slowly. "I am very disappointed in you, Nora. I shouldn't have thought you were a liar to boot."

Tears roll down my cheeks, and this time I can't stop them. I wipe furiously, swallow hard.

Miss Thompson passes me a hankie. It has a lovely lilac scent. That makes things worse.

"I'm sorry," I say after a while.

"Yes, I can see."

Her pen is tapping against the pad. She seems to be reading over what she's written. Suddenly she tears off the sheet, crumples it and drops it in the waste basket. Then she puts her glasses back on. Her cheeks are flushed.

"You may leave now," she says without looking up.

I walk slowly out of the room, taking care to hold my head high. Corinna and Judy are waiting with my sisters on the steps of the portable.

"Jeez," says Corinna, "What did the old witch do?"

"Nothing," I mumble.

They look at me puzzled. "She must've said something pretty horrible," Corinna persists.

It was horrible in a way I can't explain and they could never understand.

"Just forget about it," I say, and I walk quickly away from them.

My sisters sprint up the hill ahead of me, their knobby little girl legs pumping wildly. I'll get a pain in my side if I try to catch up.

Another Monster

Anita shepherds the boys, still half asleep, into the back seat of my car, while her new boyfriend and I arrange luggage in his car and camping gear in mine. I scarcely know Roger, a tall rangy fellow with a spotty beard who is carrying Anita off to a B&B in Mendocino for the weekend. I, being unencumbered by boyfriend or children, have volunteered to take her son and his buddy camping.

She leans in through the window of the car to stroke her son's hair. "I'll see you in two days, Colin. Bye, Stefan."

"So long, troops!" Roger offers us a mock salute. Colin stares straight ahead. But as I drive off I see in the rear view mirror that he is on his knees waving out the back window at his mother, who waves steadily back. He keeps waving till we turn a corner and then collapses next to Stefan.

The campground is shaded by oak and manzanita and cooled by the creek running through it to the nearby manmade lake where there is a beach. Aside from a few scattered RVs, it's almost empty and we find a spacious site adjacent to the stream. We wade gingerly in and splash each other. The water is cold but tolerable.

Next I pitch the tent, and the boys pound the stakes with flat rocks.

"Somebody's watching us," Colin whispers. I look around. At the edge of our clearing a small boy is poised as if ready to bolt.

"Hello," I say, beckoning him closer. He takes a quick step back. "What's your name?" I call.

"JR."

"Is that short for junior?"

He nods, sidling closer. He walks at an odd angle, with one shoulder hunched up. His hair is bright blonde and bristle cut.

"This is Colin and Stefan." The boys grunt and continue pounding at the stakes. "And my name is Ruth."

"Whose mama are you?"

"No one's. Colin is my godson."

JR looks puzzled.

"I'm like an aunt," I offer. "Are you here with your mom and dad?"

"Just Mama. And *her.*" He points back at the dirt road that winds through the campground, and now I see a patch of blue and metal.

"Who is *she?*"

"My sister."

"And what's her name?"

He shrugs.

"Juniorette," Stefan suggests, without looking up from his chore. Colin snickers.

It occurs to me that this baby has been left alone in the middle of the camp road.

"Why don't you introduce me to her," I say, and head in that direction, JR tagging along. On the road I find a towheaded infant sleeping in a stroller.

"Isn't she sweet," I coo. JR spits on the road. "She's okay," he says. "She cries a lot."

"That's what babies do, isn't it? Why don't you wheel her in here. Colin and Stefan like babies."

"Nah, they'll wake her up," he says and starts pushing the stroller down the road. "I'll be right back," he calls over his shoulder. The boy and the stroller seem to skitter over the road like dry leaves. They disappear into a clump of cottonwood.

I let the boys choose between peanut butter and jelly or Swiss cheese and tomato sandwiches. Colin opts for the former. Stefan experiments. He wants Swiss cheese and peanut butter and tomatoes, hold the jelly. And would I slice the tomatoes very thin and cut the sandwich into quarters?

Stefan relishes each bite. His cheeks are plump full moons. Colin is tall for an eight-year-old, with a long pale face. He polishes off his food and squirms on the bench.

"C'mon," he nudges.

"It's healthier to eat slow," Stefan says.

Colin huffs. He crosses his eyes on purpose.

"Delicious," Stefan says. "Nutty and juicy." Then he elbows Colin. "Speaking of nutty." They giggle and stare. I turn to see JR, minus the stroller, standing several yards away, again as if poised to flee.

"Hello JR," I call, and glare at my two boys. "Have you had lunch yet? Sit down. I'll fix you a sandwich."

JR sidles over to the bench and sits next to me opposite Colin and Stefan, who have clammed up.

"Mama's still in bed," he says.

He inhales the peanut butter and jelly sandwich.

"Another?"

He nods. No please or thank-you. His nose is running, nostrils and upper lip are snot encrusted.

"Here, blow your nose will you." I pass him a paper towel, and he blows mightily. His ribs stand out with the effort. Purple and brown bruises, some faded and indistinct, splotch his chest and arms. He wolfs down the second sandwich and drinks an entire bottle of cherry-flavored seltzer water. Even Colin, fast-food expert, looks amazed.

"You better not swim for a while," Stefan suggests. "You'll get a cramp."

JR shrugs. "Can't go to the beach till Mama gets up."

"Well, there's plenty of time left to the day," I say, and I begin to clear the table. "We'll look for you there later on."

"Can I go with you now?" JR asks.

"You'll have to ask your mama. Is she having a nap?"

He springs to his feet. "I'll ask her. Don't go without me." And off he races down the road to a small pick-up truck with a camper mounted on the bed. A metal door slams.

About a minute later a woman bursts out of the camper, a tall skinny blonde in a string bikini. She hurries across the road and into the stand of cottonwood that borders the creek, with JR trotting along behind her. We hear muffled, angry shouts, a baby crying.

They reappear. With one hand the woman is pushing the stroller in which an outraged, redfaced infant sits. With the other hand she's hauling JR along by the ear. She pauses about a hundred yards away from us, and we can hear every word, though her back is to us.

"Don't don't don't" JR stutters.

"I told you never take your eyes off her. How'd she get out of the stroller?"

"I didn't," JR begins.

"One more whopper I'll whop you really good. She about drowned. You walked away and forgot her, ain't that right?"

Her voice, low and raspy, a smoker's voice, softens suddenly. "Little Iddy Biddy," she purrs and leans over the stroller to soothe the baby, letting go of JR's ear. The boy spins away from her crazily, changes direction, starts running toward our camp.

But he doesn't get far. His mother swoops and pounces. She claws his arms with long red nails.

"You little bastard," she hollers. And while he wiggles desperately in her grip, she slaps him hard wherever she can. He sobs. "Shut up!" she screams, and keeps hitting him.

We three watch, helpless. I sense rather than see or hear Colin and Stefan urging me to do something. Stop, I think. STOP! Did I say it aloud?

The woman sees me then and looks away. She lets go of the boy. He doesn't move. He is half-crouched and shivering despite the heat. "Mama," he whimpers. "Go on now," she says. "Get back in the camper."

The boy races off without looking back, his mother following with the stroller. The metal door opens and shuts twice.

Colin and Stefan are staring at the ground.

"Get into your trunks, boys," I say quietly. They scurry into the tent.

The lake glints blue and cool in the hot sun, inviting us in. It looks like the lake where I summered as a child, where our father taught my sister and me the side stroke and Australian crawl. He swam underneath our inner tubes and pinched our bottoms. He roared like a sea monster and tossed us through the air into the lake. This was when he was in a good mood.

This beach is sparsely populated. A bored looking young man lolls in the lifeguard's high seat. His muscles gleam with oil. He is not interested in a middle-aged matron in a sensible one-piece suit with cross-straps in the back, thighs getting a bit cheesy, and two kids in tow. I'm not into teenage boys anyway. Still, they used to look at me.

We all smear on sunscreen. The water is cold, fed by the same creek that runs through the campground. I rent a giant inner tube for the afternoon, which provides a fine warm float, not that the boys mind cold water. I dive down under the inner tube and up through the middle and I gurgle and roar as best I can.

"If I were bigger and stronger, I would toss you up in the air and into the water," I apologize.

"Not a problem," Stefan consoles me.

"I can teach you the Australian crawl," I offer.

"Do we have to?" they say as one.

I assure them that they are free to play, and I will now demonstrate the crawl, should anyone be interested. Off I go, arms lifting, falling. I glide like a mermaid, or a mer-mama perhaps.

When I stop and look back from hundreds of yards out I see the two boys watching me from atop their big tube. I wave, they wave back. For a while I float lazily on my back, and then swim to shore.

"What if you got a cramp out there?" Stefan asks sternly.

"That lifeguard would have to get off his butt," I laugh.

Bored with the water, the boys explore the shoreline. "It's gross here," Stefan shouts. "It's slimy," Colin chimes in. They urge me to try it out and I inspect the marshy end of the lake with them. The muck oozes between my toes. I agree that this is "grody to the max," and retreat to our blanket and my book.

I never could read for long at the beach. The sun bakes my mind, flattens things out. I could be as simple as a lizard on a hot rock. I could be the rock.

My father's bad moods were unexpected, like summer storms that exploded out of nowhere. One morning after a thunderstorm, hail stones big as quarters piled up in the ditches on both sides of the road. I was very small, younger than JR, and I had a red bucket to fill and dump into the icebox before the stones melted. If I hurried I could save my mother 35 cents, because she would not have to put the ice sign in the verandah window. These are ice cubes from heaven, she told me.

In my haste I did not look both ways before I crossed the street. A car screeched to a stop inches away. I can still see the grillwork of that fender and the driver's ashen face, and I recall being carried off by my father, whose face was bright pink. He carried me into the cottage, sat on a chair and threw me over his knees face down. My mother put the flattened red bucket on the table.

He slapped me hard for a long, long time, stinging my behind in a rhythmic frenzy. I was more outraged by the unfairness of this punishment than the actual pain. What had I done wrong? I was only trying to help.

"I'll teach you to never never," he said, while my mother's voice murmured steadily, "Stop, please stop." I stared out the screen door though my tears at the yard where my little sister was sucking on hail stones, and all the ice cubes from heaven were melting.

"Are you asleep?" says a thin reedy voice. I open my eyes to see JR hunkered near my face, his eyes screwed up against the sun.

"If I am, then you are but a dream." I blink at him. "A dream JR."

JR snickers.

"You wanna bury me in the sand?" He has a plastic bucket and a small shovel. I sit up and look around. Colin and Stefan are playing a few hundred yards down the shore in the marsh. Their backs are to us. A hundred yards or so to the other side of our blanket, JR's mother is applying suntan oil to her long tanned legs. The lifeguard watches. The baby girl crawls across the blanket.

"Itty Bitty, you stay out of that sand!"

Itty Bitty is wearing a ruffled bikini bottom, a pink t-shirt and a sun bonnet. She stops at the blanket's edge and puts out a tentative hand.

"Let's make a sand castle," I suggest, and JR leaps up eagerly.

Together we erect a multi-towered castle on the shore. I look back surreptitiously at his mama. She is cooing at the baby, oblivious to us. Or she isn't there at all. She and the baby have gone off somewhere leaving blanket and towels behind.

We are digging out the moat when Colin and Stefan saunter back.

"It needs slits for the archers," Colin says and sets to work.

"I shall crenellate the fortifications," Stefan announces.

JR seems puzzled but pleased.

I withdraw gradually and leave the boys to play. There are other children on the beach by now and several dogs as well. The dogs, large and small, bound across the grass and splash through the shallows. They sniff each other's rumps. The little humans are more circumspect.

Now that he's older, Colin keeps to himself. When he was four he would venture out of his flat to visit me. Our street is a cul de sac with little traffic. He was cautious and brave crossing the street. He would climb the porch steps and through the letter slot shout in his deep toddler voice, "IS ANYBODY HOME?"

I usually was, the first six months or so I lived there. Then I stopped being available. I had too much work and no time to read him a story in the middle of the day. I ignored the eager voice piping down the long hall to the room where I hunched over a keyboard typing someone's dreary dissertation. Not now, I would think, try later.

What sort of mother would I have made, being so half-hearted a godmother? I don't think I'd ever hit a child. My mother never did. Anita never has. I was too cowardly and poor for single motherhood. But oh I would have buckled down and done it right, I see it now that it is too late.

The three boys play in the marsh. They're getting a bit wild, I notice. JR's mama has noticed too. She strides along the beach with the baby on one hip.

Slime balls are flying, the boys are spattered with mud. They drop their arms, seeing who is bearing down on them. Their howls subside to giggles.

"Get out of that muck, JR," his mama snaps. She looks down at her sandaled feet. "Ugh," she says. "You wash yourself off good." Then she turns and strolls languidly back to her blanket, glancing coldly at me. She sits down, lights up a cigarette, blows smoke on her baby, the bitch. I want to slam dunk her in the muck.

JR hesitates. His mother stands up again. He skitters into the water, starts splashing himself. Colin and Stefan are standing in the marsh, arms dangling, looking back up at me. What am I supposed to do now? Maybe they shouldn't be throwing muck at each other? They shouldn't be fighting each other, I decide. I gesture with one hand flat. Cut it out, I signal.

Colin moves first. He ambles into the water and squats next to JR. Stefan follows. Soon they are all washing up, then they have a water fight, fairly low key. Okay, they're still fighting. That's what boys do, I guess.

At the refreshment stand I order three large slushees.

In the dank corridor between refreshment stand and restrooms I find Itty Bitty sleeping in her stroller and her mother talking on the pay phone. This must be where they disappear from time to time. She sounds irritated. "Honey, you know I wouldn't," she says. She doesn't notice me at all. Her bright red nails tap on the receiver.

JR is being ignored by his new pals, who have retreated with their drinks to the forbidden marsh. He gulps his slushee and pesters me with questions. He wants to know how old Colin and Stefan are. He is seven but he doesn't remember his birthday exactly. "How old are you?" he asks. "Why are your legs hairy? Is your husband coming tomorrow? Where is Colin's mama? How come you don't have kids?"

"Kids are too expensive," I say. "I can't afford them. So I borrow them instead."

"Maybe you could borrow me, sometime?"

"That would be nice," I say. "We all live in San Francisco. Where do you live?"

"In the camper."

"I see. And where do you go to school?"

"Ain't no school," he says. "It's summer." I find out he doesn't know where he'll be in the fall.

Back at our camp, Colin and Stefan help me build a fire with wood that I bought from the ranger. We are all too hungry to wait for the fire to die down to coals, so I fry hotdogs in a skillet over the gas camping stove, and warm the rolls. The meat splutters greasily. I pour the boys apple juice and myself a small glass of red wine. Colin frowns. "It's good for my old heart," I tell him.

The *bonfires*! The good big fires that Daddy built those chilly nights on the lake. And then he would warm us up to singing rounds, like a magician pulling silky knotted tunes out of sealed mouths.

"Not again," we'd protest, feeling put upon.

I never did tell him how much I liked singing under the stars while sparks flew out of the fire and our marshmallows burned or roasted, usually burned. Repeating the rounds, harmonizing with my sister, I glowed with the fire, the stars seemed to hum along above us. This was a trance state, of course. We sang ourselves to sleep.

The boys bump marshmallow sticks together in the fire. Sparks fly high in the air.

"Careful," I caution. "The trees are dry."

"May the force be with you," they shout.

Clash, clash, now their sticks are laser beam swords.

"Don't play with fire, please," I say louder, and they calm down, though not for long.

"Yeeow," Colin hollers.

They have dropped their sticks. Colin is standing with legs apart and fists up, like a boxer.

"He burned me!"

The light is fading and I can't find the flashlight. All I've got in the first aid kit are band aids and hydrogen peroxide.

"Where are you burned?"

"On my leg. Stefan burned me on purpose."

"I did not!"

I can't see much of anything. I hold an icecube to where he points, then smear on some margarine.

"Is that okay?"

"It still hurts," he sulks.

"I'm sure Stefan wouldn't hurt you on purpose."

"He did so!"

"What's with you?" Stefan mumbles.

Colin turns his back on us. His shoulders quiver. Then he hurries over to the tent, unzips the flap and disappears inside. Muffled sobs emerge from the tent.

Baffled I look at Stefan, who shrugs.

"I'll see you later," he says.

"What? Where are you going?"

"Down to the creek," he says calmly.

He walks past the tent without looking in it.

Colin quiets down to an occasional hiccough, but doesn't come out.

On hands and knees I peer into the tent's shadowy interior. Colin is huddled under a sleeping bag. I can't see his face. "Colin?" I whisper. No answer.

"Colin, no one is mad at you." Silence. I think about opening the flap to stroke his head like Anita does, but I don't. I haven't earned the right.

She's left him in my charge before but I've never seen him throw a tantrum. What would she do if she were here? She isn't; she's taken off with a man who's practically a stranger. Stefan can't relate. He has always lived with both his parents.

"Check out the sunset," I say, moving back. "The sky's on fire. Sort of like you, Sparky."

Not until Stefan comes back to report that "Kids are splashing in the creek, can we too?" does Colin crawl out of the tent. Off they scamper together. I hear their voices floating up distinctly—Colin's deep pitched, melodious; Stefan's steady, monochromatic. And then crazy wild laughter, JR. They return with JR when it is almost dark and a new crescent moon is rising.

"JR never roasted marshmallows," Colin announces. He pats the younger boy on the shoulder. "Here, JR, here's what you do."

I manage to get them to sing "Old McDonald had a farm." A cacophony of animal sounds erupts. JR won't stop clucking, an hysterical chicken. I give him a hot dog to distract him and he gobbles it up uncooked. "Ugh," says Stefan. "Never mind," I say, "They are far from being raw."

The wood cracks loudly and collapses inward, the flames die down. The children grow quiet.

JR shivers. "Lookit," he points toward the road. We look at the dark trees and spooky shadows.

"What?" Colin whispers, round eyed.

"A monster!"

I see it. The moonlight has shaped a large dappled creature into being. It has a plump snaky body with plumes rippling along the ridge of its back. I click on the flashlight. Gone. Only shrubs and trees. Click off the light. There it is again. A long tail curves up, sways eerily.

"It may be the spirit of the creek," I say. "A big friendly water snake taking a moonbath."

"Jeesh," Stefan snorts.

But JR and Colin look a little anxious. I click the light back on.

"Time for bed," I announce. "I'll take JR to his camp. You two brush your teeth and get into your bags."

JR and I set off. I let him hold the flashlight. The moon is a sly grin sliding up the sky.

"Wish I could sleep in the tent too," he says resignedly.

"It's just big enough for three, JR. I'd have to sleep outside."

"Don't you like to?"

"I like a roof over my head."

"How come?"

"The stars keep me awake."

He falls silent as we approach his camp. The only sound is our feet on gravel and the creek rushing over stones.

There is no fire or hot coals. White metal gleams on the shadowy truck bed. We go around to the back. JR stands stiffly before the shut door.

"Hello!" I call. "I've brought JR home. We're all going to bed now."

The door swings open.

The woman is holding the sleeping baby in her arms. "Thank you for the trouble," she says thickly. Her face in the shadows seems very young and sad. She has been crying, I think, or drinking. Or both.

"He's no trouble," I say.

"That's good to hear," she almost whispers. "Get inside, son."

JR clambers up the steps. She takes him in her free arm. He collapses awkwardly, he seems to fold up next to her and become very small and limp.

"Could you get the door? My arms are full."

"Sure." I shut them in—JR, Mama, Itty Bitty. "Good night," I say to the shut door. No one answers.

Our tent glows in the night. Stefan has his own flashlight. I hear the boys whispering and giggling. As I unzip the flap they hide something from me, I'll never know what.

They quiet down. Now I feel like an intruder, a big clumsy adult taking up too much space. Anita would sleep outside and leave the boys their clubhouse. She prefers to sleep under the stars, free and unconfined.

She was under the stars with Colin's father, they were awake all night. Somewhere in the Anza Borrega desert nine years ago the moon was full and Anita was madly in love with a recovering junkie, a brilliant but defective man. "Good genetic material, though," she said, after he had moved on.

The boys breathe lightly, evenly. Their faces are indistinct. When the soft skin toughens and stubbles, what will they do with the women in their lives?

We three have settled in and gotten used to each other, a temporary family. I am more relaxed. Colin seems determined to keep cool. Stefan is so adult at times he unnerves me. I find myself seeking his advice.

"Do you think we should pick up JR and take him to the beach with us?"

Stefan ponders. "We'll be stuck with him all day then, instead of half the day."

"I like his laugh," Colin puts in. "It's weird."

We drive past JR's camper slowly but see no one outside. The beach is deserted when we get there but for a few fishermen several hundred yards down the shore.

JR's family arrives late in the morning and JR heads straight for me. He crouches on the edge of my blanket.

"Mama says I can sleep with you guys tonight" he spits out the words hurriedly. "I gotta sleep outside anyhow. So I put my roll outside your tent, okay?"

"Why do you have to sleep outside?"

"Frank's coming."

JR looks furtively over one shoulder and I look too. There's his mama relaxing on a deckchair, Itty Bitty sister crawling over one leg. Mama is reading a magazine.

"Frank fucks her," JR says in a piping singsong voice.

"You're welcome to stay in the tent with Colin and Stefan," I say quickly.

He gives me one of his sharp sidelong looks.

"You won't be ascared of them stars?"

"Oh no. Stars keep me awake because they're pretty. I can't stop staring at them."

"You ain't ever scared of them?"

"Only one thing in the world scares me."

"What?"

"Kryptonite." I wink at him.

That sets him off cackling. He races down to the shore to tell Colin and Stefan this joke, which of course they've heard before. "I'm Superman!" he shouts over and over.

I know I ought to discuss tonight's arrangements with JR's mother, whose name I still don't know. Aside from last night's brief exchange we have not spoken to each other. I put it off. Anyway, he's her kid, she should be talking to me.

The day passes dreamily. I read and swim. The boys swim and shout and build a new sand fortress. I bury all three of them in the sand so just their heads stick out. They pretend they are monsters bursting out of the depths. With JR's help I make a huge sea serpent out of wet sand. It has a scaly ridged back and a long curled tail. We are pleased with our work.

It might seem to a bypasser that JR is my kid, not Colin or Stefan. He hangs around me, I feed him, I show him how to float on his back. He has never learned to swim.

His mother and sister disappear frequently. Phoning Frank, I guess, or maybe phoning JR's father. Where there's a Junior, surely there's a Senior. I wonder if Frank is Itty Bitty's father or a new boyfriend.

Only one mishap mars our day at the beach. Colin steps on a fish hook in the marsh. He limps toward me without a whimper, brave little fellow. I extract the hook and present it to him. Tetanus shots, I think, everyone has tetanus shots, right. The first aid stuff is in my bag, good work. I pull out the hydrogen peroxide. "It's going to sting," I warn him. He nods. The stuff fizzes in his wound. Colin flinches slightly. JR watches with big eyes.

"Can I have some too?" he asks.

"It's for cuts, so they don't get infected."

He inspects his legs. "What about this one?" He points to some scratches, not quite healed.

"Alright," I say. I dribble it over his leg, and it fizzes.

"Some more!"

"Weird," Stefan mutters.

"Somemores!" Colin crosses his eyes and JR giggles. "You know what s'mores are?"

"Uh uh."

"Can we show him, Ruth?"

"Sure. We'll stop at that store on the way back."

Well I can't just drive off with the kid, can I? I trudge over to where his mother is reading through dark sunglasses.

I see JR watching from the beach, alert and stiff. Now I wonder if he made it all up. I stand over her. She smiles politely and lowers the magazine. The cover has a zodiac on it and the word "success" in big red letters.

"I thought I'd take JR back with us to the camp," I say cautiously.

"Yeah, that'd be fine."

"He'd like to sleep over with my boys."

Her smile deepens slightly. "That's real nice."

"He'll need his sleeping bag."

"I'll bring it over."

"Alright, then. We'll see you later. My name is Ruth, by the way."

"Kathy," she says.

Her lips compress into a hard red line. Her eyes are hidden. We regard each other warily. I nod and retreat to my blanket.

Before we leave the beach, the boys ask if they can jump on the sand monster. I agree reluctantly. It is a very fine sculpture these small barbarians wish so keenly to destroy. Of course it is foolish of me to feel any attachment to a heap of sand simply because I gave it shape. The three boys jump, shout, and pound the monster flat. It would have melted away in the night anyway.

"Hey, keep it down to a dull roar in there!"

That was my father's line. Wherever did he pick that up, I wonder, a W.C. Fields movie? Still works though. The racket drops a few decibels. "Pull my finger JR," I hear Colin whisper.

After a while I hear only their steady breathing, crickets, water in the creek. Above me the stars teem indifferently. It was a big lie I told JR. I never could sleep well without a roof over my head—not because stars look pretty to me. Even as a child after staring out a window at the night sky I slept badly. All of that remote and alien space, the mere thought of it.

I don't sleep. I wait till my bladder is really full before I get out of the sack. If I were camping alone I'd go over to the shadows to squat and pee. Instead, I trot down the road to the bathroom.

That's when I hear them. Kathy and Frank.

"You bitch, get in here. Get your ass in here now or I'll carve a piece right out of it." That sort of thing. Frank is not only a loud and mean sorry fucker, he is lightning quick. Because when I come out of the bathroom what I hear is a low bass murmur, and counterpoint her sighs. And then he rumbles: "You know I love you babe. You drive me crazy."

I get back in the sleeping bag and think of the last man I loved saying I'm crazy about you, woman, and how we made love for hours. I cry noiselessly for a while. Then I sleep.

I dream that my father is alive after being dead almost four years. He is tired and pale. And he is gentle, all the anger bleached out by his dying. "I love you all," he tells us. "I'm so happy to be home." I am happy too, at first. I have missed him terribly. But then I see my mother's discomfort. She has to sleep with Dad curled up next to her, clinging to her, and she stiffens. Oh no, I cry in my sleep, you have to love him.

The boys crawl out of the tent when they smell bacon frying, JR first, his nose runny and twitchy. I make them hot cocoa with one marshmallow per mug.

JR fidgets on the bench. He cranes his neck and listens for some sign of life over at his own camp. He is half-listening to Colin and Stefan who are talking rapidly and in a private argot about a baseball game they saw at Candlestick.

"What candystick?" JR interrupts.

"Oh Jee-suss," says Stefan. They both look disgusted.

JR's face tightens. A muscle quivers under one eye. Then he jumps up. "Stick your old candy up your ass," he says. "Stick it stick it stick it." He runs off down to the creek.

"Terminally weird," Stefan sighs.

Colin shrugs, perhaps torn between shifting loyalties.

I'm on my way down to the creek to explain Candlestick to JR when he reappears as suddenly as he vanished, zigzags around me over to the fire circle where Colin and Stefan are crouched now, and hunkers silently beside them. They ignore him.

I start to pack things up, dismantle the tent. JR watches tightfaced.

"We'll be spending the morning at the beach, then heading back to San Francisco," I explain. He nods unhappily.

"You can come to the beach with us, I'll talk to your Mom."

That perks him up a bit.

We're all packed up and in the car, and still no one is stirring at JR's camp, not even Itty Bitty. Do they muzzle her? A whisky bottle lies on its side by the fire circle.

I write a note and leave it on the table next to their camp stove.

> JR has come to the beach with us. I will bring him
> back if you don't show up before we leave, around
> 1 o'clock. Ruth Baum.

I put a rock on the note. JR watches me from the front seat of the car.

On the beach JR does not play with the two boys, though Colin seems anxious to make amends for slighting him earlier. JR all but clamps himself to me. He plops beside me on the blanket and will not budge unless I do. He hovers around me yelping like an untrained pup.

I am tired from lack of sleep. I can hear the irritation in my voice, can't he? It doesn't faze him. He's used to much worse. I know that I should disengage gently and I am bungling the job. What would Saint Anita do, I think sourly.

When Kathy, Itty Bitty and Frank appear at last, I am relieved and JR is stony-faced. It is about time for us to leave.

Frank is a scrawny little rooster of a man, not the huge brute I had imagined. He has tattoos on his arms and a conspicuous bulge in low slung swim trunks. He surveys the beach, nods curtly at JR and myself. I wave. Kathy waves back.

JR careens toward her suddenly. "Mama," he shouts. Then I can't hear what he's saying.

"You lie like a rug," she says nice and easy; she isn't angry. Frank laughs and spits in the sand.

JR saunters back down to the shore and starts piling up wet sand.

I call to Colin and Stefan. "Time to pack up and go."

"One more swim" they beg me.

JR follows them into the water part way, then stops and looks around at me. He is afraid of the water, I realize. I smile and wave, but keep reading my book.

A shadow falls across the page, JR blocking the sun.

"Lookit what I made," he demands.

It is an oval mound of sand with a deep line cut down the middle, lengthwise.

"Do you know what it is?" he asks.

"No, what is it?"

He frowns and studies my face for some reaction. I look at the mound.

"You know," he insists.

"No, tell me," I say, hoping I am wrong. Nothing in my life has prepared me for talking to a seven-year-old boy about labial lips, vaginas, the mound of Venus, cunt.

We are both silent for long, long seconds.

The muscle under his eye twitches.

Suddenly he jumps on the mound. He stomps and smashes it flat. Then he kicks the sand around. When he is finished, he watches me expectantly.

"I guess it was another monster," I say.

He shrugs. He spits on the sand.

We take a different route home, Highway 4, narrow and dusty. In the midst of farmland and orchards we discover a giant waterslide. I pull over and look in my wallet. I have enough money left to buy two tickets for one hour.

"What about you?" Colin asks. "Don't you want to?"

I do, I realize. I am 45 years old and have never gone down a giant waterslide. This could be my only chance. Maybe they take credit cards. They do.

The slide and the park around it are in an old apple orchard, with a campground adjacent. The place is packed. Here is where all the children in Modesto hang out on hot summer days, not where we were camped.

There are dozens of towheaded kids on the slide, I see JR everywhere. He hurtles down the slide clamped to me—help help help help, he was saying, and I couldn't I can't, how can I.

The Luckiest Man Alive

Dieter maneuvers the car casually down switchback curves into the Eichelbachtal, a deep crease in the dark pine forest.

"*Die Heimat,*" he announces dryly. Julie looks eagerly around. She will never have a home in this sense of the word, a place her entire family comes from.

In the far distance are snow-capped mountain peaks and below, the roofs of the two villages, Obereichelbach and Untereichelbach. She hears the creek for which the valley was named.

"Acorn Creek Valley," she murmurs. "Why didn't you bring me here sooner? It's so beautiful."

He shrugs. Uneasy, she checks her hair and makeup in the visor mirror. What if his parents don't like her? Or she doesn't like them?

Having imagined a quaint, half-timbered ancestral home, she's disappointed that Obereichelbach is a suburb of the older, smaller village. The forest was cleared and the boxy two-story houses built only thirty years ago in the early fifties.

Long terraced yards slope downhill toward Untereichelbach, and in all the yards that she can see, ceramic garden dwarves with red jackets and hats and white beards stand guard among fruit trees and flower beds. The air is fragrant with roses and plum blossoms.

Papa Steinle takes Julie and Dieter around the garden. He's tall and barrel-chested, with a full head of silver-gray hair. His eyes, faded blue and long lashed like Dieter's, seem narrower because his cheeks are pouchy. His nose is broken at the bridge.

"Now breathe deeply," he exults. "It's the freshest air in Germany."

"Just because you can't smell pollution doesn't mean there isn't any," Dieter says.

His father turns to Julie and winks. "You see how he is?"

She's elated because she can follow the dialect. She smiles encouragingly.

Dieter falls silent. The older man launches into a rhapsody over the plum trees and the extraordinary plum wine made by his wife. "Now here is the special garden dwarf who protects the plum trees, *Fraülein*."

Julie drops to her knees to examine the figure. It is unlike any other she has seen, carved from wood, its costume painted forest-green. The face — not cast from the same puckish mold as its ceramic brethren — is somewhat gloomy. It seems to stand slightly off balance, as if about to stagger, and in one hand brandishes a tiny goblet.

"Dieter made him," he tells her.

"Oh, he's sweet," Julie cries. "Have you had a little too much plum wine, Herr Garden Dwarf?"

"I paint his coat and hat every spring," Herr Steinle says, with a sidelong glance at his son. "I'm a painter, too."

Inside the house, Frau Steinle is working at the kitchen table alongside Dieter's sister Sybelle. They are large women wearing flour-smeared smocks over their party clothes.

"Try this *Wurst*," Herr Steinle urges. "My wife made three kinds of *Wurst* and three breads. It's hard to say which is best. Try some of each."

Frau Steinle smiles shyly. Her face, plump and unlined, is flushed from the heat of the kitchen. Her hair is pulled back in a neat gray and blonde knot.

"She made seven different cakes," her husband adds. "You'd better loosen your belt, *Fräulein*."

Dieter shows Julie the room where she will sleep, his sister's former bedroom. It's small and dark with a narrow bed under a sloped ceiling and one window hung with white, ruffled curtains. Sybelle's stuffed animals are still carefully arranged across the pillows, though she hasn't occupied the room since her marriage.

They look at Dieter's old room, too. It's larger and lighter, its windows overlooking the garden. On the wall opposite the bed hang some charcoal sketches and watercolors of the village, all by Dieter, and a framed, tinted photograph of him as a small boy with a shock of white blonde hair and red lips. He is dressed in *Lederhosen* and almost but not quite smiling.

"You never told me you wore *Lederhosen*. You were adorable."

He frowns. "It was mandatory. Every boy in the village had a pair."

He opens the window and they sit on the sill. Dieter rolls a cigarette and Julie takes one puff and passes it back. She watches his full lower lip, the way he savors the tobacco. Their knees are pressed together.

"I'm really glad you came with me," he says.

"I thought you didn't want me to," she murmurs.

"Of course I did."

"You made the party sound like an obligation."

"Actually, it is." He smiles at her. She can't tell if he's serious or not.

"Don't you like your family?"

"Sure, I like them. But we have absolutely nothing in common. *Scheisselbachtal* is a real time warp."

"Shit Creek Valley? That's a joke, right?"

"It smells of pig shit."

"It does not."

He toys with a lock of her hair. "Stick around a while, *Liebchen*, you'll see."

"Not if I can't sleep in the same bed with you." She pouts and he laughs.

"We'll sleep together somehow, I promise." He puts out the cigarette and takes her in his arms and kisses her slowly.

Today is Papa Steinle's 66th birthday. A *Schnapszahlfest* in his honor is being staged in the large front room, whose windows are open to the street. Two long tables are laden with platters of *Wurst*, loaves of bread, several cheeses and bowls of ripe plums. Another table is dedicated to the schnapps, which appear to be any kind of consumable alcohol.

Schnapszahlfest is dialect. Julie can't find it in any dictionary. *Zahl* means number and double digit birthdays are lucky, Dieter said. It means "lucky number party," she decides. She is already planning to invite everyone they know to a *Schnapszahlfest* for Dieter's 33rd birthday.

Guests arrive with bottles of wine, beer and liqueurs. After they shake hands with Eugen Steinle, they buzz around his son. What have you been up to, they ask. A worthwhile sabbatical in Italy, we hear. Sly glances at the American fiancée. She smiles and sips her wine. Dieter drinks thirstily and greets the men with back slaps. His father too grows merrier. The more he imbibes, the more difficult conversation with him becomes. She asks whether oak trees grow in the nearby forest. He replies, "The old town once had a wall around it."

Aunts, uncles, cousins, neighbors stream in and out of the room. Dieter introduces her to everyone. She can't remember names, but does manage basic conversation. People speak slowly for her benefit.

She meets the *Burgermeister* of Untereichelbach. "I have a cousin in Chicago," he tells her. "Oh, so do I," she replies gaily. "Perhaps we'll meet again at a *Schnapszahlfest* in Chicago."

A tiny white-haired woman was Dieter's first teacher. "What a rascal, our Dieterle. His earliest drawings were graffiti. But so clearly gifted. Did you make that dress yourself, *Fraülein?* It's very pretty."

"The natives are friendly," Julie whispers in Dieter's ear.

"I told you there's nothing to worry about," he says. "You're the star of the show."

Sybelle passes her fat rosy baby to its grandfather, who attempts to perch the infant on the edge of the schnapps table. It slumps over and drools on his hairy fist. "Here Dieter, you need the practice," Herr Steinle chortles, and hands the baby to his son. The baby squeals. Dieter holds it gingerly before passing it back to his sister. "The kid is soaking wet," he says, and everyone laughs.

"Good health," Dieter cries. "To healthy babies and dry bottoms." And he drains his glass.

A tall slender woman in jeans and T-shirt looms up on Dieter's arm. She is his cousin, "Little Emma."

"I remember Emma with pigtails and braces," he marvels.

To Julie's relief, Emma speaks perfect English. Her face is a pale oval, eyelashes so blonde they disappear behind thick-lensed glasses.

"She's another Shit Creek Valley survivor," says Dieter *sotto voce*. Emma looks pleased to hear this. The cousins flank Julie, talking excitedly in a mixture of English and German. She thinks they're as elegant and well matched as racing horses. Dieter roars with laughter from deep in his throat, and she feels an upsurge of desire for him so keen she's relieved when he rushes off to greet someone else.

Emma explains she is a university student on vacation. "I hate it here," she says flatly. "I can't wait to go back to Stuttgart."

"But it's so beautiful," Julie demurs.

"It's totally boring. Next summer I'll travel in Italy. Dieter said you were living in Verona. Why Verona?"

"I got a job teaching English there. Then I found a flat in the old town and it had a balcony overlooking an alley. It was perfect. Friends would stand in the alley and shout my name. 'Hey Giuliatta! Giuliatta!' I'd never have left if not for Dieter."

"How did you meet him?" Emma asks. "Did he happen to walk down that alley?"

"And see me on the balcony? That would have been too perfect. I was in a church looking at frescoes and so was he. After that, I saw him everywhere."

He had followed her into the church, she learned later.

"Why?" she asked him.

"Because you were sailing across the piazza toward me and your dress was della Robbia blue. I wanted to paint you."

"Paint me?" She scoffed. "Is that what you were thinking?"

They spent a good deal of time in bed with the shutters drawn. Friends stopped calling her name from the alley and phoned to arrange their visits. She'd had a few lovers from among the Veronese, but took no one seriously until Dieter Steinle dropped into her life, as if by some enchantment, tall and fair and radiating passion. He didn't want to leave without her once his Sabbatical had ended, and he couldn't afford to stay. He had to return to his job in Karlsruhe, where it's so gray and soggy she feels they're living underwater.

She promises Emma she'll mail her names and phone numbers of friends in Verona and elsewhere in Italy. "You'll have the best time, believe me. The only way to know a country is to live in it."

Emma's pale skin flushes. "I may stay there, if it's as good as you say."

Julie shrugs. "You never know what might happen in your life."

They look across the room at Dieter. He is talking with great energy and both hands, and Julie laughs. "You see, he's an honorary Italian."

Herr Steinle insists that Julie sit next to him at the long banquet table and Emma quickly takes the seat on her other side. Dieter retreats to the far end of the table to play pinochle with his sister and brother-in-law.

"*Prosit!*" Herr Steinle clinks his glass against Julie's. His face is mottled red.

"How do our women put up with these besotted oafs," remarks Emma with a pleasant smile.

Julie looks around nervously.

"Don't worry, no one else understands English."

Several conversations are in progress simultaneously.

Herr Steinle and his cronies talk rapidly and she strains to recognize words. Emma says in her ear, "You can't imagine how many times I've heard these idiotic war stories. I can't tune it out like Dieter does."

War? She thought they were discussing a soccer match. She glances at Dieter. Brother and sister are hunched over their cards, speaking a private argot. He must hate these stories, she thinks.

But of course all these old men once were soldiers. One stooped and grizzled fellow wearing a Tyrolean cap with a limp feather in it looks old enough to have served in the war to end all wars. Soldiering may have been the only remarkable passage in their lives.

Herr Steinle refills her glass to the brim. She gets at most a tenth of what he's telling her. She hears: soldiers, fight, bombs, hungry, escape, lucky (or happy? It's the same word in German).

When he pauses to drink again, she asks Emma, "Is he describing his escape from enemy forces during the war?

"That's close enough."

"It must have been terrible for you," she manages.

"Terrible," he agrees. Then gabbles on. She imagines a young, plucky Eugen, dodging bullets and grenades. The young Eugen looks like Dieter, with sandy hair, nose not yet broken.

"Uncle Eugen, speak slower," Emma urges.

"I don't understand what happened in Vietnam," Herr Steinle says thickly. "Americans aren't good soldiers anymore. What do you think, *Fräulein?*"

Everyone is listening. Dieter grimaces and slaps down a card.

"I don't know," Julie replies carefully, "I think at least thirty thousand American soldiers died in Vietnam."

He repeats the number, slurring. "*Dreishigtausen?*"

She nods. He thinks for a moment, then asks, "Is it true that thirty percent of Americans are Jewish?"

Her heartbeat quickens. Could she have misunderstood?

"You said *thirty* percent?"

"*Dreissig,*" he repeats slowly. "So I have heard."

"That is false," she tells him. "It's closer to *drei*. About three percent of Americans are Jewish."

There is an awkward silence. Emma studies her curiously and Julie feels her face grow warm.

"Only three percent? Very interesting," Herr Steinle goes on. "It is also well known that Israelis make excellent soldiers."

"So do Palestinians," Emma puts in.

Her uncle ignores this. He describes two boyhood friends who were Jewish. They were clever boys who worked alongside him in a factory in Pforzheim. But he lost track of them.

"I don't know what became of them," he says sadly.

Dieter looks as glum and off kilter as the garden dwarf. She wants to signal somehow, "It's you I love, I don't have to love your father, too." But his head is bowed, his eyes closed.

"Let's get some fresh air," Emma suggests.

Julie nods and follows her out the front door.

It's good to be outside. The air in the house is thick with tobacco smoke. They walk briskly past homes identical to the Steinle's, large and prosperous looking with their entrances close to the street. Neighbors stroll by or lean out of windows to greet them.

"*Grüss Gott!*" they chorus.

"*Grüss Gott!*" Julie and Emma reply.

"Can you understand now why I want to leave?" Emma gestures at the houses, the people. "They're all fascists."

"You can't be serious."

"But I am. Doesn't Dieter tell you anything?"

"He never talks about Obereichelbach unless I press him. What are you saying, Emma? Is there a neo-Nazi movement here?"

Emma looks shocked. "Oh no, nothing like that. It's the way they think. My uncle, my father, everyone."

"That's not surprising in their generation, is it? My father says stupid things about Germans. Some of his cousins won't get in a VW."

Emma drops her voice, though she's speaking in English. "Are you Jewish?" she asks, shyly.

"I'm Italian, mostly, some Irish. One great grandmother was Jewish. So that makes me, what, 12.5 percent Jewish. One-eighth *yiddisches Mädel*."

"Dieter should have told them."

"But why? It doesn't matter to him. Or to me."

"That's nice," Emma says and falls silent.

Julie thinks uneasily of her parents. They'll never come to Obereichelbach, she decides. She can't imagine the Steinles in California. She can't even imagine them in Karlsruhe.

When she comes back into the front room, cheeks flushed from the brisk walk, Dieter's mother smiles at her from across the long table and murmurs to a woman nearby. "*Shayne Mädel, gel?*"

It's what her grandmother used to say, the fifty percent Jewish nana who taught her a dozen Yiddish words. *Pretty girl.* She smiles back and Mama Steinle beams, showing a gold-capped tooth.

The sky is turning indigo blue and guests are still coming and going.

Mama and Sybelle carry in tureens of dumplings with sauerkraut and roast pork for dinner. This is served with the local beer and followed by coffee, *Kuchen,* and the de rigeur plum brandy.

Never before has Julie reached this pitch of intoxication and remained upright. Perhaps it's because Emma has pressed mineral water upon her between rounds. Still, the room is beginning to wobble. She hears Emma's voice in her ear analyzing the aftermath of the Iranian hostage crisis.

Papa Steinle holds forth with both hands and also his feet, which he stamps as if marching. His monologue lurches on unabated in Julie's other ear. She can't see Dieter's face now; it's cradled in both his hands. She hasn't been able to speak with him in hours, it seems.

Emma peers at her uncle from narrowed eyes. "You'd think nothing else happened to him since Berlin."

Corpses everywhere, Julie hears. The Reichestag on fire. *Alles kaput. Alles.*

Then she loses the connection again.

"Sounds like he had a close call," she says to Emma.

"He was luckier than he deserved to be."

"What do you mean?"

Emma doesn't answer. She looks around for Dieter, but he's disappeared. There's a fan of cards before his empty chair.

Papa Steinle leans against Julie's shoulder.

"I was a good soldier," he says. "Yet they would hang me by the balls."

"Eugen!" his wife protests.

He begins to talk instead about a cousin who wound up in a Russian prisoner of war camp.

Emma lowers her voice. "My uncle served in the elite bodyguard of the lunatic Austrian painter. Understand? I can't say the name. It is never mentioned."

Julie recoils a little. Dieter's father, Hitler's bodyguard?

The room starts to spin and she focuses on the ruddy broken nose. He looks like a punch drunk boxer. Or a clown.

"He was one of a hundred men," Emma whispers. "He got picked because of heroism on the front. Which was due more to luck than courage, he says so himself." She pauses to listen and Julie glances at her. Emma's mouth is a prim line.

"He's bragging about how lucky he's always been," she translates. "Lucky to get out of the bunker alive. Lucky not to wind up in prison like cousin Eckhardt. Lucky to avoid denazification. Oh oh, he's not supposed to talk about that either. Aunt Maria's upset again. Lucky to have married Maria, of course. Lucky to still be alive."

"*Glücklich!*" roars Herr Steinle. "I'm the luckiest man alive."

Mama Steinle escorts Julie to Sybelle's bedroom. She fusses and clucks. "Sleep well," she says, pausing at the door for a last concerned glance.

Julie pulls off her dress and collapses on the bed. She knocks the stuffed animals to the floor. Dieter? He must have crashed in his old room. In the dark, muffled shouts swoop up from below.

She dozes fitfully. The sounds of the *Fest* buzz over her, fade away. She dreams the bed is in a cemetery. It's a busy place, she senses rather than sees, because it's pitch dark. All around her, unseen but audible, relatives of Dieter who've been dead for centuries, are drinking and laughing and droning on about their lives, their sicknesses, the circumstances of their deaths. She is annoyed to discover that death is one long party, an unlucky number party. All she wants to do is sleep.

Toward dawn the door creaks open.

"Shh," Dieter whispers. He tiptoes to the bed, wearing only jockey briefs, and slides in beside her, smelling of beer and stale cigarette smoke.

"You're still drunk." She turns her face away.

"I promised you, *cara mia,*" he breathes in her ear. She is bone dry, but Dieter doesn't seem to notice. He bites her shoulder to muffle his moans.

"That was super," he says, then rolls over and falls asleep, pinning her at the edge of the bed.

"Wake up!" She shakes him. "The bed's too small."

"I'll sleep on the floor." He topples off onto the rug. She looks at the white curve of his buttocks.

"You could join me," he yawns.

She throws a blanket at him.

"Tell me about your father's job with the *Führer, Liebchen.*"

"Oh *scheiss,*" he groans.

"A little bedtime story, *bitte.*"

"What should I tell you?" He wraps himself in the blanket. "It was the best job he ever had. It was away from the front. He's a stupid peasant."

They are quiet. He stares at the ceiling.

"I never think about it anymore. It does no good." His voice trails off wearily. "I would have told you some day, honestly."

"You should have told me before today."

"I didn't want to spoil your visit. Besides, it has absolutely nothing to do with you and me."

"It's a big part of your life you're not coping with."

"Nonsense," he says, and turns his back to her.

"*Schlaf gut*, Dieter."

In a few minutes he's snoring. Julie lies wide-eyed and sleepless on the narrow bed as the sky in the window turns gray, then pink. The stuffed animals are watching her from the floor with bright little button eyes, as if to say, we never think about it either.

Eyes Wide Open

My father died at his Friday night poker game, holding a winning hand. But not until I see my mother, a solitary figure waiting at the end of the jet gangway, and no Daddy hopping up and down beside her, shouting my name, creating the usual commotion, wearing out his heart, do I believe his number was up.

My mother waits quietly at the gate, silver hair haloing a still unlined face, clothing rumpled, dark shadows under her eyes.

She hands me the car keys.

"I'm a nervous wreck, Ruth. Daddy did all the driving, you know."

When I get behind the wheel, I can smell his skin, faintly. The head rest is stained with sweat.

It's a long drive to the small house on the canal where my parents moved after my sister and I left home. Miami seems to go on forever, a colossal blight, sprawling ever farther westward into the Glades. When I left, I thought I'd never live here again.

"I'll stay as long as you need me" I tell her. "I can find work here same as anywhere."

"That's good," she says. "I've never done any of this before."

My sister and her family fly in that evening from Mobile and I drive back to the airport to pick them up.

Anna looks like she's still in college, in part because she's wearing a varsity t-shirt, but also, like our mother, she'll look young when she's a grandmother. I envy that sun-bronzed desert complexion. I'd like to know how my father's family got so bleached out in the Diaspora. What axe-wielding, short-lived Viking hordes lurk in our DNA? Meanwhile, the family is evolving in new directions. I hug my sister, then bend over to embrace Billy and Grace, who have their mother and grandmother's dark eyes and hair and Roy's round rosy cheeks and turned up nose. And they all have drawls, even Anna.

"Mama, look," Grace points at a group of Hare Krishnas. "Bald hippies!"

Anna giggles, eyes me and then blushes.

Roy's eyes are red rimmed. I hug him, too. Even though he thinks I'm a hippie and I'm sure he's a redneck, suddenly he's like a real brother. He seems more upset than Anna, or less constrained about showing it.

"Your Daddy was one of a kind," he says.

Anna told me Roy had been "scared to death" to meet Daddy and ask him for her hand in marriage. Roy is a country boy and devout Baptist. His prospective father-in-law was raised in an urban ghetto by orthodox Jewish immigrants.

So when Daddy said, "You're asking for my blessing?" Roy didn't know if he was puzzled or appalled, and Anna was no help. She was ready to bolt if things went downhill from there. On her wedding day, she would tremble from head to toe.

"I'll rephrase that, sir," Roy pressed on. "I love your daughter and I'm fixin' to marry her. So I'm asking for your approval."

"Fine. What'll you give me for her?"

Roy didn't miss a beat.

"I believe it's supposed to be the other way around, sir. What might the dowry be for your daughter?"

They laughed and shook hands, and Daddy said he was relieved to get one daughter off his hands. He'd never thought the tomboy would go first and he'd given up on the hippie chick.

My next task is to phone the aunts and uncles.

It isn't too difficult, since almost everyone suspects something bad has happened as soon as they recognize my voice. Why else would I call them? My father's brothers and their wives are stoical; my mother's siblings, more given to emotion. I save the worst for the last, figuring by then I'll be a practiced bearer of bad news. The call I most dread is to Mum's oldest sister, Aunt Estelle.

"Ruth, honey," my aunt says, the voice itself like honey until I explain why I'm calling.

"Oh my God," Aunt Estelle shrieks. "Oh no! Poor Dorothy."

"She's too upset to talk to you now," I tell my mother, who folds her arms across her chest and frowns. "How come she's upset? She and Ben never got along."

At night I lie next to my mother in the dent my father made in the mattress. We pretend to sleep. I watch the digital clock and think, he was right here, he was alive and warm and sleepless, watching this clock, 48 hours ago.

I said goodbye to him in a deli only two months ago. He shouldn't have been eating that corned beef sandwich. He relished every bite, all the while, gazing steadily at me, as if afraid this time I'd vanish forever. It was embarrassing to be loved so openly and intently. I couldn't wait to get away.

Next morning, two aunts, one uncle and a cousin fly in from Toronto. More relatives arrive in the afternoon. The two-bedroom house fills quickly, also the RV. Rooms are taken at a nearby motel.

Later that afternoon, neighbors and friends stream in with platters of sandwiches, tuna casseroles, booze.

"Is it like a party?" Billy asks, puzzled.

"It's like a wake," Roy explains.

"Awake? You mean instead of asleep?"

"That would be you and me," I say aside to Mum.

My paternal uncle and his nephew embrace each other in the small back yard. Uncle Nate and Jerry haven't spoken in years, and I have no clue why they quarreled. Now they are sharing a motel room. At twilight we sit on deck chairs under the magnolia tree where Daddy set up his workshop—shelves full of seedlings and tools, red geraniums spilling out of white urns, and a crown of thorns, spiky and pink. The canal glimmers under a harvest moon. It's balmy, not humid, one of those magical autumn nights my father reveled in. A door opens and shuts and I look up, half expecting to see him or his ghost. But it's Anna bearing a tray of iced tea and bowl of chips.

My uncle marvels. "Where'd he get his green thumb? We never grew nothing back home."

"Uncle Ben had a gift for life," Jerry says solemnly. "He could make flowers grow and a stone laugh. He could've done stand-up comedy."

"He wasn't always funny," I observe quietly.

"He was, too," Anna says. "Most of the time."

"He ran hot and cold," I remind her, but she looks away.

"You got that right," Uncle Nate says. "One minute he's telling jokes, the next, get out of his way."

"No one can be funny all the time," Jerry counters.

Our uncle persists. "Happy as a clam or Frosty the Snowman. You ask me, Ma spoiled him on account of he was the first one born over here."

"So who asked you?" Jerry says

Uncle Nate glares at his nephew. "Ruth brought it up, not me."

"Just kidding, Unc. I know it was rotten in that shtetl."

"He really was a natural entertainer," I say quickly. "He could work any room. Like that time we went to court together, do you all know that story?"

"Who got busted?" Uncle Nate asks.

"Me. Nabbed in a bar, underage, with fake ID."

"Oh ho, chip off the old block, eh?"

"Oh no, not that again," Anna says.

"Tell us, already," Uncle grouses.

"I was guilty as charged. And the judge says, 'Young lady, you've caused a lot of people a lot of trouble, that'll be forty dollars or twenty days.' And Daddy says, 'Your honor, how about twenty dollars and ten days?'"

"That's just like him." Jerry laughs.

"What, he was going to let them throw his daughter in the klink?" My uncle sniffs.

"No, of course not. The whole courtroom cracks up, except the judge. He pounds his gavel and says, 'You pay the bailiff over there, Mr. Baum.' I never was so proud of him."

Anna giggles with her hand over her mouth, eyes scrunched up, just like when she was small. She recovers and clasps her hands together.

"Don't you remember, Ruth, how he'd say, 'I'll bet you girls anything I can make you laugh. What d'you want to bet? No matter how hard I tried not to, I'd fall down laughing."

"Yeah, and it wasn't always funny," I add.

"What I mean," Jerry concludes. "He had the timing down."

The funeral parlor supplies a rabbi, who calls Sunday night. "What kind of man was he?" the rabbi fishes. "Well, he had a gift for life," I say. "He was the life of every party. He sold life insurance."

"Did he have hobbies?"

"He loved to garden and fish and play cards."

"Anything else?"

"Children, he loved any child."

What I don't say: he treated his wife like a child.

I don't tell the rabbi about the time my father picked up a knife and threatened my mother with it because she'd "talked back." Those were her words, as if she'd been a child acting out. We were all at the kitchen table having supper and though I was old enough to remember the incident, I don't. It's my mother's retelling of it I remember. I see the scene clearly, two frightened little girls, their mother cringing. He realizes what he's doing and puts the knife down and storms out. "It was just a butter knife," Mum said. "He never lifted a hand against me again."

Anna and I were hit plenty, though, when we were small, usually with the flat of his hand, sometimes with a yardstick he kept next to the fridge. If we didn't tidy our rooms or jump up fast enough to clear the dishes off the table, and he was in a bad mood, he'd haul out the yardstick. The last time he hit me, the yardstick broke in half and I laughed, involuntarily. His face seemed to drain of blood. I thought he looked mad enough to kill me. I ran out of the house and would have kept running if a neighbor hadn't beckoned me into her home. Mrs. Gonzales fed me milk and cookies and told me not to worry, he'd calm down soon. Everyone on the street must have heard the shouting. That was when he slammed his fist into a door and cracked the wood. Later, Anna put a bandage over the crack.

A large candle supplied by the mortuary and guaranteed to burn for a week flickers in the kitchen, sending eerie shadows under the bedroom door.

"Are you awake, Ruthie?"

"Yeah. I can't sleep."

"I feel so strange. I'm numb inside."

I stare at the ceiling, at a loss.

"You can tell me anything you want," I say finally.

"I can't cry for him. You understand?"

"You're angry. He was mean to you sometimes. But he did love you, I'm sure of that. Aren't you?"

She sighs heavily. "I don't know."

I lie awake for hours, even after my mother's breathing deepens. I try to focus on what will happen tomorrow and the next day. But what keeps coming up instead is: how dare you die so soon? I'm not finished with you.

My father was in high spirits when I last visited. He'd survived a heart attack, lost weight, looked vibrant. He didn't even pretend to be dismayed that I was divorcing my husband, whom he'd never liked much.

Then Aunt Estelle phoned with bad news about an old friend, and he wanted to be in on the call. "I'm talking to my sister long distance," my mother snapped. "Stop telling me what to say."

He turned around and stalked out of the house.

After the phone call, Mum and I watched him from the kitchen, sitting on a deck chair facing the canal with his back to us.

"He kept interrupting me," she complained. "And I can't say boo because of his heart."

I managed to calm her. Then I went outside and pulled another chair up next to his. He stared at the stagnant water in the canal.

"Your mother hates me," he said.

"She loves you," I protested. "She just gets irritable sometimes."

"Her whole family hates me. My own family uses me. And my so-called friends. I run all over for them, what do they care? My kids are out the door, I never hear from you." He didn't sound angry. His voice was flat, listless. "What's the point of going on?"

How many tantrums had I endured and Anna forgotten? But this was different. I'd never known him to be paranoid or suicidal, and it frightened me.

"Nobody hates you" I insisted. "Everybody loves you. How can you think we don't?"

His face was pale. "You don't know anything about it. I'm a punching bag for people."

"You're too smart a man to believe that," I said, desperately.

He glanced at me then, surprised. Trumped him, I thought, and plunged on.

"You're not at all the sort of man people like to hate, and you know it. You know this kind of moping around isn't good for your health, Daddy."

He nodded slowly.

Within half an hour, the gloom had lifted and he was cheerful again.

It was the one time I got through to him. Now I'll never know if anything might have changed, if only we'd had more time. To do what? He thought therapy was for crazy people.

My mother has opted for a closed coffin. Then Roy asks for the lid to be open so the children can see their grandfather one last time. I phone the funeral director and arrange a private showing in an anteroom, after which the coffin will be closed in deference to my mother, who tells us, "I don't think Jewish people have an open coffin." Anna seems bewildered. I'm not sure I want to see him stone dead and cosmetically refurbished. I'll decide when I get there.

The funeral is scheduled for one o'clock. We gather early for a breakfast of salmon salad and a rye bread Jerry fetched from a nearby bakery. I decide to prepare Daddy's favorite, onions and eggs, but my mother is looking glum.

"That was his last breakfast," she says. "He wasn't supposed to eat eggs. Maybe it killed him."

I sauté the onions slowly till they are translucent and golden brown before adding the scrambled eggs and cooking those slowly, just like Daddy did, so they are soft when served on a large pre-warmed platter.

"Here it is, the Benjamin Baum memorial breakfast," I announce.

Uncle Nate is pleased. "I couldn't have cooked it better myself," he declares. He eats noisily, smacking his lips.

"You got any fresh garlic?" Jerry asks. "Your father loved to smear garlic and butter on bread."

"Just powdered," Mum says.

She and her sisters, Aunt Estelle and Aunt Rose, being three generations removed from the shtetl, breakfast on tea and toast with jam. I tuck into everything. I've never been so hungry.

Anna and Roy got up at dawn to jog and now they are at the Busy Bee diner with the children, where grits and sausages can be had.

It does not occur to anyone until Anna and Roy return that today is Halloween. Grace and Billy have acquired small plastic pumpkins filled with candy and Anna announces she's packed costumes for the children.

"I figured they could trick or treat around here tonight," she says, large eyed, still half-child herself.

"You did what?" Roy splutters. "I don't believe you sometimes, girl. It's your father's funeral and you packed costumes?"

"But I promised them they could." Anna stares at the ground.

"You'd best unpromise them. It just ain't fittin'. They need to learn respect."

"What's all the fuss about?" Uncle Nate demands. "I can tell you my brother wouldn't mind in the slightest. Religion's the opiate of the masses. On that we've always agreed."

"What about their grandmother?" Roy stares him down. "They should show their Bubbie some respect."

"Oh dear," Bubbie Dorothy murmurs. "I don't know what's right. I've never been in this situation."

"Of course, they have to learn respect," Aunt Estelle declares. "We're sitting *shivah*. No one's supposed to go anywhere."

"But they're not going to the funeral in costumes," Anna protests.

Everyone starts talking at once.

"Ben was never observant —"

"They're little children, for crying out loud —"

"How could she even think of such a thing —"

"He'd have taken them out himself —"

Little Grace tugs on her grandmother's sleeve.

"Bubbie, is Zaydie a ghost now?"

My mother shivers and folds the child in her arms. "That's it. Quiet everyone." She raises her voice, and it trembles slightly. "I'm the Bubbie and I say they can trick or treat."

Roy shrugs. "Your Zaydie is in heaven with the angels," he tells his daughter.

"Shooting craps in paradise," I murmur and Roy shakes his head, exasperated.

Two black limos pull up precisely at noon and whisk us all up Dixie Highway at what seems a less-than-funereal pace to Royal Palm Chapel in Coral Gables. Our mother is in the first car with Uncle Nate and the two aunts. In the second car with my sister and her family, I'm taking deep shaky breaths. "Don't get hysterical," Anna pleads. She gazes anxiously at her children. I swallow hard and stare out the window.

At the chapel we're escorted to a side room and asked to wait there until the private viewing room is ready. Everyone is given small black ribbons to pin onto lapels or blouses, and the men and boys get yarmulkes. Several minutes go by. Billy peeks out and reports that the main room is full. Someone spots our group and people get up and file in to pay respects. Here are my two ancient great aunts, amazed that they've outlived their niece's husband. And PJ Lanahan, his fishing and poker buddy. He's a large red-faced man with a big belly. "I'm sure going to miss that son of a gun," he says. "I tell you, there was never a dull moment with Ben on board. That crazy loon." He wipes his eyes with his sleeve.

One by one the mourners move around the small room and press hands or kiss cheeks. All these people really did love him, I realize, astonished. If only he could have known. I glance at my sister. Her face, perhaps mirroring my own, glows with pride. Her eyes are damp.

But shouldn't this be happening afterward?

The funeral director's assistant rushes up distraught. "We're beginning the service right away," he says. "Everyone take your seats, please."

"What happened to the private viewing?" I ask.

He lowers his voice. "I'm sorry, ma'am. We couldn't get his eyes shut."

"That's how he was in the ambulance," my mother stage whispers. "Eyes wide open."

Anna gasps and Roy puts both arms around her.

"I'm very sorry." The assistant clears his throat. "We have another funeral scheduled at 2:30."

Aunt Estelle bursts into loud sobs.

Organ music swells up and the casket is wheeled in, draped with black cloth and flowers. Inside it, my father is staring death in the face. Blah blah, the rent-a-rabbi drones, and I can't concentrate, I'm sleep-deprived and tears are leaking.

Suddenly the doors to the chapel are flung open, and I see a group of strangers in black waiting to come in. What is this, a drive-through mortuary?

It's another long ride to the cemetery in Liberty City. This is where members of the Grand Order of Israel and their spouses are buried, a ghetto within a ghetto. It has a seedy appearance, its granite stones streaked with rust. I watch the casket lowered into the ground and Uncle Nate and Jerry and Roy shovel dirt over it, and I'm pissed that Anna and I can't do it, too. God, I hate this religion, I'm thinking, just as that annoying guy from Royal Palm skulks up to me and with a small pair of scissors cuts the black ribbon on my blouse. I understand this is in lieu of rending garments, but my heart has been sliced. I weep silently then, shoulders heaving.

My mother puts an arm around my waist.

"I still can't cry," she tells me.

ACKNOWLEDGMENTS

I am especially grateful to Ruhama Veltfort for helping me select and edit the stories in this collection, some of which she read in their earliest incarnations as a member of my former writers' support group in San Francisco.

Writer friends have given me invaluable support over the years. In San Francisco, in addition to Ruhama, they were Sally Abbott, David Belden, Naomi Cooper, Melinda Dart, Henry Hitz, Mark Lapin and Irwin Rosen. In Sonoma County, they are Sarah Amador, Nancy Bourne, Wray Cotterill, Judith Day, Marko Fong, Eve Goldberg, Richard Gustafson, Courtney Smith and Amanda Yskamp. Thank you all for your astute critiques and encouragement, as well as the pleasure of your company.

I am indebted to teachers who inspired me to write, beginning with Lester Goran at the University of Miami, and much later in the Bay Area, Bob Gluck, Guy Biederman and Daniel Coshnear.

Without the support and love of my family, who have made it possible for me to have time and space for writing, this collection would not be in print. My deepest gratitude to my sisters, Louise Rosen Franco and Ava Rosen Rich, and brother-in-law, Richard Franco, who also proofed the manuscript. And to one special friend, who is part of our family and has lent me unflagging support over many years, Carol Adair.

Last, but never least, I thank my mother, Mildred Sandy Rosen, who taught me by her example the love of reading.

ABOUT THE AUTHOR

Jo-Anne Rosen's stories, from long to flash fiction, have been published in print and online journals in Canada and the U.S., including *The Florida Review, Other Voices, Summerset Review, Prick of the Spindle, Pithead Chapel, Flashquake* and others.

Born in Toronto in 1944, transplanted to Miami, Florida at age 13, she was awarded a scholarship and fellowship to the University of Miami and earned an MA in English literature. In the 70s she traveled all over the U.S. and Europe, by thumb and camper van. She lived and worked in San Francisco almost 30 years, as well as in Oregon and Germany. Her home since 1998 has been in Petaluma, California.

Jo-Anne is self-employed as a book and web designer and small press publisher. She established Wordrunner Publishing Services in the 80s, a print chapbook service in the 90s, and the literary zine *Wordrunner eChapbooks* in 2008.

In 2007 she was awarded a two-week writing residency at Soapstone in Oregon. She is presently co-editor of the Sonoma County Literary Update.